Hardesty

X3

www.BarbarianSpy.com

WARNING: This book is for sale to **ADULT AUDIENCES ONLY**. Contains graphic gay male sex, multiple partners, anal sex, double penetration, rough sex, interracial sex, bondage, ritual sex, BDSM, and gay romance and love, all of which may be considered offensive by some readers.

All sexually active characters in this work are at least 18 years of age.

BarbarianSpy
Toronto, NSW
Australia

Hardesty

X3

habu

Table of Contents

Introduction

Hardesty is an unusual Vice Homicide detective in Washington, D.C. Although he is a straight arrow in obtaining justice for rent-boys who have been done to death no matter how powerful the perpetrator in the hedonist and power-wielding capitol city is, he is himself addicted to the very rough sex vice he is charged with stopping. He both protects and uses the young male prostitutes of the city.

This is a collection of three works, previously published separately in e-book, in chronological order, of Hardesty's world of solving male-on-male crime while satisfying his own lusts for young, blond, submissive men.

In the initial Hardesty story, *Gotta Keep Trying*, Hardesty cruises the gay male clubs of Washington, D.C., to check out the ages of the young men dancing the poles. When he focuses on Todd, a lithe young-looking dancer with a blond Mohawk and a provocatively placed gecko tattoo marking the young man's erogenous zone, he is enticed to go beyond just checking out Todd's age. Lost to his desire and his developing determination to settle down with just one man, Hardesty pursues the young man, who, possessed by indecision and his own demons, runs hot and cold on him. When Todd turns up as a key offering on an interactive video sex site, Hardesty is forced to the edge of frustration in driving his Vice squad colleagues to keep trying harder to bust the male prostitution ring and free Todd.

In the election tale, *Snitches*, when a U.S. senator is named as a possible vice presidential running mate, all hell breaks out in his attempt to hide that he has a weakness for sadistic sex with rent-boys. When his thugs mess up an attempt to silence one in a D.C. hotel, snitches descend on D.C. Vice cop Hardesty, not a stranger to vice himself, particularly with snitch rent-boys. Hardesty's attempts to figure out what is what and who is doing who are complicated by his own partner's decision to add freelance blackmail to the situation and to cut down on the competition in the process. Hardesty's efforts to save the one rent-boy who isn't snitching leads him on a merry out-of-town chase.

In *Retribution* Christmas Day isn't being kind to D.C. Homicide Vice detective Hardesty. Called to a crime scene at the Georgetown University boathouse on the Potomac River, he is taken aback at seeing the face under the ice of a man he only hours earlier was partying with at an exclusive, full-service gay male brothel. Immediately thereafter identifying a body in a Mercedes in the boathouse's parking lot as a rent-boy from the previous evening who Hardesty has known (biblically) himself, the plot thickens as the Secret Service descends on the boathouse looking for someone else altogether. A very important and very secret personage, the owner of the Mercedes, is missing. It's going to be a very busy Christmas week for Hardesty, not just in trying to solve a murder mystery against the opposition and possible complicity of the Russian mafia and the U.S. government itself, but also in keeping his own connection to the male brothel under wraps.

Gotta Keep Trying

Chapter One: The Pole Dancer with a Blond Mohawk

The dancer on the pole looked too young. That's why Hardesty zeroed in on him. Hardesty was looking for them young. The others were working the crowd. Leering back, throwing dirty words into the crowd in response to what was being called out to them and making suggestive motions with their bodies on the poles. But this one, the small, lithe guy, not more than five foot five, Hardesty estimated, with the blond Mohawk and the fluttering eyelashes, was dancing the pole to the slow music in a shyer, more introspective way. That didn't mean that he didn't have guys zeroing in on him like Hardesty was—but for different reasons, Hardesty told himself.

It's just that he was an enigma.

What was he doing here at all, Hardesty wondered. He kept going back to the guy looking too young, too innocent—wholesome under an attempt to play the part—but sexy at the same time. Really, really sexy. His body was boyishly perfect. The Mohawk wasn't extreme—he didn't look punk. He was a dyed blond. The hair was auburn at the roots, but it looked like he'd let it go that way on purpose, like the hair was just frosted. He had hardware—a small ring in his eyebrow and one in his navel—and a tattoo of a gecko or some lizard or something disappearing down under the waistband of the gold G-string he was wearing. All you could see of the tattoo were a tail and some hind legs in green. He wasn't heavily muscled, but there wasn't any fat on him either. His stomach was flat and his hips thin, but his buttocks flared out into perfect bubbles.

The face was boyish too, almost pretty. His eyes were hazel or blue, Hardesty couldn't really tell which in this light. But he didn't care that much about the eyes—more that he looked young, too young, and that he was dancing within himself. Very sexy, but as if he was too innocent to be in here. Too vulnerable.

Patrons were coming close to the stage and stuffing fives and tens and even a few twenties in the waistbands of the G-strings of the other two dancers, and the dancers, in turn, were blowing kisses and making lurid movements to fit the mood. But none of that was happening with this one dancer. There was some sort of barrier around him that the boisterous men couldn't penetrate. He had more than his share of admirers, but they were worshipping him from a distance, most of them sitting there, lost in watching him, no doubt spinning in their minds what they'd like to do with the small, lithe, vulnerable body. Occasionally they'd come up and put their bills on the surface of the stage below where he was dancing. So he was getting his share of the tips. They just weren't touching him. It was like they were afraid he was too young to touch, not legal. They fully appreciated what he was doing, but they sensed a danger in treating him like the other two dancers.

This is what caught Hardesty's attention more than anything else. He took out his wallet and extracted a fifty-dollar bill and laid it down on the table in front of him. He made sure the young dancer saw him do it, which he did, and then Hardesty pushed the bill a nudge, just a nudge, toward the dancer on the tabletop and gave the dancer a meaningful look.

Putting a ten in a dancer's G-string waistband was showing one form of appreciation in a bar like this. Showing a fifty on top of the table told the dancer something entirely different. And all of the dancers here were on call for those fifties. Hardesty knew it was part of the contract.

Fifteen minutes after the end of the set, the dancer was walking through the beaded curtain at the back of the room and slowly making his way to Hardesty's table. He was managing to perpetuate the enigma. He was wearing low-rise faded jeans—the hind legs and tail of the gecko were still disappearing down into his pants at the crease where the sculpted edge of the under curve of his belly joined the lop of his right leg—but he was wearing an open green plaid flannel shirt and a yellow-gold baseball cap with the word "Lions" embossed in green above its bill. Some sort of high school team cap was Hardesty's first thought. The kid looked that young; the baseball cap certainly didn't make him look older. It was like there was a basic innocent, boy-next-door aura about the individual pieces of clothing he was wearing. The thing was, though, that the plaid shirt was open in front, showing his perfectly formed, honey-colored, boy's torso, and he was wearing thin-strip sandals and no socks. He looked both innocent rural high schooler and sex on wheels all at the same time. Hardesty wondered what was real and what wasn't with this guy. He'd have to push the envelope to find out.

They were hazel. His eyes were hazel. He was only half smiling when he sat down at the table, across from Hardesty, and he looked half embarrassed too, like this was all new to him. He placed a couple of fingers on the fifty-dollar note and cast his eyes down, on the bill, as if he couldn't say what he did to Hardesty face-to-face.

"You want to come into the back?"

"I have a room—at a motel," Hardesty said with a low growl. "There will be more than the fifty. Quite a bit more. That cool with you?"

"Yeah, that's cool," the young man answered, although even in this he managed to send confusing signals. He said it like he wasn't completely sure—like he hadn't really been through this routine before and didn't know if leaving the premises was permitted. Like he didn't know whether he should pin down what "quite a bit more" totaled out to.

Hardesty just wasn't sure. He had to be sure. He could have made the young man say the words here and taken care of it all right here. But he just wasn't sure. And there was something about this young, vulnerable-acting guy that spoke to Hardesty. That aroused him. He didn't want to think about the consequences of that, thought.

Perhaps he should have.

* * * *

Hardesty showered first at the motel room. He'd wanted to take off his suit coat a long time before now. The young man—especially when he was sitting so close to Hardesty in the car—had heated Hardesty up. Once they got in the motel room, he couldn't wait to get into the bathroom and take that coat off.

He could have taken care of it all in the car—just like he probably could have right there in the bar. He could have let the young man offer to suck him off there. It seemed that the kid was going to do that. But he hesitated in making the offer—that innocence and uncertainly forcing its way through the studied sexy exterior again—and Hardesty had overridden the start of an offer with questions about the young man, most of which were diverted or answered in the least-revealing way the kid could manage.

"Twenty-one," the guy had said. He'd been smoking a cigarette and rolled down the car window and flicked the butt out when he'd said that. He face was turned away from Hardesty, who was trying to keep his eyes on the road and on Todd at the same time. The guy had already said his name was Todd. Hardesty gave him his own real name.

"Just Hardesty. Everyone calls me just that. No first name needed."

Turning away from him like that when giving an age told Hardesty it was a lie. But just how much of a lie? That was the crux of the matter. That's what mattered with Hardesty. He was looking for them young, real young.

"Gotta piss, so I'll go first," Hardesty said as soon as they got in the door of the room at the seedy nearby motel that he'd already rented that afternoon. No issues with checking in, even if this was the type of motel that gave a shit how many and of what variety occupied its rooms—more likely by the hour than the night. He'd used this motel before.

For a split second Hardesty was afraid that Todd was going to ask to go first—or, more likely—for them to shower together. But Hardesty had business to do that he didn't want the kid to see.

Once in the bathroom, he stripped his coat off, and pulled the gun holster out from his arm pit and over his shoulder. He looked around. If nothing else, he could wrap it up in the folded clothes when he came out of the bathroom. But he wanted it well out of the way. He saw the gap between the wall and the back of the toilet tank, and the gun fit in there, out of sight, just like it was built for this need.

He showered quickly, not wanting to lose the mark, not wanting Todd, who continued to seem skittish about the whole deal, to fly the coop. But Todd was there, naked, and stretched out on the bed, his eyes on the bathroom door, when Hardesty came out, a bath towel wrapped around his waist and knotted in place.

Todd's eyes knitted and his mouth formed a little O when he saw Hardesty, which Hardesty knew would be the case. He was pretty nondescript in build in the specially fitted suit, but seen only in a towel revealed he was a cut bodybuilder. Hardesty knew that when he dropped the towel, Todd would have another reason to widen his eyes and squirm a bit.

"Your turn. And clean yourself out real well while you're in there."

Todd stood up from the bed in a fluid motion, not hiding anything, all innocence—or purposeful posing. Hardesty couldn't discern which. He took his breath in, though. The gecko tattoo hadn't just been scurrying into the guy's pants. It was stretching out into his groin and its red tongue was flickering out and around the base of Todd's cock. Even here Todd was boyish. The cock wasn't small but it wasn't anything to crow about either, its innocence proclaimed by being flaccid and uncut. The balls were pert. The evidence of studied intention, though, was hinted by the groomed pubes. They were trimmed short and shaved into a V down into the root of his cock and had the same dye job as the Mohawk on his head—auburn underneath blond highlights.

Hardesty wondered how Todd had managed to do that as he watched the bouncing little butt cheeks move toward the bathroom. He supposed that could be done at home with a toothbrush.

While Todd was showering, Hardesty took the small tape recorder out of the pocket of his folded suit coat, turned it on, and placed it in the top drawer of one of the nightstands. Before closing the drawer, he took a small can of lubricant out of the other suit coat pocket and put it in the drawer too. Then he fished three condom packets out of his folded trouser pocket and a wad of fifties and deposited them in the drawer. He stood up from the bed and walked over to where Todd had carelessly dropped his clothes on the floor next to a chair.

"Teenagers," he muttered. Then he stiffened at the thought of just how much of a teenager Todd was. And, delving deep into his secret of all secrets, he felt his cock hardening.

This was a point where he could have—probably should have—dressed and walked out of the motel room. And he thought briefly about doing that. But how he reasoned his way out of that was to recall that his gun was in the bathroom with Todd, concealed behind the toilet tank.

Instead, he fished Todd's wallet out of the lad's jeans and quickly searched it for forms of ID. He found a couple, including a driver's license. Todd wasn't twenty-one—surprise, surprise—and he wasn't Todd either. All of the ID cards were for a Toby Drake. Hardesty wondered why he found the name "Todd" more comforting in this role he'd taken on than "Toby."

He wasn't twenty-one, but if these IDs were to be believed, he wasn't underage either. A couple of them gave a birth date that put him a couple of months above nineteen. Still a teen, though. But that part of what Hardesty was looking for was by the boards. The ID went back into the jeans. Either the guy was a neophyte to be carrying around real ID, or he was really clever. And if he was being really clever, then it was likely that he was underage after all. Hardesty decided he had to stick with his line of approach.

Todd walked back in the room, rubbing his Mohawk with a towel and walking along, naked, just like he was in the boy's locker room back at school. No self-consciousness, no attempting to be provocative or sexy. But, in that, being very sexy.

He walked over to the bed and sat down on the side of it, facing Hardesty.

Hardesty, standing across the room, turned to him and dropped the towel from his waist. Todd's eyes went big and he gave a little gasp, as Hardesty knew he would. And Hardesty was barely half hard yet.

"I need to know what I'll get for fifty dollars," he said.

"I thought you said it would be more."

"It will be if I'm satisfied with what I would have gotten for the fifty. We can work our way up from there."

"What is that you want?" Todd asked.

"Tell me what you'll do for that."

"I'll suck it and fuck it for fifty dollars—but just one of each. Repeats or anything kinky would be more."

Another chance to end it. But Hardesty didn't take that opportunity. He had the fifty-dollar bill wadded up in his fist.

"Guess we'll start with the basic and see if that satisfies enough to build from there."

He opened his fist; smoothed out the bill; walked over to where Todd's clothes were piled; rummaged around, and put the fifty in the pocket of Todd's jeans. He lifted the jeans from the floor and deposited the bill dramatically so Todd could see he wasn't palming the fifty. Then he came back to the bed and stood close to Todd.

This was the point of no return for Hardesty. He chose what he wanted to happen over duty. He decided to go with the age on the ID.

Todd put his left hand on Hardesty's waist, cupped Hardesty's balls with his right hand, and opened his mouth over the head of Hardesty's cock.

While Todd was sucking his cock—with Hardesty still uncertain whether the guy was proficient at this or was a bit awkward, which only made Hardesty go harder and enjoy the blow job more at the thought he was working with a neophyte here—Hardesty leaned over, opened the nightstand drawer, took out the three condom packets and the can of lubricant, and put them on top of the nightstand. He also took out another fifty and placed it next to the can of lubricant, making sure that Todd saw him do this. While his fingers were in there, he turned off the recorder. He had what he needed if he wanted to use it. And he didn't want what would happen now recorded.

He had already decided what he wanted to do.

"Belly to bed," he directed in a low, commanding bed. "And scoot up on the bed."

Todd turned and went up on the bed on his knees and stretched out on his belly. He gave a sigh like this was all just a nighttime "going to bed" routine for the little guy.

He had no idea how arousing that was, Hardesty thought. But then maybe he did. The jury was still out on that.

Hardesty straddled Todd's hips on the bed and massaged the young man's back and shoulder muscles and arms, feeling the tension slowly draining out of the teenager. Todd was giving little mewing sounds like he was enjoying it. Hardesty glided his hands up Todd's side and into his pit on one side, finding that he had groomed himself to short tuffs of hair there and wondering if Todd had frosted what little pit hair he had as well. He'd have to check that out later. He pushed his arms under Todd's chest from both sides and lifted the young man's torso off the surface of the bed. Hardesty's hands went to Todd's pecs and he massaged Todd's nipples with his fingers until Todd was groaning and Hardesty could feel the younger mans pelvis raise a bit from the surface of the bed and move in a slow rhythm, stroking the underside of his cock on the bed.

"Please, man."

"Please what?"

"You know."

Yes, he knew. But it was arousing him more that Todd didn't seem to be able to say it. Young, innocent, vulnerable. Hardesty decided to go slow. The underside of his own cock was wedged inside the cleft of Todd's buttocks. Hardesty started to stroke slowly across Todd's hole while still massage his nipples and playing with the nipple ring. Todd whimpered and groaned. His fists had bunched up wads of the bedspread over his head, and Hardesty watched the young man bring the bunching of his fists into rhythm with the dry-fuck stroking of his cock.

Letting Todd's torso descend on the surface of the bed, Hardesty started kissing his way down the youth's spine while moving his body down below Todd's. He kissed and nibbled at Todd's cheeks before pulling them apart with his hand and blowing on Todd's hole. It puckered right up for him. Hardesty kissed the bud and ran his tongue over it. He blew on it a couple of times. Todd sighed and the hole opened. Hardesty stuck his tongue in it and it opened more.

He felt his muscles tighten and a flash of anger come up from his belly. He tongued it again and now could see a couple of inches up into the channel it had widened so much. Why, he could get several fingers in there. He could drive a Mac truck up that channel.

Hardesty growled. The little fucker was a poser. This hole was in regular use.

He stood up from the bed and with hands trembling in anger tore open a condom packet, rolled the condom on his rock-hard cock, sprayed lubricant on his cock and on the puckered hole, and came back down on the bed between Todd's spread legs.

Todd didn't know a thing in the changed plans on the length of the foreplay until Hardesty was pulling him up to his knees with an arm grip under his chin and was stuffing his cock inside Todd's channel with the other hand.

Todd howled his surprise and the roughness of the invasion of Hardesty's cock.

"Ayieee, you're huge. Oh, fuck, you're splitting me."

Hardesty knew that he, indeed, was huge, but he had seen the slackness of that hole. He knew the young man could take him.

When the cock was fully buried and Hardesty started to piston hard, Todd, with groans and whimpers, relaxed and let Hardesty have his way with him—which was a very rough, hard, deep, and demanding way.

He was docilely taking the hard, rough fuck until Hardesty started working his torso with his free hand. Nothing unusual happened while Hardesty was giving him nipple play, or when he played with the ring in the young man's navel, or even when he pulled on Todd's cock and balls during the fuck. But Hardesty moved the palm of the hand to where Todd's right leg joined his torso, and Todd suddenly went active.

He started begging for the fuck. "Yeah fuck. Get it, get it! Fuck me. GiveittomegiveittomegiveittoME!" with his body writhing and his pelvis counterpunching Hardesty's thrusts.

Todd shot out on the bedspread and went limp, and Hardesty, ready to blow himself, let Todd fall in a heap on the bed, pulled the condom off his cock, and masturbated for six or seven strokes before ejaculating on Todd's back.

Todd was panting heavily, his shoulders were heaving, and Hardesty couldn't tell or not if he was sobbing into the bedspread. He had rolled into a fetal position.

Hardesty's anger had evaporated, and he was ashamed of himself. He had no right to be angry with Todd. Christalmighty, he was a rent boy. It was Hardesty making out something innocent and vulnerable in him. The kid hadn't led him on—other than adding at least two years to his age in what he'd told him. Of course his hole would be well used. That's how he was trying to make a living.

All of the innocence stuff was in Hardesty's mind. Although maybe not all, if the guy had been reduced to a sobbing pile of hurt.

"I'm sorry, I don't know what came over me," Hardesty said in a low voice. He placed his hands on the arm and thigh of Todd. Todd didn't shrug him off. "You were just so desirable at that moment," Hardesty continued. He was too embarrassed to tell the truth. "I just wanted to have you so bad."

Todd was still trembling, but Hardesty could feel him relax a bit and his breath become more regular. He lightly rubbed the areas of Todd's body he could get to for a good ten minutes more, while the ball Todd was in slowly untightened. Hardesty managed to run a hand down between a thigh clutched to a stomach and Todd's belly and reach and encircle the youth's cock. He played with Todd's balls and did a squeeze and release on Todd's cock, which the cock seemed to appreciate.

"Let me make it up to you," Hardesty said. He moved over and opened the drawer to the nightstand. He extracted another fifty-dollar bill from the small wad. Waving it in the air where Todd, untucking his head, was now watching Hardesty display the fifty dollars.

"As you see, the insurance fifty is still on the nightstand. I'm going to walk over and put this one in your jeans. If you don't tell me to stop, then you'll let me make love to you again—love this time, not like what I just did."

Todd's eyes were wide and he sniffed. "You're hard again."

"Yes, I am hard for you again. That's how much I want you." He continued on to Todd's jeans, tucked the fifty in, and turned toward the bed again. Todd hadn't told him to stop. Instead, he had unclenched his body and turned over on his back, raising his torso on his elbows.

Hardesty looked up the whole sweep of the lithe, boyish body and moved quickly to the bed and came down on top of Todd, careful to take his muscular weight on his elbows and knees rather than crush the small man. They went into a deep kiss, and their cocks rubbed against each other as they both moved their pelvises in harmony.

Hardesty kissed slowly down Todd's body, paying particular to his nipples and navel ring. When he reached Todd's groin, he kissed him in the fold of his torso into his left leg and then repeated on the crease on the right, where the gecko was. Todd moaned and grabbed Hardesty's hair with both of his fists.

"Yeah! Fuck yeah!"

Hardesty kissed him again there, and Todd groaned and shouted out another "Yeah! Fuck it!"

The older man moved his lips to Todd's cock. He pushed the foreskin down with his teeth, lightly scrapping the sensitive glans, and flicked his tongue in Todd's piss slit. Todd groaned and arched his back. "Yes, yes, YES!"

Hardesty sucked the cock for several minutes as Todd's body went stiff and he raised his pelvis and pumped with his cock. Testing a theory, Hardesty moved fingers to the gecko tattoo and started rubbing it. Todd went wild with his pelvis and shot his load.

The lips of the older man went to the gecko and he was licking and sucking there.

Todd writhed under him, even more aroused now than when he'd ejaculated. "Fuck me, Fuck me! Getitgetitgetit!"

Careful to keep his fingers rubbing the gecko, Todd went up on his knees; pushed them under Todd's buttocks so that Todd's thighs were on his hips and his torso streamed out below Hardesty; and slowly, this time, buried his cock in Todd's hole.

Todd was beside himself with passionate response as Hardesty pumped his channel—and rubbed the gecko.

Hardesty had obviously found Todd's erogenous zone.

Later, asking almost too late, as they were well into the wee hours of the morning with the two of them stretched out and Todd spooned into Hardesty's pelvis, Hardesty murmured, "Can you stay the night?"

"I have no place else I need to be," Todd answered. The way he answered it made Hardesty think that he had no place else he could have gone that night.

In the night, Hardesty woke from a very pleasant dream in, he thought, the same spoon configuration they both, exhausted, had dozed off in. He realized that the transition from the dream to reality was that there was a mouth working his cock—exactly what had been pleasant about the dream—and that they weren't really in the same configuration. They were in a 69 position. So, while Todd sucked him, he sucked Todd. In the dark of the night.

He felt the mouth pull off his cock.

"Hardesty?"

"Yes?"

"I want to make love to you now. I want to fuck you."

"I don't . . ."

"You don't understand. Here, sit up on the edge of the bed."

He did so and Todd moved around and sat on his thighs, with his legs, bent, on either side of Hardesty's hips. He placed his hands around Hardesty's neck, clenching his fists together, and rolled his hips up. "Here, put it in me."

"Just a sec," Hardesty answered. He took the last condom packet off the nightstand, feeling the regret that it was the last one he had, extracted the condom, and rolled in on his engorged cock as it rested against Todd's navel ring. Todd raised himself up with the strength of the leverage of his heels and his knotted fists, while Hardesty slowly entered his channel with his cock.

22

"Hold still. Let me do it all," Todd whispered. He then started to stroke his channel on Hardesty's buried cock.

Hardesty couldn't keep wholly still. After a few minutes, he placed his hands on the youth's thin waist, making sure that a thumb could reach the gecko tattoo on Todd's right side. He started to rub. Todd threw his head back and howled to the ceiling and began riding the cock like he was a jockey in the Kentucky Derby.

They came almost simultaneously.

* * * *

All during breakfast at a greasy spoon down the block from the motel, Hardesty couldn't think of much else other than that he was stupid to have come with only three condoms. The kid had wanted to go two more rounds in the night. He was stupid for other reasons too, but in for a penny in for a pound on that, he decided.

It had been a chore shrugging back into his suit this morning, especially getting the piece in its holster under his armpit again, when all he wanted to do was have another go at Todd. But he'd only had three condoms. The fact that he'd never been able to get it up more than three times a night before—and not even that many times—wasn't something he was going to let comfort him. With Todd— pure innocence under that great, pliable body and a hole that could take him easily—he felt like he could go all night.

He wasn't stupid about everything, though.

"No, I can't take it. That time was for me. I'm just sorry you didn't have more condoms. I shoudda brought some. I knew I'd forget something."

"No, Todd, you're not a charity, and you need it more than I do. So, here, take this fifty. I want to be on good terms with you." He stuffed the fifty-dollar bill in Todd's pocket to go with the hundred the guy had outright earned. He had that green plaid shirt buttoned now, and suddenly he looked just like any other nineteen year old having breakfast with an older brother.

Well, uncle, maybe, Hardesty thought. Despite the pleasures of the night and the prime condition he was in, Hardesty's muscles felt all of his thirty-two years this morning. That's not to say that he wasn't ready to go again.

"So, you usually remember to bring condoms?"

"Yeah," Todd said, looking down at the tablecloth as if the whole topic was embarrassing for him.

"And you do this often—go with a man who watches you dance at the club?"

Todd looked up at the corner of the ceiling now. "Often enough."

"How long have you been dancing at that club?"

"Just a week. I'm just filling in for a friend. The manager wants me to continue, but . . . well . . . I don't know."

Hardesty could well imagine that the club manager wanted Todd to continue working there.

"So, what's 'often enough,' Todd? If you've only been dancing at the club for a week, how many times have you gone with a man in a week?"

"Once." Todd looked like he was ashamed to admit it.

Hardesty momentarily regretted again having been so rough with him the first time. But then he remembered how slack Todd's hole was—how quickly it had opened to his attentions. The young man hadn't just started doing this in the last week.

"What do you do, then, Todd, if you aren't a regular dancer at the club."

"Ummm, this and that."

"And do your parents know you are doing this and that?"

Todd flared. "I'm twenty-one. What do parents have to do with it?"

"Uh, right," Hardesty said. What he thought was a more sarcastic, yeah, right. "It's OK. I just worry about what you're doing."

"It gets me by."

Hardesty was "this close" to asking Todd to go home with him. To throw all of this over and to be with him—just him. But he stopped himself. He already was off the reservation here. He couldn't fall for a kid like this.

"We have the room until noon," he said in a low voice, watching Todd closely for his response.

Todd looked at him, smiled slightly, and then looked down at the fifty-dollar bill again.

"Yeah, fifty each time," Hardesty murmured, and then when Todd didn't say anything, he continued, "Maybe I'm too old and ugly for you. Maybe you didn't like it?"

"What's not to like?" Todd lifted his head and shot back. "You're not nearly as old as much of the men coming to the club and wanting something extra. And you've got a hard body and a gigantic cock. What's not to like about that?"

"And fifty dollars each time," Hardesty said. But then he felt that was unfair. Todd hadn't wanted to charge him for the third time, the time that Todd had initiated it and done most of the work. "Sorry, I didn't mean that," he said, then he rushed on. "I have to take a piss, and we need more supplies. Give me a minute and we'll go back to the room. There will be a rubber machine in the john, I'm sure."

He stood up and turned and headed toward the toilets at the back of the diner. He didn't really have to take a piss—but he did anyway as long as he was there. What he really wanted was the machines he knew were in the men's room of this diner. He'd eaten here often. He'd used the motel down the block often even. Just never quite the way he'd used it last night.

He put his coins in the machine and a condom packet dropped out. Screw this place for selling only single packets, he told himself. He hesitated. Then he searched around in his pockets and found enough change to have another go at the machine. He had condoms at home—lots of them. But, well, they were at home, and it was 9:00 a.m., and they had the room until noon. Although he didn't know what the other guys would say if he didn't drag into work until after noon. Fuck 'em on that, though. He was already so far out of bounds that it didn't make a rat's ass of a difference.

He only had change enough for a second condom. They'd just have to make do.

He came out of the men's room to find that Todd was gone. He wasn't at the motel either.

Chapter Two: The Mistake of Making It Personal

Hardesty wasn't in the best of moods when he got to the precinct, and the guys and gals there didn't help it any—as he knew they wouldn't.

"Had a hard night?" he was greeted at the door, accompanied by a snigger.

"Found it hard to get to work today, Hardesty?" boomed a voice from one end of the Vice squad room.

"Hard morning, Hardesty?" another voice chimed in from the other side.

They all knew Hardesty fucked men, and they also knew that any day he dragged in after noon was likely to mean he had been on such a binge the night before—that he'd been hard and pumping most of the night. Some of them had seen what he was packing and the rest had heard about it. What they didn't think, though, was that he was out screwing a target rather than dragging him in for prosecution. They didn't think this because that was strictly taboo.

That's how far Hardesty had gone off the reservation with Todd—or Toby—or whoever the little blond piece's name was. Hardesty was OK in going to the bar. That's what he did, and the fact that he was gay himself made him far more useful to the department on male-on-male sex crimes. He looked for illegal activity; that was his job. That included underage prostitution. And it included solicitation itself if there was a campaign against it going on. They couldn't always put the screws on it; there weren't enough Vice cops on the whole East Coast to close down prostitution—female or male—in this city.

What he wasn't OK with was, first, not backing out once there was more evidence the target was of age than there was that he was underage. Second, if he was going to pursue the point, he coulda/shoulda brought Todd in on the solicitation charges—before actually engaging in a sexual act. That's what the recording was all about. He didn't. But where he mostly wasn't OK was that he fucked the target and didn't do any of the above. He could have brought him in, even on suspicion. What he shouldn't have done was fucked him three times in the same night first—and would have done it twice more the next morning if he'd had the opportunity to.

Hardesty was too good a cop for this. And he knew he was. He spent the better part of the afternoon trying to figure out for himself why he'd done it. He came up with two possibilities: He increasingly was lonely and wanted just one guy to be coming home to and Todd had all the attributes of a guy Hardesty would want to come home to, with the dangerous edge being that Hardesty was aroused by young-looking guys that he could feel like he was overpowering.

And if it wasn't one or two of those, or both, Hardesty thought he should get out of Vice and go to another unit. If he started getting soft on these guys or using his advantages over them to get laid, it probably was time for him to move on.

The thought that he was looking for someone more permanent—and someone like Todd to boot—scared him, though. By the end of the afternoon he'd convinced himself that he just saw something in Todd that he wanted to save before it was too late—not just that he looked for young-looking men, but also that he looked innocent and vulnerable young men. He thought back to when he got angry. It was when he thought it was already too late to turn

28

Todd. He didn't know what had happened after that to change his mind, if he had. All he knew was that he went gaga at the prospect of fucking Todd. That gecko tattoo business was something else. He'd known guys who had erogenous zones, but Todd lost all control at the mere touch of his. Hardesty had found that very, very arousing.

That evening and the next found him at the bar where he'd picked up Todd. He didn't see Todd again, and he didn't see anything else illegal going on there either. But he told himself he was doing his job by going there. Todd looked underage. What if the manager had taken him on without checking?

But the manager was vociferous in claiming he had checked Todd out. And, if presented with a subpoena, he said he'd be happy to give Hardesty a look see at the evidence he had that Todd was eighteen, and thus legal. Hardesty did a little double-take. What the manager's evidence was put Todd even closer to the illegal edge than either what Todd said or what his own ID showed—but it still didn't put him below the level. The last thing Hardesty wanted, though, was to create evidence that he was checking Todd out. He still hoped to find Todd again, and . . . yes . . . to fuck him again (and again).

It wasn't professional now; it was personal. And there were things he could do with Todd on a personal level that he would hold back from if it was professional. He'd be going crazy thinking about what he could do with Todd now until he found him again.

The club manager backed what Todd had told Hardesty on one point. He did regret that Todd wasn't working there permanently—indeed that he hadn't completed the gig he'd contracted for.

When Hardesty pressed for information on where Todd might be, suggesting that he could make scrutiny hard or easy for the club, the manager just gave him a sardonic look and said, "You might try the movies."

Hardesty didn't think—at least at that time—that this was very helpful information.

He didn't just check in at that club. He went to others as well and fit in doing his job while also looking for Todd. He also checked the streets in the gay male tenderloin district. It was during such a check that he found Todd again.

Hardesty was out on patrol with one of his partners, Phil, three evenings later when he next saw Todd. The young man was working the streets. He was leaning on a wall under a lamppost with a couple of other guys when Hardesty and Phil pulled up by the curb beside them. Todd, wearing his open green plaid flannel shirt, his tight faded jeans, and his thin-soled sandals, wasn't looking out at the street. He was talking to another guy who wasn't looking at the street either.

Thus, when Hardesty and Phil had gotten out of the car, with Hardesty saying, "Let's ruffle these guys," Todd and the guy he was talking to, a young black guy not much bigger than Todd, just stayed in place and continued talking. The others sauntered away as quickly as they could without showing the panic they were in.

The young black guy saw the two Vice cops first and pulled off the wall and started to walk quickly away.

"You get that one," Hardesty told Phil. "I'll talk to the other."

"Saving the chocolate for me," Phil muttered, as he took off after the black guy at a fast walk. "Nice. Don't wait up."

There really wasn't anything you could do with these guys unless you caught them making an offer for money. But the Vice cops did what they called "rousting" them every once in a while just to let them know they were being watched.

"You," Todd said, accusingly, when he turned and saw Hardesty approach him. "You're a cop."

Phil already was out of earshot, walking briskly down the street behind the guy Todd had been talking to. Phil was gay too, and Hardesty knew that he had even fewer scruples about taking advantage of that than Hardesty did. The little black guy had been cute. Hardesty figured he had some time to talk to Todd.

"Yeah, I'm a cop. A cop with a soft spot and a hard dick for you. I could have arrested you and brought you in back in the motel room. You solicited me; I got it on tape. You're not very good with this solicitation business, are you?"

Todd turned to walk away, but Hardesty grabbed him by the arm and held him against the wall.

"How long have you been working at this? The truth now."

"A couple of weeks."

"But you've been reamed well. You might have been for rent for only a couple of weeks, but you've been doing it for a while. What's up with that?"

Todd gave him a venomous look, but then he shrugged and looked resigned. "Why the hell not. It don't change anything. My mother's boyfriend. Thane. Thane Moore, the black bastard. I just got sick of it after a while and left."

"And that's why you don't have parents to go home to?" Hardesty said, his voice softer now.

"Bingo. As long as he's screwing my mom, she doesn't give a shit that he's screwing me too. You gonna take me in?"

"I can't very well do that, can I? It's a bit late to turn that tape in. I erased it anyway. And you're not doing anything wrong right now. I could take you in for loitering and they could give you the usual 'you don't want to do this because we'll rough you up like this' treatment back at the precinct. But I don't want them to know about you."

"Why not?"

"Because I still have a hard-on for you. Haven't you figured that out for yourself yet? I'm hot for you. And as long as you let me fuck you, I can protect you—but not if they know about you and me down at the precinct. Understand?"

Todd didn't say anything, but he looked like he understood that quite well. Which was interesting to Hardesty, because he didn't really understand it himself. He had just blurted it out without a thought behind it. If anyone at the precinct had heard him say that, his career in Vice would be toast. What was the hold that this guy had over him, he wondered. The power of the gecko? Was Todd's erogenous zone just as much his own?

"You OK with that?" he asked.

"Yeah, I guess so," Todd said. He was looking at the streetlamp, though, not at Hardesty.

"You want my cock? You want me to fuck you?"

Todd hesitated.

"Fifty dollars each time. Like before. I accept what you are." There was no pride in Hardesty's want.

"Yes," a little more definite now.

"OK, I got another hour on my shift. You go over to the coffee shop down the street there. You see it?"

"Yeah."

"Here's a ten spot. You go in there and drink coffee and nurse it, and I'll be back in a little over an hour."

"And then what?"

"Then I got a place we can go. OK? I've been aching for you. I've got a whole box of rubbers at home."

"Yeah, cool."

Todd was already down the street and in the coffee shop and Hardesty was leaning on the squad car before Phil returned, stuffing his shirt tail down into his pants and whistling happily.

"You get your wick dipped to your satisfaction?" Hardesty asked. He didn't like the smug look on Phil's face."

"He had a nice, soft mouth, if you must know," Phil answered. "And don't tell me you didn't get something set up with the blond kid. I know you like 'em young."

Hardesty couldn't tell Phil he hadn't, so he just gave a low growl and moved to the squad car. "Come on. We've got more territory to cover in our shift."

"And you can't wait for your shift to be over to get your cock polished, can you? You show it to him? You get him all hot and bothered by it?"

Hardesty didn't answer. He let the slamming of the car door answer for him.

When Hardesty drove back nearly two hours later in his own car and in civilian clothes, Todd was not to be found. He didn't panic. He had half expected this. He just cruised around the tenderloin district more. Todd was new to this game, and Hardesty had seen it all.

It didn't take him long to spy Todd again, leaning against another wall, under yet another lamppost. He pulled his car over to the curb, but outside the circle of light the streetlight was casting. He was close enough to Todd for Todd to know someone was here for him after a couple of minutes had passed by and the driver hadn't gotten out of the car.

A few more minutes after that Todd pushed himself off the wall and sauntered slowly toward the car. He took a pack of cigarettes out of his shirt pocket and extracted one before putting the pack back. As he approached, Hardesty pushed the button that lowered the passenger window.

"Got a light, buddy?" Todd said as he leaned down to the passenger window sill. Hardesty shot a hand out and gripped Todd's wrist.

"Get in the car, Todd."

"You again. Look, man—"

"Just get in the car, Todd. We'll just talk a few minutes." He leaned over and popped the door open himself. He grabbed for the other wrist as the door opened, so that at no time was Todd completely free. He got into the car, though, without any trouble.

"Why are you like this?" Hardesty asked. "We're good together. I know you want the cock."

"It's too complicated," Todd said as he folded himself into the passenger seat and Hardesty put an arm around his shoulders. "You're a cop and all."

"You want my cock or not? It has nothing to do with me being a cop."

"It has everything to do with—"

Todd didn't get the sentence finished, though. Hardesty had used the hand on the arm around Todd's shoulders to turn Todd's face to his for a possessive kiss. At the same time his other hand palmed Todd's belly and then moved to Todd's right side and slid down on top of the gecko tattoo. He started to rub the middle of that, and Todd, moaning with a sound muffled by the possession of the kiss, began to writhe under him. His hand first went on top of Hardesty's, trying to pull Hardesty's hand off the tattoo. But when that didn't work, he shuddered, relaxed for the time it took Hardesty to release his lips and work his nipples for nearly a minute while Todd laid his head back and moaned softly.

When Hardesty's lips went back to Todd's, his fingers still working the gecko tattoo, Todd reached over and grabbed Hardesty's engorging dick through the material of his trousers.

Hardesty disengaged from the kiss, gave a low laugh, and said, "You want the cock or not?"

"Oh god, yes," Todd whimpered. "Here, now. Fuck me."

"That would likely get us both arrested," Hardesty said. "But I've got a place." He let Todd loose but put the car in gear immediately and moved the car out onto the street. He hit the "lock all doors button" as he did so.

The place turned out to be Hardesty's house, a two-bedroom bungalow in not the best part of town. But it was home to Hardesty and it was private to him. He'd never brought anyone here he'd picked up while in the line of duty. He didn't know for sure why he was bringing Todd here now. There were motels he'd used that they drove past in getting here. He knew it was significant that he was bringing Todd to his house, but he filed that away in his mind for examining later. He also found himself planning far enough ahead that his hold over Todd would get past continuously having to pay him for it—or him going back on the street for it. But nothing much formed around that thought.

He was too much in heat now to think about any of that now.

He managed a "four for" this night. He had plenty of condoms in the house. Only exhaustion got in his way for the fifth. Passion for the small Mohawked blond moved Hardesty to pound his ass hard, and his inability to gauge his energy brought him to exhaustion. Todd sucked him off trying to bring him up again the fifth time, but, although Hardesty managed a weak ejaculation, it didn't qualify as a fuck.

The four before that were pretty spectacular. They did it in the shower the first time, with Todd standing and bending over and grabbing his ankles and Hardesty pounding him from behind, holding Todd's waist with his hands, the palm of one hand rubbing on the gecko tattoo. There was a nipple-chewing missionary position taking and then, after a doze, there was a side split. The fourth was Hardesty flat on his back and Todd riding the cock in a cowboy position. Each time, Hardesty made sure he had rubbing contact with the gecko tattoo.

In the morning, Hardesty woke up to an empty bed. He wasn't surprised. If Todd was good at anything, it was disappearing. Four of the five fifties on the dresser were gone too, but a deal was a deal. At least Todd was honest in not ripping him off for more than he got—no matter how hard Todd had tried for that fifth bill.

As he drank his morning coffee, Hardesty walked around the house, looking for what might have to be changed. He stood in the doorway of the second bedroom and assessed the furnishings. Would Todd want a separate bedroom? If so, for how long? What colors should he redo it in? If his clothes were any indication, Todd seemed to be partial to green and gold.

He shook his head then, as if forcing the cobwebs out. Would he have to buy a lock and chain too to keep the kid here? He didn't think so. Todd was really into the fucking the previous night. Hardesty didn't think it would be that long before he would come around to the whole ball of wax. It was murder out on the street.

Hardesty would just have to keep trying. "You gotta keep trying," he said out loud as he went into his own bedroom to get ready for work.

Chapter Three: Always Wanted to Be in the Movies

A week without locating Todd anywhere, and Hardesty was beginning to question whether he'd ever find him. He'd either gone to ground or to another city—or maybe home. Maybe Hardesty would need to find a way to get information on Todd's background out of the manager of that club where Todd had been dancing the pole. Maybe Hardesty would need to lean on that guy a bit.

He spent more time at the club, but although it was running along the edge of legality, Hardesty wasn't able to find it on the wrong side of that edge. He did get the name of one guy from the other dancers there. Todd had said that he was substituting for someone. A couple of the dancers were able to tell him that it was for a guy name Nathan.

"Nathan. Nathan Winston," one dancer said.

"No, honey," one of the more effeminate dancers broke in. "That would be Winstead."

"Does Nathan Winstead still work here?"

"No, sugar," the more effeminate one said as he looked Hardesty up and down like he was a candy bar. "He's gone."

"So, do you know where he went?" Hardesty asked, focusing his attention on this dancer. He touched the dancer's arm and then when the dancer shivered for him and gave a low moan, Hardesty let his hand trail up the dancer's arm.

"I'm not sure I remember," the dancer said, conveying that the bidding had opened.

"What would it take for you to remember?" Hardesty asked, placing his other hand on the dancer's waist.

Hardesty fucked the information out of the dancer, such as it was, from behind, as the dancer was bent over the back of a straight chair in the dancers' dressing room. Nathan Winstead seemed to be into live-action Internet porn now. The dancer had no firm answer on where Nathan was, but he'd heard something about a studio up 16th Street somewhere. And, oh, yeah, there was also some middle-aged, but well-preserved, rich guy in construction who used to come sniffing around for Nathan. He'd stopped coming around when Nathan stopped dancing here. And, yes, of course, for future consideration, the dancer would be happy to keep his ears open for where Nathan lived now and who the construction man was.

"I had him one night when Nathan was home sick and the construction man had ants in his pants. One strong cocker, honey—but not a candle to you, sweets."

When he went to the precinct the next day, Hardesty found a bunch of the other Vice detectives gathered around the equipment of one of their Internet techs, Charlie.

"Damn," he heard Charlie say as he walked up to the group. "Lost it again. Almost had it. West by northwest of here is the best I can do. At least for now."

Hardesty walked around behind him. The screen everyone was staring at was blank.

"The screen is blank, you idiots," he said.

"Doh," said one detective.

"It wasn't a few seconds ago, dumbass," another said.

"Roll your recording of it back, Charlie. Show Hardesty what we had," said another.

It was a scene set up in a room with a big bed in the center of it. There was no attempt to hide the lighting equipment in the areas at the sides of the bed. The bed was centered on an exterior wall, or so it seemed. There were windows on either side of the bed. Unusual windows. There was a tall center pane, with a narrow pane on either side and then a short pane running over the top of all three windows. There were no drapes on the window. There was a light-blue coverlet on the bed and several pillows. The sheets were a glossy dark blue and were a bit mussed up.

Hardesty caught all of this in a glance. But he didn't look at it for long, because his attention was riveted to the figure of a young man on the bed, face and toes toward the camera. He was saying something into the camera, but Charlie didn't have the sound on.

"Turn the sound on, Charlie. Now," Hardesty commanded.

"My name is Tyler," the voice was saying to someone off camera, who was asking him questions in English with a slight German accent.

"And how old are you, Tyler?"

"Wouldn't you like to know?"

"Ah, saucy, boy. We'll see how saucy you are at the end the session." This was said with some amusement, not threateningly. "Where are you from Tyler?"

"From somewhere else but here. From a farm."

"And do you have animals on this farm?"

"Yes, big ones."

"What is your favorite animal on the farm, Tyler?"

"One named Thane."

"You have an animal on your farm named Thane?"

"Yes. He's big and black. And he's my mother's boyfriend."

"And does this animal play games with you?"

"Yes. He fucks me. And he's rough."

"Do you like big, black men fucking you rough, Tyler?"

"Yes."

"Show us what you have, Tyler, and maybe in the next segment we can get one of our big, black viewers to come in here and fuck you. I'm sure our members would like to see that. Would you like that?"

"Yes."

With that, the small youth with the blond Mohawk on the screen, who Hardesty knew as Todd, slowly stripped off his jeans—all that he had been wearing—and laid back on the pillows, still facing the camera.

"Very pretty, Tyler. Nice tattoo. What is it?"

"It's a little lizard."

"Very nice. Can you show us your hole, please. If a big, black man comes in here to fuck you in the next segment, we need to know if he'll fit."

Todd held his legs out and rolled his hips up to show his hole.

"Very nice, Tyler. I think our viewers will have fun with that. Now, can you make yourself come for us?"

"Turn it off!" The command cut through the room like a cannon blast and everyone turned and looked at Hardesty. Until now he'd been mesmerized and in shock. But he couldn't take any more. "Wait, roll it back to the beginning and run it again."

"Which is it, sport?" Charlie asked, more than a bit sarcastically. "Turn it off or let it roll?"

"Just do it," Hardesty barked. Then he softened. "Please. Please reroll it."

"Whatever you want, dude," Charlie said. He reran it and Hardesty looked at it real closely this time. Some of the other detectives drifted away, having seen more than they wanted to see the first time.

After the second running—the third, actually, Hardesty having missed out on the first one, Hardesty was back on the attack. "Where is that signal coming from? We have to stop that."

The squad's captain slid over to join the group. "That's just one of several, Hardesty. And it's not obvious it's child porn. It might actually be marginally legal. But the guy looks young enough that we can investigate on the assumption he's not of age. But not front burner. We've got too much on the plate already."

"We gotta do something. We gotta keep trying," Hardesty said, trying to keep his shock and anger in control. They didn't know, and there's no way he could let any of them know. "You gotta trace down where that Web site is broadcasting from, Charlie."

"We're doing what we can, Hardesty," Charlie said. "But let's keep it in perspective, buddy."

Hardesty was about to explode, but he couldn't do that. He willed himself to cool down, to sound reasonable. "Thanks, Charlie. I know you're working on it. Let me know if you locate it, and I'll keep my ear to the ground as well. Maybe I can come up with something that can help."

He turned and went back to his desk, and the rest of the detectives dispersed too, now that show-and-tell was over. Several of them wondered to each other what had set Hardesty off, though, and the answer, as it was for all of them, invariably was that Hardesty was working too hard and getting too attached to some of the cases. It happened to all of them eventually, they said. No one stayed on Vice forever, and Hardesty had already been in the unit for several years.

After everything simmered down, Hardesty moved in a circle back to next to Charlie's desk.

"I have heard about something like this, Charlie. The next time you see them on, start looking up high on 16th Street. It may be nothing, but it may connect with something else I'm working on."

"Thanks for the tip, Hardesty," Charlie said.

"Sorry about blowing like that, but—"

"No problem, I know how it gets. And guys like you have to go face-to-face with it on the street. I just click on buttons on this computer."

You don't know the half of the going face to face with it, Hardesty thought, as he picked up his jacket and headed for the tombs. He had to start checking this Nathan Winstead name out.

One key issue Hardesty thought was present in that tape, but one he couldn't voice without revealing he knew more about this "Tyler" than he should, was that it didn't sound quite like Todd. He was slurring his words slightly. And his eyes looked a bit dull. Hardesty was convinced that Todd was drunk on the tape or drugged at least slightly. But it didn't come out enough for anyone who didn't know Todd to be able to see.

Chapter Four: It's Just Business; and Business Is Good to You

"Come on, Charlie, run it to ground."

"Shhh, you're distracting me."

Hardesty; Crane, the squad captain; and a couple of other Vice squad detectives who weren't otherwise engaged were gathered around Charlie, who was seated in front of the computer screen and madly clicking away on the keys.

The scene was the bedroom with the unusual windows. A smaller screen was inset in the bottom, right corner. This showed just a running text of gibberish but evidently was program data Charlie was chunking away at, trying to get a fix on the origin of the signal.

The screen image was moving between three cameras, one at the foot of the bed and the other two at either side of the bed. As the camera angle changed, the other video cameras, on tripods and unattended, could be seen at the margin of the screen shot.

"What can you tell us?" Crane asked impatiently.

"Just so far that this appears to be live," Charlie muttered, his fingers still dancing on the keyboard. "The ones caught earlier today were recordings. They apparently are firing these off periodically in short bursts. These apparently are only the teasers, advertisements."

The scene was of Todd on his back on the bed. His arms and legs were stretched to the four corners of the bed and elevated, being held in straps hanging from a frame out of camera shot above the bed. A big, black stud of a man was on his knees between Todd's thighs, his hands grabbing Todd's waist and pulling the young man's pelvis up to his. He was fucking Todd in long, deep thrusts. The black guy had a black balaclava—a form of cloth ski mask—over his head. But he was wearing nothing else except an elaborate, multicolored tattoo covering one shoulder and arm down to the elbow—what tattoo artists called a sleeve. The cameras were picking up the action from behind the black man's back, with attention focused on the contracting and expanding of his bulbous glutes as he fucked Todd. They also were picking up on the root of his cock inside Todd's hole and the bouncing of the black guy's balls. The side angle on one side was focused on the long slide of the cock and, on the other side of the bed, on Todd's face, which was turned toward the camera, his mouth formed in a big "O" and both the contortions of his facial muscles and the expression of his eyes showing the pain-pleasure of each thrust. The soundtrack in the background, which Charlie had turned down low, seemed to be canned panting and "fuck me, fuck me, give it to me" phrases that didn't go with the movement of lips in the live show.

It also didn't sound like the voice of the Todd that Hardesty had well set in his own mind from when he was fucking Todd.

"The sound?" Someone behind Hardesty asked.

"Probably canned for the teasers," Charlie said. "Some shorts have live audio; some have this canned soundtrack. Damn, signal's off again. They seem to have these things timed for protection."

The screen had gone blank. Well, not exactly blank. There was a bunch of gibberish posted to the screen now.

"They're back." Crane pointed out to Charlie.

"Nope, that's from another signal location. Breaking in. It won't last long either."

"But is that some sort of foreign language?" The squad captain was asking the questions.

44

"I don't think so," Charlie answered. "Best thing I can work out is that's code for how members of this club can buy a copy of the whole segment—that what we have seen is just a teaser, an advertisement, for a full session."

"Members. You said members. What is this insidious animal?"

"I think it's a club," Captain. "I think men join—I've found a chat room connected to the site, but Steve is working on breaking that down. I think these are men who like to watch—and maybe have a go—at a stable of young models—they call them models. They get teasers on this Web site, and they can order full videos, or, I guess, set up an appointment. On the video we had of this young guy with the Mohawk cut yesterday, the invisible announcer seemed to be inviting big, black men to step up to the plate. And here, today we have a big, black guy who's doing that. I don't know how they get signed up, though."

"We'll have to check into that," Crane said "Try to get someone signed up and get inside. That blond guy didn't look legal age to me."

"We can't wait for that, Captain," Hardesty broke in. "We've got to do something now. That young guy . . ."

Hardesty stopped himself from spilling that he knew Todd just in time.

"These things take time and hard work," the captain said. "This one doesn't look like it's going anywhere for a while. It's deeply entrenched."

"Well, we gotta keep trying," Hardesty responded lamely.

"We will, Hardesty. That's the business we're in. Look, Charlie, the screen's come back on."

Charlie turned back to the screen and started racing with the time on the keyboard again. "This is a rerun. Saw this short earlier today," he said as he worked.

The scene was in a different room, but there still was one of the unusually shaped windows in the background. A young dark-headed man with dark, curly body hair, a real pretty-boy type—a shock of curly black hair, alabaster body, only lightly muscled, boyish, was on his back in a sling suspended from the ceiling. His wrists and ankles were cuffed high on the four chains. His head was pulled back and down at one end of the sling, with an olive-skinned man, middle-aged it seemed, but in good shape, feeding his cock in the young man's mouth. The man's head was covered with a black cloth balaclava. He otherwise was naked.

"The one at the head looks Hispanic," someone from behind Hardesty said.

"No tattoos that I can see," said Crane. "Maybe late forties."

At the other end of the young man was a gaunt white man, with ropey muscles and veins standing out on his arms. He too was wearing only a black balaclava—and a thick leather band around the base of balls and of a cock that must have been quite long, as it was taking a long time to enter and then pull out of the young man's hole. This time the soundtrack was of heavy panting and slurping noises.

"Curly-cued tattoo framing on the back and down the spine of the one behind," someone watching said, as the shot panned around to behind him. The scrolling on his back extended from shoulder point to shoulder point, came down to a V and trailed down to his waist.

"Damn!"

They'd lost the signal again, to be replaced with a screen of code.

"There must be a way to identify some of these young men," someone said. "We could approach it from there."

"Ssst. It's back," Charlie said. "Another rerun."

A voice in the background on screen again.

"You know why you're here, don't you, Peter?"

"Yes, I guess so," a young Asian man was saying. He was sitting on the end of the bed of the other location, huddled in on himself. He looked unsure. The voice was understandable but had an Oriental accent to it—probably not born in the USA.

"You guess so? We told you what we want and that we'll take care of you, didn't we?" The German accent Hardesty had heard from the first film.

"Yes."

"What are you doing in D.C., Peter? Tell these men here and the ones out there, watching you."

"I'm a dancer."

"And we told you all of these men were going to fuck you, didn't we?"

"Yes."

"Have you ever taken eight men at one time?"

"No." And the way he said it made Hardesty believe him.

The questioner with the German accent seemed to appreciate that answer too. His voice had a smile in it when he asked the next question. "And you are here of your own free will?"

"Yes." A little hesitant.

"Is that Chinese guy on drugs?" someone at the back of the viewing pack asked.

"Probably," the captain answered in a grim voice.

Back to the scene and the slightly German accented voice. "Don't be shy, Peter. Lean back. Let all of the men out there get a good look at you. They'll all want to be your friends, I'm sure. Will want to be good to you, like I've been good to you. I've been good to you, haven't I, Peter?"

"Yes, you've been good to me." The Asian guy went back on his elbows. It seemed like he'd ended that by saying a name, giving an identity to the man with the German accent, but any audible evidence of that had been wiped off the videotape.

"Heels on bed, Peter, and pull your cheeks apart. Let us see what all of these men have come to fuck—what all our viewers out there would like to fuck."

The young Asian man did as commanded. His hole was puckered, open. He was well used.

This reminded Hardesty of Todd, and that made what the young man said enter his consciousness. He'd said he was a dancer.

The figures of six or seven naked men, a few young looking, more tending toward middle age, the black shoulder-tattooed man from the earlier film among them, appeared at the edges of the screen. They were all naked, save for the balaclavas on their heads. Most of them were pulling on their cocks.

"Have you cleaned yourself out as I asked and lubricated yourself well?"

"Yes." The voice sounded trembly, uncertain.

"Good. And tell all of the men out there, Peter. Have you ever been gang-banged before? They will want to know. They will be especially interested if this is your first experience."

"No," the trembling voice still.

"No, what, Peter?"

"No, I've never done this before."

"The boss first then, shall we, gentlemen? Then line up by size, biggest last, please. We'll give him a progressive drilling effect."

The back of a man came into view from the center of the screen. A black cloth balaclava covered his head, as with all of the rest. The framing tattooing across his back identifying him as the man at the bottom of the sling in the earlier sequence. A brief shot from the side showed an unusually long cock, leather band around the root, in full erection. He had several leather strips in his hand.

Looking somewhat scared and dazed, the young Asian man was pulling himself up farther on the bed. But when the tall, gaunt man reached him, he turned the Asian man, belly down to the bed, snaked an arm around his waist, and pulled him back so that his feet were flat on the floor. The white man towered over the Asian and he quickly manhandled him, doing it dramatically for the camera so that it could see his wrists being tied together in front of him and his legs being bound close together with straps around his ankles and thighs. The effect obviously was to tighten his hole to accentuate the restriction of the room for a cock inside his channel. Then he was bent over the bed. He cried out—no canned soundtrack here—as the gaunt white man split his buttocks with a thrust of his cock. Three thrusts, accompanied by cries from the Asian and the screen went blank.

All who were watching just stood there, transfixed, no one able to say anything for a minute—until the screen changed to the coded message.

"Gone again, in time," Charlie muttered. "These last two have run periodically all day. The third one should go into reruns soon."

"If only . . ." the same detective started to say who had mentioned trying to track the "models" down.

"This last one—the Asian guy—said he was a dancer," Hardesty said. "And I think I've seen the first one on the poles somewhere too."—this was as close as he could come to saying he knew Todd—"I think I have an angle we can work."

"So do I," a voice from the back of the group piped up. Hardesty turned to look at where this had come from. It was Phil, his partner from that night he'd rousted Todd on the street. Phil was looking directly at him.

Oh, shit, Hardesty thought. He must have remembered Todd from that night. Now I'm in the shit.

But Phil didn't refer to that when he spoke. "I recognize the tattoo on the black guy in the second clip we saw. He's a pawnbroker up off Connecticut Avenue. I say we give him a visit. Having a member of the club in hand would be a good start."

No one asked Phil under what circumstances he had seen the torso tattoo of a pawnbroker who liked to fuck young white guys on camera. They knew Phil too well and were too excited about the solid lead he was giving. They were all shaken by what they'd seen in these short teaser films—and by what could be going on in the longer versions.

"I can go get him now. Anyone with me?"

"Yes, me," Hardesty boomed out before anyone else had a chance to respond. He'd follow the dancer lead later on his own.

Chapter Five: Busting It Up

"I don't need no warrant to tell you to take off your shirt, Alfonse. And I don't really need for you to take off your shirt for both you and me to know that you have an all-color arm sleeve tattoo, do we?"

The black pawnbroker stood there, behind the cash register in his junk-packed store and stared belligerently back at Phil. There was a touch of fear in his face too—which was disconcerting, because he was a big bruiser of well over six foot and probably tipping out at over 250 pounds of pure muscle.

"Don't know what that's got to do with anything," the man answered. His fists were balled up, but one of them was moving slightly forward, below the counter—right at the level a pawnbroker would keep his weapon. "I told you that little punk would lead you on a merry chase."

"Keep your hands in view, good buddy," Phil barked, as he unbuttoned his gun holster. "I could drop you before you got to anything, and you don't want this grief. This is business. This don't have nothing to do with business between me and you. I wouldn't want to have to drop you."

"No time for sweet talk, guys," Hardesty interjected. "Where is the Web site studio, Mr. Barkley. Just give me an address, we'll sit on you for a couple of hours, and then we'll let you go."

"What studio?" the black man said, turning his wary eyes to Hardesty. The Vice cop could see that Barkley was assessing how deep a hole he was in. He'd tensed up significantly at the mention of a Web site studio and had backed up a step, like he'd gotten a body blow from an unexpected direction.

"We saw you on the video with the tied-up blond trick, the one with the Mohawk," Phil said. "We're ready to assume he's underage, which puts you in a world of hurt. Not a piece I think you'd forget doing—like earlier today." Hardesty blanched at this characterization of his Todd. His Todd. The thought made him angry too and he slammed his fist through the head of a drum hanging from the column next to him.

This startled both Phil and the pawnshop owner, but they quickly looked away and were at each other again. Still, Hardesty thought if that rattled the black guy and made him think they were on the edge here, that was probably good.

"And we saw you getting ready to join in a gang-bang of a Chink," Phil continued. He wasn't known for his delicacy or political correctness. "Don't ask me 'what studio' again. Maybe you'd rather talk downtown, though."

"An address. Now, Barkley. We don't have time for this," Hardesty impatiently interjected.

"I want to talk with my lawyer," Alfonse Barkley answered, his eyes narrowed, his chin dropped to his chest in an "ain't gonna say anything stance."

"OK, we'll meet up with your lawyer downtown, Alfonse. You can call him from the squad car, when you're hooked up. Come out of there nice and easy now, big guy. Hands showing above your waist."

As they were hustling a handcuffed pawnshop owner to the squad car outside, Phil turned and muttered to Hardesty. "Good going. The strong-arm approach worked a charm, didn't it? And don't think I don't remember you talking to the blond Mohawked guy in the film out on the street the other night. Took him home with you that night, I'll bet."

"Shut it," Hardesty answered. But after they'd gotten the black guy in the back of the cruiser, Hardesty put a hand on Phil's arm before they got into the front.

"Yeah, and I remember you strutting back to the car, tucking in your shirt, and whistling to the tune of 'I Just Got a Blowjob on the Job," Hardesty shot back. "The guy you poked in an alley OK? Maybe I should go look for him and count the bruises?"

"Well, you obviously got ants in your pants yourself for the blond cutie," Phil said. "The others can't see it, but I can see that you're going nuts over him being in those videos."

"So what if I am? What are you going to do about it?"

"Nothing. We're all in this together. Not my watchout that you're getting too personal with it—but, if you are, you are. I've got your back—just as long as you've got mine. Just remember that."

"Thanks, Phil. Glad we're squared away. So, you're taking this guy to the tombs?"

"Yeah, but maybe not a part of the tombs where his lawyer will find him real fast. I think I can work this guy?"

"Maybe like he's worked you?" Hardesty said.

Phil gave him a level stare. "Yeah, well, you had your chance. If this guy gets put away, maybe you'll fill in his slot?"

Hardesty didn't answer that. He just got in the driver's seat and almost had the car on roll before Phil would slide in beside him.

* * * *

Hardesty went up to the Vice bullpen while Phil took Alfonse Barkley downstairs to the tombs. They hadn't given Barkley his call from the squad car. Hardesty had no idea how soon Phil would give the pawnbroker that call, but he had a feeling it wouldn't be until after they'd had a more intimate chat—if Phil didn't get sidetracked by that guy down in Transportation he was trying to hook up with. Sometimes Phil let his dick get in the way of his concentration.

His phone was ringing when he got to his desk.

"Hardesty?"

By instinct and well-oiled practice, Hardesty slapped his hand over the phone receiver and called out, "Phone trace; my phone," in a booming voice. He knew that someone would be on duty to jump right in on that. Then he was right back to the phone.

"Todd. Where are you? I've been worried."

"I just had to call. I'm sorry that I walked out on you, but, you know . . . I'm not used to . . . you're too nice to me. And a cop. I don't deserve anyone being nice to me that way. I've really fucked it up."

"Where are you Todd? I'll come right to you. I've got a room set up for you at home. In green and gold. Those were your school colors, right?"

There was a pause on the other end. Hardesty welcomed it and didn't break into it—both because it meant Todd was considering what he said and because the longer he kept the young man on the line, the more likely the call could be traced.

"I don't know. I've got something good going now, I think. A steady gig with good money. They're good to me. They're my friends."

"I'm your friend, Todd. I can be just as good to you. I care for you. I don't think anyone else you're with does." He couldn't go further than that. He couldn't let Todd know they'd been watching him being taken. That surely would tip the scales on this call.

"I don't know. It's good here. I'm not on the street. You left me on the street."

"No, I didn't, Todd. Think. I offered you something else. You walked out on me. You went back out on the street on your own. God, Todd. I've been tearing my hair out looking for you. I'm asking you to come home. I . . . I . . ."

"Home? I don't know. So many want me. Some of them just like Thane. I just don't know. You talkin' 'home' sounds a lot like control again."

Hardesty was aghast. He'd almost said it. He'd almost told Todd he loved him. He'd never said that to anyone else. Why was he almost saying it to Todd? Was it true or was he just being dogged and willing to do anything to get the youth out of the business?

"Todd. It doesn't have to be any way you don't want it. You can make all your own decisions—but maybe better when you aren't so confused. Why are you calling me if you aren't sure that I care?"

"Umm, I . . . I just want to thank you for trying for me. You're the first guy since I hit D.C. that treated me right—well after . . . you know."

"God, Todd, I'm sorry. You don't know how sorry I am about how it started. But . . ."

He didn't complete that sentence, because the line was dead.

"Trace?" he yelled out.

"Sorry. A disposable," shot back the answer from across the bullpen.

* * * *

"Nice to see you, sugar. I was just thinking about calling you. I could use some of you. But I thought you'd like to know that I saw Nathan at the club last week."

"Nathan, at the club," Hardesty parroted back to the dancer calling himself Freddie—the effeminate one who had told him that Todd had been substituting for Nathan.

He wasn't sure he'd heard right. They were at the back of the club room, but the sound system was on full blow, and the crowd was cheering the three dancers on the poles.

Freddie wasn't one of the dancers in this set. Hardesty had seen him when he'd entered the bar, still in his G-string and sitting on a burly guy's lap. When Freddie saw Hardesty, though, he rose from the lap—much to the disgruntlement of the man he'd been working—and motioned Hardesty to another, empty table.

"Yes, he was gone before I could speak to him. He was talking to one of the new dancers, Ping, though, before he left. And the next day Ping took off too. Didn't appear for his set, and I haven't seen him since."

"Ping. That's a peculiar name."

"Not for a Chinaman, it isn't, sweetie. Ping was Chinese. American now, but not from here. Good dancer too. All of the really good ones seem to be moving on quickly . . . except for me, of course." Freddie gave Hardesty a brilliant smile, fluttered his false eyelashes, and put his hand on Hardesty's thigh, really high on this thigh, and not on the outside either. He had an index finger on Hardesty's crotch and was rubbing something cylindrical inside the material. It was stirring in there for him too.

Freddie was a disposable type for Hardesty. When he was randy and he didn't want anything complicated, he'd just stroll down any street in this district, and the Freddies of the business would be pulled into his wake. A quickie in that motel room he used and tensions gone for a couple of days with no threat of attachment.

"And were Nathan and this Ping talking serious?"

"They seem to be—them and that construction guy I told you about."

"He was here too?"

"Yeah. You asked about his name. It was Gunther."

"Gunther. It sounds German."

"He sounds German too. It's fun to hear German words when someone is fucking you. Do you speak German, Mr. Hardesty? I could give you some words you could use."

Bingo, Hardesty thought—not for Freddie's blunt proposition, but the German accent. His spirits soared. It was all coming together. "This Gunther have a last name?"

"I'm sure he does. But we never got around to sharing last names. We share other things, though. Are you in the mood to share, Mr. Hardesty? I rather think so. Sharing might help me remember more."

There was no denying that Hardesty could share. Hardesty's cock had far less taste than his brain did. Freddie was cupping his basket now and continuing to stroke his cock with an index finger inside the material of his trousers.

Hardesty tried to ignore that—for now. He had to concentrate. He was on the trail. Things had to happen fast from here.

"Is he a tall, thin guy, but good muscles, veins standing out on his arms, and a winged tattoo all across his back."

"Don't tell me he fucks you too, darling. That would be a shame. Such a waste of a magnificent cock—yes, I can get its measure, big boy. But, yes, that's him—not that I've ever gotten a good look at his back, except at the beginning, when he's undressing."

"And you'd be able to pick him out—and Nathan—and Ping—on videos?"

"I don't see why not."

"And will you come down to the precinct with me to look at some videos? No hassling, just some IDing of men."

"I have videos that would knock your socks off back in the dressing room, doll. I'd like to take your socks off myself."

Hardesty sighed and threw a brain wave at his hard-on that he'd gotten the message—but only, he told himself, in the line of necessity. "Later. I'll give you something special later, if that's what you want—if you'll go down to the precinct with me now and do this one thing. Just a couple of minutes of your time. I can book a motel room on the way over, if you want some sort of assurance."

"Eight inches of assurance?"

"If that's what you want. Maybe more."

The dancer visibly shuddered. "Let me get something more than this on, lover. I'll be only a minute. This isn't really the right attire for a police station performance. Will there be a lineup? Can I give specifications of the men I'd like to see lined up?"

* * * *

The Web site was on the air when they got to the precinct. The captain raised an eyebrow as Hardesty, pulling Freddie along with a hand on the dancer's arm, slid into the semicircle of detectives looking at the film.

It obviously was already near the end of the film clip. One naked, balaclava-helmeted bruiser was on his back on the bed. Todd was draped on top of his chest, looking up at the camera. The man's cock was inside Todd, and Todd was moaning and looking dopey at the camera. The man's legs laced through Todd's and lifted his out and up. A second man, with a balaclava on, a little more pudgy and older than the first, came down on the bed on his knees, he walked on his knees to between Todd's spread leg. A side-angle shot showed him entering Todd's ass with his cock—on top of the cock already there.

The man on top was whispering something lost to the camera, and Todd answered in a thick voice, "Yes, it's OK . . . I can . . . oh, shit."

The man on top was beginning to stroke inside Todd. He's taken Todd's ankles in his hands and was holding the young blond's legs up high and spread well apart.

"Say it. Tell the viewers you want it. That we take care of you. That we're good to you." An off-camera voice with a German accent.

"Yes," Todd conceded in a slurred voice, "You're all good to me. You're my friends."

"And you want other friends from out there, beyond the camera too. Invite them to join the bid to share you."

"Yes, I want it again," Todd murmured.

But then his eyes snapped wide open and he grabbed out for the shoulders of the man on top. He began to writhe between the two men and to cry out, "Yes, yes. Fuck me. Both. Harder! Getitgetitgetit, Give it, Give it . . . Oh, God, YES!"

Hardesty had seen where the guy on the bottom had moved a hand to Todd's gecko tattoo and was rubbing it.

"Turn it off. Turn the fucking thing off," Hardesty said.

"Can't. Working here," Charlie answered, his fingers dancing on the keyboard.

The captain pulled Hardesty aside. Hardesty, in turn, pulled a wide-eyed Freddie with him.

"Calm down, Hardesty," the captain hissed. "This isn't like you."

"We've gotta keep trying, captain. We've got to bust these guys."

"I know we do. We're all working on it. And who's this you've dragged in?"

Dragged in wasn't far off the mark. Freddie was dressed so flamboyantly that there was little question what he was or what he'd do for money.

"A dancer. I think he can ID—"

"That was Todd," Freddie blurted out.

59

"I'm sorry you had to—" the captain started to say. But then he turned to Freddie. "That was who?"

"God, I wish that was me," Freddie murmured, lost in his own little world. "That was Todd. He danced with me at the club."

"So, he knows the blond guy," Hardesty said before the captain could react. "I thought that might be the case. Let's show him the other tapes and see who else he can identify."

"That's Nathan, yes. Nathan Winstead. He's a dancer, yes. and he's with Gunther—and the Hispanic is called Leon. Boy, can he cock. That's Gunther again, the one obviously in charge. He's in construction, you know. Somewhere up 16th Street, I think is where Nathan told me his offices are. No, I don't know his name . . . or where on the 16th Street. And Ping. The Chinese guy is Ping. He is a dancer too. And, oh my, oh my. I think I'm going to faint. Somebody give me a fan."

"Perhaps a glass of water," The captain said, motioning to one of the detectives.

"Oh, no, sugar. That's just a figure of speech. I think I might faint in a good way."

The captain looked perplexed, like he didn't know what would be appropriate to say. He fully understood that the weird gay guy was providing useful information and that he, the captain, needed to stand back and not get in the way of the flow.

"So, that's it? That's all you recognize?" Hardesty asked.

"Well, the rest are mainly muscles and hood ornaments and dicks, honey, but I can tell you that those people are having one hell of a good time. Now, Mr. Hardesty, if we're done here, you said you'd give it to me."

"Umm, do we need to go tap the snitch fund, Hardesty?" the captain asked.

"No need, captain. I got this. I'll take Freddie back to the club and be back in a few."

* * * *

"Oh, honey, honey, you horse-hung stud. Oh, Yes. Be good to me. Give me your sugar. Yes, just like that. It's not the long arm of the law; it's the long cock. The thick, looooong cock. Oh, Fuccck, yes. Keep pumping me like that and I'll tell you anything."

Hardesty had Freddie kneeling on all fours on the bed in a room in the same motel he'd taken Todd to that first time. He was crouched over the figure of the little dancer close, his cock buried to the hilt, fucking in hard, pistoning action, short jabs, deep. He'd snaked an arm under the small man's waist and was slow pumping his dick.

His mind was wandering as Freddie babbled. The fuck was OK, but it wasn't Todd. And it was just paying off an informant—at least he told himself that. He knew it was idiotic, but his cock liked fucking the Freddie types. They seemed to appreciate it and fucking them was uncomplicated. There was nothing personal in it for any part of him other than the cock, though. And, yes, he did sometimes think of his cock as a different personality all together. It certainly seemed to have a mind of its own from time to time.

So, he was as much a prostitute as Todd was. He was just as prone to sell himself for what he wanted in return. That was sort of comforting to think of. It took the complication out of his perpetual randiness. Freddie was small. Todd was small. Both Nathan and Ping had looked small. Were all pole dancers small—and boyish? Did they all babble and squeal when they were being fucked like Freddie did? Not Todd. Well, not until his tattoo was rubbed.

"Oh Sweetfuckingjeesus! You're makin' me come." Hardesty had stopped the pistoning temporarily and was revolving his hips slowly, moving his cock in a circular fashion deep inside Freddie's ass. Freddie's groans and the way his body was shuddering indicated he loved this attention. Hardesty pumped hard a couple of more times and Freddie's body jerked and he came inside Hardesty's fist. Hardesty moved that hand up to Freddie's mouth, and the little dancer licked the cum off it.

Hardesty began to pump again. "Oh, lover, yes. Hard. Deep. Like that. Gotta take care of daddy." He clenched his channel, and it was Hardesty's turn to groan.

"Now, don't you come before telling me you're ready. But you can fuck me like this all day. You're amazing. Fuck me all day. Oh, Sweetfrigginggod, don't you come now without telling me."

"I'm telling you."

"What?"

"I'm telling you. I'm about to . . ."

Freddie was quick as a rabbit. He pulled away from under Hardesty and turned and scooted down all in one fast, fluid movement. He jerked the condom off Hardesty's cock and reached up to twist Hardesty's nipples as his mouth closed over Hardesty's dick. He was just in time to collect all of Hardesty's ejaculate.

Hardesty rolled one way onto his back and Freddie rolled the other way, both stretched out flat on their backs on the motel's king-sized bed. The bed was the only quality piece of furniture in the room. Hardesty had always thought that was so the springs would be solid, wouldn't squeak and disturb the fuck games of those in the neighboring rooms. Truth be known, though, this is why he rented at this motel so often himself.

"You give good fuck . . . for a cop," Freddie murmured. Then he laughed. "Sorry, just joking. You give great fuck for anyone."

He turned toward Hardesty and came up on an elbow, with his hand cupping his chin. "You're sweet on Todd, aren't you? You're not just asking about him because you're a cop and it's your job, are you? You care for him."

"Yes," Hardesty answered with panting breath.

"I could tell by the way you asked questions about him—and by the way you reacted to those videos."

"Yes."

"That's why I told you what I did. I'm not usually a snitch, you know. But I could tell you cared about one of us."

Hardesty didn't answer that. He was processing it.

"That and because I could tell you had a monster cock and could fuck. And you do and can. And I wanted it inside me. Even if you're a cop. And a Vice cop, too I think. Worst kinda cop. But what a way to go. Cuff me and haul me off. But fuck me in the back of the squad car. That's what a lot of the Vice cops do."

Freddie laughed again and even Hardesty managed a chuckle.

"You said, during sex, that you'd tell me anything, Freddie."

"I'm not accountable for anything I say during hot sex. But OK. What do you want to ask?"

"Back there, at the precinct, when you saw Todd being doubled. You said you wished it was you."

"Yeah, I sure did. Do you know how I can get into movies too, sugar?"

"Doing that?"

"Hell yes."

"Having other men do that to you?"

"Why not? Why do you think I'm a pole dancer? Did you think it paid well? There's nothing wrong being addicted to cock, honey. That's me. And guys like Todd. And Nathan and Ping. You think they don't know what they're getting into? They're just addicted to the cock. Some

63

of them are addicted to bad boys too. That's Todd, I think. But I think you can be a bit of a bad boy too. I'll bet you went into Vice so that you could fuck honeys like me in the back of your squad car. And when they can have a monster cock like this . . ." Freddie had rolled over to Hardesty and had Hardesty's cock in his hand. The cock was noticing the attention ". . . they make the most of it while they can. People like me and Todd get old too. If we're addicted to cock, we get the most of it we can while we can. And what if men get off on thinking they are in control and getting it by force or sneak, if that's their fetish? If men will pay for that, all to the good."

"But Web sites like that. The danger. The degradation."

"Some men like the danger, even the degradation. For some, it's more arousing. Didn't you see how Todd stepped it up several notches when it was getting really tough. It's a high he was reaching for. I'll bet he gave it to you good in the back of your squad car."

More like in the front seat of his own car, Hardesty thought. But he didn't want to tell Freddie that it more was that Todd had an incredibly sensitive erogenous zone and someone had stenciled a gecko on top of it to point the way.

"So, you think that someone like Todd isn't going to settle down?"

"Sure he would. If he had the right cock inside him twice a day. One like this one." Freddie had worked Hardesty's cock up hard again, and Hardesty was slow panting, trying—without any success at all—not to show he cared. "And someone who eats his Wheaties like you do, lover. My, my, you've come back fast. And big. You like me; you really like me." Freddie laughed before continuing. "What is it, hon, seven and a half or eight by two? I keep statistics, you know."

"Something like that," Hardesty said through heavy breathing. "I haven't bothered to measure it."

"Liar, all men measure themselves." Freddie gave the cock a little slap, and Hardesty jerked in surprise and short-lived pain.

But he knew Freddie was right. And of course he knew how big he was—to the centimeter. And he was a little miffed that Freddie had guessed on the short side. "What if cocking doesn't seem to be enough?" he asked.

"It's enough for someone like Todd, trust me. You just have to get his full attention first. And give him the security he needs. And cocking twice a day. If you want to find him in your bed in the morning, keep your cock inside him all night. It's just the way it is with guys like Todd and me. And speaking of cocking twice a day . . ."

"I can't, Freddie. I've got to get back to the office. I've given you what . . ."

"Yes, you've given me the cocking you promised. And you gave it to me good, better than you had to. But your cock doesn't agree with you. You're hard again, all eight and a quarter inches of you. Didn't think I could measure with my eyes, did you?" He laughed again and then moved on top of Hardesty, pinning him to the bed. "And now I'm going to make love to you, and there's nothing you can do about it."

Freddie was straddling Hardesty's thighs, and Hardesty had thrown an arm across his face, knowing they were going to fuck again, that once again his cock had won over his resolve. "Ahem," Freddie said, and Hardesty took his arm away from his face and looked up at Freddie, who opened his mouth in a grin. It took a few seconds for Hardesty to realize the young dancer had a condom pellet in his mouth.

"Freddie, no."

Freddie leaned down over Hardesty's pelvis. He gripped Hardesty's balls with one hand and squeezed hard enough to convince Hardesty just to lay there quietly and Freddie unrolled the condom on Hardesty's cock with his lips and teeth. Hardesty groaned his imprisoned arousal.

Still gripping Hardesty's balls, Freddie moved up, straddling Hardesty's pelvis, skewered his ass on his chosen pole, and slid down it to the root. He lowered his lips on Hardesty's nipples, and his long, blond hair, having escaped its pony tail, was brushing on Hardesty's chest and shoulders. The small man grabbed Hardesty's upper arms and pressed them out to his side. That was only symbolic. Freddie didn't have the strength to hold Hardesty's arms down if the big man didn't want him to.

But Hardesty just laid there and moaned. Freddie was doing something with the muscles of his channel that had Hardesty in thrall. His mind flipped to what Freddie said about big men and their fetishes and the fetish of being in control—and he realized that he wasn't in control now. Freddie had him imprisoned in the prison of lust, of the male need to get his rocks off.

Hardesty groaned and gave into it. He easily freed his arms, reached down and cupped and squeezed Freddie's buttocks cheeks. He pulled his feet up flat on the surface of the bed, raising his pelvis for a deeper penetration of Freddie's channel, which caused Freddie to moan. And then, using the leverage of his heels, he began to stroke hard and deep.

"Oh, Sweetfuckin'jeesusss!" Freddie cried out. "You're killing me. And don't you stop doing it! At least eight and a quarter—maybe more! Give it to me. All of it. Oh, god, closer to nine. Oh fuckin' shit, honey. Work me, baby." Freddie dug into the mattress with his knees and started rocking back and forth on the cock, groaning and moaning and breathing too hard to comment further . . . until after he'd shot his load and was working Hardesty's nipples with his mouth and teeth again while Hardesty was still stroking. "Tell me before you come. You gotta let me know before you come."

Afterward, as Hardesty was dressing and Freddie was still laying on the bed, on his back, legs splayed, and playing with his cock with his hand, Freddie said, "Hauptman. The construction man. His name is Gunther Hauptman. Hauptman Construction Company. The guy on the tapes telling everyone what to do. The one with the wings tattooed on his back and speaking with a German accent."

Hardesty gave Freddie a hard look.

"I had to be sure. Todd is a lucky man. Go find him. And remember, just keep him well fucked. Keep it inside him all night. Nine inches of cock should do it fine. And I know you can't wait. Go ahead. I'll get back to the club on my own."

And then to Hardesty's retreating back: "If you find out how I can get into those movies, you'll let me know, right?"

And as almost a whisper when Hardesty was through the door: "And if Todd doesn't want you, come back to me. I do."

* * * *

The first bad news accosted Hardesty as he hit the stairs hard up to the third-floor Vice bullpen. Phil was standing on the second floor landing, looking dejected—and very guilty of something.

"What did you find out from . . . ?" But Hardesty didn't finish the sentence. From the guilty look Phil was giving him, he knew the crux of the story already.

"He's gone. His lawyer had him out of here before I could get him booked."

"Gone? Blakely's gone?"

Phil didn't answered.

67

"How the shit can a perp be gone even before you get them charged? We didn't give him the phone call for his lawyer in the car. We conveniently forgot to give him that."

No answer.

"Oh, fuckin' A. You got down to the tombs and put him in a cage and then you went to the motor pool, didn't you? Let that big guy in dispatching dispatch you on his desktop, didn't you? Took all the time in the world doing it too, right?"

"We know where he is. We can just go back and pick him up."

"And what the hell good would that do, Phil? He's on the loose. He knows what we were dragging him in for. First thing he did, I know, is to call Gunther Hauptman."

"Gunther who?"

"Oh, shit, Phil. You may have lost them all for us just because of your need to have a cock inside you—and your attention deficit disorder."

Disgusted and panicked, Hardesty pushed the other detective aside and hit the stairs running. Moving fast past Charlie's position en route to his own desk, Hardesty had a sickening thought.

"Charlie, I told you the other day to latch onto the upper 16th Street corridor at the beginning of your race with the clock on tracking that Web cam location. Did you?"

"Oh, shit," I forgot. "Very next time, I promise."

As he passed a researcher's desk, he said—almost yelled—"A Gunther Hauptman of the Hauptman Construction Company. Can you get an address stat, Cleo? Should be on 16th Street."

"Will do," a young woman said, all business, as she swiveled back to her computer terminal.

The message light on Hardesty's phone was blinking.

The message was short; it couldn't have been traced even if someone had picked up on it live.

"Hardesty. It's me again. I've been thinking. Maybe you're right. Maybe you should come pick me up. I'm at . . ."

That was it. The message had been cut off.

"Oh, fuck."

This matched an "Oh, fuck" floating up from Charlie's position as well. "Captain. Guys. Hardesty, you'd better come watch this. I'll rewind."

The scene on the screen was the Hispanic, his black cloth balaclava in place, standing on the bed, feet spread. Todd was suspended from his middle, their pelvises glued together, Todd's torso swung down in front of and away from the torso of the Hispanic, the young man's wrists, in handcuffs, dragging on the bed. His legs were wrapped around the Hispanic's hips and, with his ankles cuffed together.

The coverage apparently was live. The Hispanic was gripping Todd's waist on either side, with the fingers of one hand rubbing the gecko tattoo.

Todd, sounding nearly spent, his cum already dribbling down his chest, was murmuring. "Deeper, harder, you're so big. Do it, do it. Getitgetitgetit! Oh, god, you're so good to me. FUCKFuckfuck." From there, Todd's voice was reduced to a slow-motion babble.

As they watched the screen in horror, a tall, thin figure came into the playing field from the right margin. He was clothed, and he kept his gray, buzz-haircut head turned away from the camera lens, but Hardesty didn't need any proof to know that it was Gunther Hauptman.

Hauptman barked "It's busted. We have to leave." The accent was German.

He had a white cloth in a hand and he knelt on the bed and placed the cloth over Todd's face. Todd squirmed briefly and then was just hanging there until the Hispanic pushed him down onto the bed. Hauptman backed to the camera and knocked it to the floor, where the only visual was the bed skirt. There briefly were sounds of a weight being hauled off the bed, but then the camera was switched off.

A female voice called out from across the room: "2315 16th Street. Home address in Bethesda, Maryland, if that helps. 6472 White Oak."

Hardesty turned and looked at the chalky-white face of Charlie. "She's right," Charlie said almost in a croak. "It ran long enough the first time to get a fix. 2315 16th Street."

"Captain!" Hardesty called out, but Captain Crane was already there.

"I know. We gotta keep trying," he said. "16th Street it is. Mount 'em up, crew."

Phil was there now, all guilty looking and wanting to do something. "I'll go back and pick up Alfonse Barkley. He'll just have gone back to his shop."

"Suits me," Hardesty said with a hard edge to his voice. "I don't think you deserve this bust anyway."

* * * *

The address was right. Hardesty knew that as soon as they pulled up outside the building. The windows were the dead giveaway. Two thinner panes beside a central, long pane. And another one running across the top of the three. Windows like that all across the upper stories of the vintage building.

It wasn't that hard to find the suite of offices assigned to Hauptman Construction, either. The suite number was on the listing in the lobby. It was harder to find the Web site video studio, and they only did so when the hidden staircase in the closet in Hauptman's construction company office was discovered and led them up to a series of three rooms above. Only the bed frame was in the one room, and only the ceiling hooks here and the one in the room that had held the sling were still present. The third room also had the frames of single beds in it—five of them. There was a refrigerator and hot plate, and a bathroom. This was the only room that wasn't entirely cleaned out. From the pizza boxes, miscellaneous pieces of clothing, and gay male magazines strewn around, it would have taken a bulldozer to sanitize this room.

Hardesty stood there, in the middle of the room, seething and holding a baseball cap in his hand that was a yellow-gold with the word "Lions" embossed above the bill.

"Damn that cocksucking Phil," Hardesty muttered under his breath. And then he set his shoulders and called out. "Let's hit the Bethesda house. He hasn't had time to clean out here and there both."

The captain was at his side. "Bethesda's out of our jurisdiction, Hardesty. We'll have to call in the Maryland police."

"So, call Maryland, Captain," Hardesty said. "They can meet us there if you can get them off the pot. In the meantime I'm taking a ride into Maryland. Anyone going with me?"

"I know, I know. Gotta keep trying," Crane said. Then he shrugged his shoulders and joined the exodus for the door.

It was true that Gunther Hauptman didn't have time—on the schedule that Hardesty had set—to clear both locations out.

He met them at the door to his Bethesda house, only opening the door a crack, putting on a brave front.

"Is there something I can do for you today, officers? I'm afraid you can't come in. My wife has cancer and she's just managed to—"

71

Hardesty socked the smug man in the mouth, and trucked right on into the foyer, letting Captain Crane lunge at the man with the German accent in an attempt not to let him fall back on his head on the marble floor.

The raiding party caught a glimpse of Nathan Winstead at a secretary in the living room, feeding paper into a shredder. He spent an instant too long looking like a deer in the headlights. With a flick of his wrist Hardesty had sent two officers off to grab him.

Hardesty hit the stairs to the second floor, taking them two at a time. He accosted a naked Alfonse Barkley outside a closed bedroom door and pushed him into the arms of a couple of more cops. He momentarily enjoyed the grim satisfaction that Phil wouldn't even get this bust.

He burst into the room. Todd was on the bed, naked and on his back, and his wrists handcuffed to the headboard. His legs were spread, with his ankles cuffed with leads to the corner posts at the foot of the bed. His pelvis was elevated by pillows, and there was cum dribbling down his inner thighs from his hole. There wasn't much question what Alfonse had been doing before he came out into the upper hallway.

Todd was babbling as Hardesty managed to get him released.

"They were going to kill us. I heard them talking about it. You were right. They weren't my friends at all."

"Shush, Todd. It's over. Just be quiet and relax. I'll take you home soon."

"Home?"

"Back to our house. Don't think about it now. Don't think about anything. Just rest."

"Ping. Where's Ping? They said they were going to kill us, get rid of the evidence. Not Nathan. He's one of them. Their procurer. But Ping . . ."

They found Ping in another bedroom. They had to disarm the Hispanic who was wielding a knife first. Ping hadn't been as lucky as Todd had been, thanks to the Hispanic's knife.

It was only then, when all of the Web site gang that were here had been ferreted out and disarmed, that they heard the sirens.

"Ah, the Maryland police," Hardesty said, sardonically. "I wonder what they'd have found if these guys had had a little extra time."

"I'm sure we can smooth it over," Captain Crane said. "It won't help having you mouth off, though. And I take it you want this Todd guy kept out of it for the moment—it can't be for long, of course. Get him out of here. I don't want you here either. Out the back door. He's on the tapes and he'll be needed as a witness, but—"

"Captain."

"Yes."

"Thanks. Just thanks." Hardesty didn't even want to know how Crane knew—or why Crane was helping him and Todd this way. He figured Crane wouldn't want to talk about it, so he wouldn't. But anything Crane wanted him to do from here on out, he'd be there doing it.

He found a pair of jeans that fit Todd and had him out the back door, while Crane was still dealing with the Maryland police at the front of the house.

"I'm taking you home and you're taking a hot shower and then sleeping for two days before anything else," Hardesty said on the ride back to his place. "You'll have to give statements and be at the trials and all—there will be a lot of trials. It will take us some time to roll up all the direct participants and then the club members. But I'll do what I can to keep you out of the worst of it."

"Hardesty."

"What?"

"My name isn't Todd. It's Toby."

"Yeah, I guess I had that figured out. That's how I knew you were pretty innocent to all of this too. You were walking around with true identity cards on you."

"You looked."

"Yes. That first night."

"So, it was just a job."

"Looking was just a job. The fucking that followed—that was personal. And I don't think either of us knew it at that time, but I think, for me, at least, that was lovemaking."

"Oh." It didn't sound like he was fully convinced. What could convince him?

"My name is James," Hardesty said. "But you can call me Jim. Just you, though. Everyone else has to keep calling me Hardesty."

"Jim?"

"Yes?"

"The shower sounds nice. But after that, I want you to fuck me."

"After all you've been through, you want the cock?"

"Yours, yes. I want you to make love to me with that huge cock of yours. I want to know that someone will take me who just wants me—who isn't taking advantage of me."

Hardesty's thoughts went back to what Freddie had said. Some guys just naturally live for the cock. Freddie said that Todd was one of those guys. And Freddie said that if Hardesty wanted to keep Todd, he'd have to keep him with the cock. Suddenly Hardesty understood. This, of all times, was when he needed to pin Todd to the bed with the cock—and to keep it inside him until Todd lost any instinct to run.

"Sure, if that's what you want."

They were on Hardesty's bed in the master bedroom. He had shown Todd the other bedroom, redecorated for him in green and gold, and Todd had said he liked it and would use the room, but he wanted to sleep with Hardesty in the king-sized bed in the master bedroom.

Hardesty had always been pretty much of a "fuck 'em and then go home to my own bed alone" type of guy. But then he thought of Freddie's advice again: *If you want to find him in your bed in the morning, keep your cock inside him all night.*

Toby was on his back in the center of the bed, his legs hooked on Hardesty's hips, Hardesty's knees up under Toby's buttocks. Hardesty was pulling Toby's channel back and forth on his cock.

"You're so big. And so thick," Toby murmured. "That's what I remembered about you. All of those men. So many men and so often, and what I remember is you deep inside me. Deeper than anyone else. Thicker than anyone else."

"I had someone tell me it was nine inches once," Hardesty said, in jest. He laughed to mark it as a joke.

"I think it must be. Hard. We should measure."

"It's busy now," Hardesty said.

"It certainly is, and I won't give it up for measurement."

If you want to find him in your bed in the morning, keep your cock inside him all night.

Hardesty felt Toby's hand on his, the one gripping Toby under his pec on the right side, and tried to move it down to the gecko tattoo.

"No, Toby, not tonight."

"I want to go wild with you tonight. That's my spot. That frees me."

"Who told you that was your spot?"

"Thane. My wife's boyfriend."

"And he had you tattooed there?"

"Yes. It almost didn't happen. Thane had to hold me and the tattooist had to fuck me while he was doing the tattoo."

75

"Toby, you are free to go wild with me any time you want. You don't need a crutch of any sort. Let's see what we can do without the tattoo."

"OK," Toby answered in a small, unconvinced voice.

Hardesty lowered his mouth to Toby's and took him in a long kiss. Toby sighed for him. Hardesty moved his mouth to Toby's nipples and the nipple ring, and Toby moaned for him. Hardesty move a hand down, between Toby's thighs and worked three fingers inside Toby's channel alongside his cock, and Toby groaned.

All the time Hardesty was slow pumping him.

"Ah so deep, so deep," Toby whimpered. "It's got to be nine. Don't stop. Please don't stop."

Hardesty was still chewing on his nipples. He started moving his cock inside Toby with his fingers. Combining rotation with the in and out, in and out pumping. Toby arched his back and howled, "Yes, YES! Give it to me, Give it to me. God, sooo deep."

Hardesty pulled his finger out and found Toby's cock. He slow pumped him with Toby babbling and writhing under him.

"This is as good as finding the tattoo. I can feel your passion."

"Yes, yes, fuck me hard."

Hardesty began doing just that, and he increased the stroking of Toby's cock—until Toby jerked and spouted up in the space between their quivering bellies.

"Thank you," Toby murmured.

"It's not done," Hardesty whispered. "For one thing, I haven't come. For another I am staying inside you all night. And I am going to be hard much of the night. And I'm going to fuck you constantly . . . through the night."

"Oh, god," Toby whimpered. But it was a happy whimper.

Hardesty began pumping again and Toby answered him with a counterpunching of his pelvis. Hardesty reached in the folds of the sheet and brought out a flexible dildo. "This really is nine inches," he murmured. "We'll do our measuring inside."

"Oh, fuck, oh, shit." Toby groaned. But he brought his feet up flat on the surface of the bed, dug his heels in to elevate his pelvis more, and widened his stance.

Hardesty began working the dildo in on top of his own buried cock. Toby cried out in passion and set his pelvis in motion, grinding hard against Hardesty's groin. They came almost simultaneously.

Hardesty let Toby free to roll away from him, while he pulled his spent condom off and dropped it over the side of the bed into the wastebasket.

"Your turn to bring it back to life," he said as he pulled Toby down toward his thighs.

Near dawn, Toby stretched out on his belly and Hardesty covering him, his dick still deep inside Toby's channel, the young man murmured sleepily.

"Jim."

"What?"

"I think we're going to need to get a bigger wastebasket in here."

"That or stop investing in rubbers," Hardesty said. "If I'm the only one in there, we don't need rubbers."

Hardesty felt Toby shudder—but, more significant, he felt the tears in the hollow of his neck. It wasn't long before he knew Toby was asleep by how regular and shallow his breathing was. But Hardesty himself didn't sleep a wink that night in his determination not to let himself slip out from inside Toby on at least this night.

Chapter Six: Down on the Farm

"You promised you could keep his photo and name out of the papers," Hardesty growled. His fist came down hard on the assistant district attorney's desktop.

"I know, we tried. But this has dragged on for months. Mr. Drake isn't a minor, you know. He may look like one, but he isn't anymore. We were doing this as a special favor to your unit. The accused have a right to face their accuser, you know. We just didn't know there would be press at that exit of the court house."

"You just didn't know. You don't know the trauma this young man has gone through. He was dragged into this." Hardesty was improvising off in lala land now, and he knew it. The Vice cop inside him told him that Toby walked into it all willingly. The number of times he had to cock Toby still—in the day and all through the night—screamed what Toby had willingly done for the cock.

But Toby was his Toby.

They'd been good for well over eight months now as the trial formed up. Freddie's advice had been right on. If Hardesty kept his cock inside Toby through the night, Toby was just as normal for the rest of the time as he could be.

The blond Mohawk was gone. Even the blond was gone. The eyebrow ring was gone. Hardesty had asked him to keep the nipple and navel rings, though, He liked to play with those himself.

Toby had admitted that he had done all of this punking up to himself just so that men would notice him and want him.

"I don't think you have any trouble with men wanting you," Hardesty had answered. "What you need to do is regiment what you are willing to give them."

Hardesty had been quite clear in not demanding monogamy of Toby, and although Toby seemed to have appreciated his suggestion that they might become monogamous with each other to the point of dispensing with condoms, he had only mentioned that the one time. And he was secretly relieved that Toby hadn't wanted to carry through with that. Hardesty had no idea whether Toby was being fucked by other men when he wasn't there. But he hadn't stopped fucking other men himself. Hardesty couldn't make the same pledge, not only because sex was a possible need in his job, but also because he occasionally had to have some variety himself. He had met with Freddie in the motel room four times in the eight months, for instance. Freddie amused him. He gave him a great ride, and he initiated expert and inventive positions that were completely out of the realm of Toby's experience.

Most of all, Hardesty wanted Toby to know that he could make his own decisions, that he wasn't trapped by Hardesty in that regard.

The gecko tattoo was still there. Hardesty had said that Toby probably would have had a continuous orgasm and die of sex in the process of someone trying to erase it. Toby had laughed. And then Hardesty had touched the tattoo and rubbed it and Toby had wrapped his legs around Hardesty and ridden him down onto the bed and begged for the fuck.

So, the effect of the gecko was still there—and Hardesty used it occasionally, often when Toby showed signs of despondency, especially at the slow movement of the trial and all of the statements he had to give.

When Toby had shown up to the trial to testify in person, the press had waylaid him outside the courthouse and splashed his name and photo across the media.

Toby's response was to withdraw into the house and refuse to see anyone but Hardesty. That's when he had let his hair grow on the sides and he'd stopped coloring it.

Hardesty knew that this was not a good turn of events, but he was wholly unprepared for the evening he came home from work—and Toby was gone.

He'd taken practically nothing with him. But this was the Toby of old—the Todd who had escaped from adversity, had been willing to shut Hardesty out, to not think twice about what Hardesty wanted and needed in the relationship.

"Some relationship," he muttered to himself on the third evening alone in the house. He wasn't completely alone, though. He had a bottle of bourbon to comfort him.

It wasn't long, though, before all of the liquor in the house had disappeared down his gullet. He was enough in control to realize at this point that liquor wasn't the answer for anything.

He sought Freddie out at the club, and Freddie willingly accompanied him to the motel, where he babbled happily while Hardesty fucked the stuffing out of him.

After they were done, though, Freddie said, "You fucked with anger and panic this time. This time it is about Todd, isn't it? That he's gone again?"

"Toby. His name's Toby. And, yes, he's out there someplace."

"Did he tell you he was leaving?"

"No, but he didn't do that before either."

"But that's when he was Todd. As you said, now he's Toby. What did he take with him?"

"Nothing."

"Doesn't that raise your suspicions?"

"It hasn't until now."

"Did you follow my advice? Did you keep him fucked—and keep him filled through the night?"

"Yes."

"And you think with what you're packing, and with those muscles, and that face, you can't keep him that way?"

Hardesty didn't answer.

"What was it you used to say when you were looking for him before? That you gotta do something."

"That we gotta keep trying."

"Yes, right. You don't know what's happened to him. So, why did you stop 'keep trying'? You don't want him anymore? Cause, if you don't, baby, you can have me—any time you want me. Of course you can have that anyway."

That hit home. The next day Hardesty began to put his detective skills to work. He hit pay dirt in the first hour.

"That young boy you have living with you?" the nosy neighbor across the street asked, her prejudices streaming down her sleeve. "Yeah I saw him leave a few nights ago. A big, black man took him down the walk and put him in a truck and off they went. You know, this is a nice neighborhood; you shouldn't—"

"Took him, Mrs. Nolan? You used the word 'took'."

"Yeah, well, the way the black guy had him by the arm and was dragging him down the walk, I don't think he was all that happy about going. My Dennis said it was probably Child Services, and I'll tell you—"

"Thank you, Mrs. Nolan," he said as he turned and briskly walked off.

* * * *

"A subpoena? For the records of a male strip club?"

"You still need Toby Drake for his trial testimony, don't you?" Hardesty asked.

"Yes, we've got a summons out for him. We have the transcripts, but the actual live testimony pins the case down better."

"Well, before all this happened, I tried to get a look at the employee records of that club. Toby had just started working there. The club manager indicated he knew about Toby's background. I have reason to believe he's been kidnapped—and not for anything related to this case. So, if you want him back, get me a subpoena to look at the strip club's employee records."

"We can do that," the assistant DA said. "We do need him back."

"And check out a Thane Moore, black, drives a truck and lives on a farm. And maybe some woman with the last name Drake. I think Toby might have been taken back home."

"I thought you said you thought Toby Drake had been kidnapped."

"If I'm right, he has been. By his mother's boyfriend."

"His mother's boyfriend?"

"Yeah, the guy who abused him sexually to begin with. The guy who caused Toby to get into all of that trouble."

"Oh. Right away then."

* * * *

The three police cruisers rolled up to the Virginia farm shortly after dawn, with sirens and lights off.

Hardesty was the first one out of the squad cars. He intercepted a big brute of a black man who answered "Yes?" when Hardesty spoke the name "Thane Moore," and Hardesty decked him without warning. He left the man, on the ground, rubbing his jaw with two shotgun-armed deputies standing beside him.

When Moore went down on the ground, a basket hit the ground beside him. Somebody's breakfast had been inside and spilled out on the ground.

As the other deputies swarmed around the yard and into the house to see who else they might find, Hardesty stood and scoped out what was in line with the direction that Moore had been walking in. Not the barn, but a large shed near the barn.

Toby was huddled in a fetal position inside a cage in the shed.

"You came for me, Jim," he whimpered, as Hardesty looked around and found heavy-duty wire cutters.

"Of course I did," Hardesty said, trying not to cry. "My nights have been too cold. My cock missed its sheath."

And then, having cut through the cage wire enough to help Toby, wearing only jeans, out of the cage, "You didn't walk out on me this time."

"No, I wouldn't do that. My nights are too cold too."

"How did he know?"

"He was a member of the club. And he'd been following the case closely, worried about when or if they'd catch up with him. He saw me on the videos. He just didn't have time to do anything about it before the bottom dropped out on that business. He knew about the club I'd worked at, saw me on the TV coverage at the court house, and paid the club manager to tell him I was with you."

"I'll have something to talk to that club manager about," Hardesty said. "Got any shoes around here?"

"No."

"I'll carry you to the car."

"They'll see."

"I don't give a shit what anyone sees. Did Thane fuck you after bringing you here?"

"Yes. A couple of times."

"But not through the night?"

"No."

"Good. We'll add that to the charges, though. Taking you home now."

"Home. That sounds so good."

"Just one regret."

"What?"

"Thane dropped your breakfast on the ground when he fell."

"That's OK. Thane's breakfasts weren't worth shit."

Snitches

Chapter One: Day One

He should have known. He should have known that Hal Etheridge wouldn't have had him brought to a fleabag hotel like the Downtowner on 14th Street. Chaz and Fred, two of Etheridge's minions—goons, really—had met Jason at the elevators on the 12th floor and virtually frog marched him down the corridor to a room off the back of the hotel.

"Is he here? Is Etheridge here?" Jason asked with a shaky voice. He didn't like it that it was Chaz and Fred. They'd always leered at him when he was brought someplace to service Etheridge.

"What d'ya care as long as you get paid?" Fred asked. "You don't care who uses you as long as you're paid."

"Shh, keep your voices down in the corridor," Chaz admonished. Chaz was the leader of the two. Neither of them was really bright enough to be considered a leader. But they both were just the type of muscle a politician like Hal Etheridge needed to do his dirty work and cover it over, when needed.

Jason only now was getting the idea that maybe he'd been moved to the "cover-it-over" phase. Maybe he'd gone too far in his snit with Etheridge the last time they'd trysted. He didn't know then, though, that a candidate likely to get a party's nomination for president had already name U.S. Senator Hal Etheridge as a vice presidential running mate.

They stopped by a door at the end of the hall next to a window with a fire escape outside it and the brick wall of yet another building, probably built in the thirties as this hotel had been, across the alley. The neighboring building probably was as dreary and outdated as this hotel was.

"Inside," Chaz growled as he turned the lock of the door to a room with an old-style key. The door swung open, and Jason saw a smallish sort of hotel room with scruffed up furnishings, a window overlooking yet another solid brick building wall, and a tired-looking bed with a brass head and footboard and a yellowing white chenille bedspread.

It wasn't the sort of room vice-presidential contender Hal Etheridge would pick for a sex session with a regular servicing rent-boy like Jason Stuart. He didn't go in for hotel rooms at all. He required special equipment to scratch his itch—and insulated walls. Jason was trained to serve these needs. The young blond was a real looker—a male model, minor porn star, and barista in a trending coffee bar. With blond hair, a small and perfect body, and boyish facial features, he didn't have any trouble keeping his dance card filled in. Hal Etheridge might be his most prominent client, but he wasn't the only up and coming politician Jason serviced.

"Where's Senator Etheridge?" Jason asked in panic, well knowing the answer to that.

"Inside, I said," Chaz repeated and pushed Jason inside the room, making the young man stumble forward.

As the door clicked shut, Fred voiced the obvious. "The senator isn't coming. He's busy with more important matters. We're taking care of this for him. We're your clients tonight. Who's first, you or me?" he said, turning to Chaz, who had Jason contained with one arm around his neck and the other around his waist, holding Jason into his body. Jason could feel that the big bruiser was hard.

"Show him the cash. My back pocket."

Fred pulled a wallet out of Chaz' back pocket while Chaz was working Jason's belt buckle and zipper. Jason moaned, but he didn't struggle. He did it for money and they were talking money. Fred fished four fifties out of Chaz' wallet and went over and slapped them down on the top of a scruffed dresser.

Quickly making Jason naked, Chaz draped him bent over the back of an upholstered, low-backed boudoir chair. Fred stood in front of the chair, holding Jason's wrists captive and face fucking Jason with a meaty cock he'd pulled out of his unzipped pants, while Chaz knelt behind Chaz and ate his ass out while pulling on his own cock.

When he was ready, Chaz did a circle of the room holding Jason in front of him, Jason's knees hooked on his hips and Jason's fists locked behind Chaz' neck, while the big bruiser crouched a bit, held Jason's slim waist between his hands, and bounced Jason's channel up and down on his hard cock until he'd ejaculated. Jason had come first.

Jason was calming down. This was his world, what he did for men. He even fell into the "Yes, yes, you're so big. Give it to me; be good to me, daddy" routine he used to inflame johns. His eyes were on the money on the dresser. They had shown the money.

Chaz then dropped Jason on the bed on his belly, and before Jason could respond—even if a response were possible with these two muscle men manhandling him in the small hotel room—he had been trussed up with three pair of handcuffs—two on his ankles, chained to the corners of the brass foot rail, with his legs spread and the other pair handcuffing his wrists behind him. Chaz stuffed the young rent-boy's mouth with his own briefs.

Jason started to struggle with Fred when he was handcuffing his wrists, but a fist to chin sent Jason sprawled with an "ooff," lashes to his buttocks and back again and again and again with Jason's own leather belt subdued him to whimpers and ended any fight he had in him. Even this wasn't beyond the zone yet. The fetishes Jason served—indeed what he took with the senator—included the lash and a bit of beating.

"You love the strap," Fred hissed at him. "Almost as much as you love the fuck."

"Your turn. I'm gonna take a shower," Chaz said.

"Where do you think . . . afterward? Down river or a public dump near Baltimore."

"Shut your yap," Chaz admonished. "He's still got ears."

"Won't do him much good though, will they?" Fred asked. They both laughed. "So, you wanna do him again, or—?"

"Naw. Not time for that. You can finish him. I'm taking a dump and then a shower. Nothing we have to clean up later, or you have to do the cleaning."

Now they were beyond the zone.

Jason, paralyzed with fear, heard the door to the bathroom close and Fred's belt buckle thump on the threadbare carpet. Then Fred, all 230 pounds of him, was on top of Jason's hips, his knees gripping Jason's thighs and the palms of his hands pressing down on Jason's shoulder blades. He was thicker than Chaz had been, so it took him a minute to bury his cock in Jason's ass, but once saddled, he began to ride Jason hard.

Jason's moans and groans from the thick, deep fuck were drowned out by the mechanical scream of the shower being turned on in the bathroom. After a few minutes of pumping him from behind and above, Fred wanted to change position. Jason felt the big man pull out of his ass, lift his weight from Jason's buttocks, and move off the bed. The handcuffs at Jason's ankles were undone and removed, and Fred came back up on the bed on his knees. He obviously wanted to do Jason in a missionary for a while. Surprisingly, he unlocked the handcuffs imprisoning Jason's wrists as well.

Jason's head was turned to the side and he could see a garrote strap laying on the bed. He no longer was paralyzed. There wasn't any doubt what these two goons had in mind—or why. Now that Etheridge was a national candidate, it was cleanup time on his background. Jason gathered all of the adrenaline that he could to unleash in one stroke. It was now or never.

With only one wrist out of the handcuffs, he now had a weapon of his own. He swung the loose cuffs at Fred's head in a desperate lunge that, nonetheless, worked a charm. Fred's eyes went large in surprise and pain as the metal of the free metal cuff slammed into his temple with the sickening sound of crushed bone. He toppled off the side of the bed and onto the floor with nothing louder than an "Ooof," which was covered from the bathroom with the grinding noise from the shower head.

Jason walloped him again on the side of the head for good measure, but the goon was already down for the count. Jason scrambled around on the floor, finding the key to the handcuff and freeing his other hand. It was only a matter of seconds before he'd pulled his clothes back on, grabbed up the money from the dresser, and scooted out into the hall.

He couldn't chance the elevator and the lobby. Who knew that these two goons were the only ones who had been sent to capture and eliminate him? He had seen the fire escape through the window at the end of the corridor when he'd been shoved into the room. The window didn't want to cooperate on opening, but, feeling infused with superhuman strength fueled by the survival instinct, Jason muscled it open and had scrambled down the fourteen stories of metal scaffolding before Chaz had turned the shower off in the hotel room.

Did he dare go back to the apartment on R Street in Northwest D.C., near Logan Circle, that he shared with three other rent-boys to at least gather his shit together before he escaped town? Had he ever told the senator or any of his goons where he lived? He didn't think so. The goons had always picked him up on the street—on 13th Street—when the senator wanted to be serviced—just like they had tonight.

Yeah, he thought he could chance it. He'd been stupid, though. In that last argument he'd had with Etheridge, he not only had revealed that he knew who Etheridge really was, but that this gave him some form of control over Etheridge. But he'd never have snitched on Etheridge—not that the senator could or would count on that, Jason now realized.

* * * *

Hardesty was cruising the old Impala along 14th Street in Logan Circle gay district, his eyes peeled for trade. Despite what he was out here for, he was looking for something special—in size and type. He was always on the lookout for something special in that regard. He had the tape recorder attached to his wide black leather belt on the driver's door side. He was dressed the part—black jeans and black leather boots and a black leather vest over a black muscle T, showing off his bodybuilder musculature. A black knit stocking cap was pulled down over his buzz-cut hair, hiding the gray that was starting to show here and there.

He was forty and would have looked it if he wasn't so muscled up. He had a close-cropped mustache and beard too, but the gray there didn't show in the not-long-past twilight in his dark Impala out on the street, as he pulled over by a group of young men standing near an alley entrance—one that opened at the other end for a quick getaway, as needed. He knew he looked like a thug, which he could easily be, on demand or when he got wound up. His gray eyes had a steeling, piercing look to them and the nose had obviously taken a few too many hits. Otherwise he looked good—if what you were looking for was a little danger and more than a bit of the rough.

It was hot enough that he didn't really need the vest, but it hid the piece in the holster in his left armpit. he was right-handed.

A couple of the rent-boys moved away, either down the dimly lit street or into the alley when he pulled the Impala over. Maybe some of them recognized him or the Impala. The guy who had caught his attention hadn't. Young and short, but very well formed. A look of innocence and nervousness. Hardesty hadn't seen this one before. He wasn't blond—he was at least partly Hispanic— but he was a pretty boy and looked like he'd be fun to break, and Hardesty knew he couldn't have everything. He turned the recorder on, hit the roll-down button for the passenger door, leaned over, stared the young Hispanic down, and called out, "You. Come here."

The young guy jerked, turned his full attention to the Impala, squinted, and squeaked out a "Me?"

Neophyte, Hardesty thought. Think I caught this one early, on the rise.

"Yes, you. Come here."

"Yes, sir, can I do something for you?" the Hispanic said as he came, leaned an arm on the sill of the passenger door window, and got the front of his face into the car. His arm was trembling, the expression on the young guy's face went through a couple of permutations, like he wasn't quite sure the look he should be taking on.

"You just loitering with friends or are you looking for company?" Hardesty asked.

"What did you have in mind?" the Hispanic asked. He'd obviously been told he shouldn't bring up the deal— like that would give him some protection or anything.

"What services are you offering? You look pretty green. You sure you're—"

"I'm old enough," the guy said.

There, the first barrier crossed. Hardesty asked, "And experienced enough?" That, legally, could mean just about anything.

"Yeah, I can do it all."

Pulling him out—like taffy. There wasn't much question what that meant.

"What's it all? You take it or give it?"

"I can give a good BJ and can take a big cock."

Bingo. "How much each way?"

"Twenty and thirty. Best on the block. Just see if you can get better."

Proof he was new to it. Hardesty and any other john certainly could get better. "Get in." Hardesty switched off the recorder. He'd gotten what he needed and he wasn't that wild about recording any of the rest of it.

He got onto P Street headed for 16th. The guy really was small. He was dressed in short shorts, sandals, and a tight T-shirt. As Hardesty got back onto the street, the guy turned his torso toward him and reached over and palmed Hardesty's crotch. "Holy moly," he mouthed breathily. Whether he'd say that to any john or not didn't bother Hardesty. Hardesty knew he was packing.

"You said you could take it big, kid. And old Dick here has been cruising around looking for it." He dipped into his pocket and pulled out a fifty-dollar bill and slapped it down on the dashboard. "Just so you know I'm good for it," he said. As he'd fiddled around with his pocket, he'd unstrapped the recorder and let it slide down between the seat and the driver's door. Chances are good he wouldn't be using it.

There came a decision time for a guy like Hardesty—either to do strictly what he came out here to do or to approach it from another angle and get his enjoyment out of it too. This guy wasn't what he normally liked, but he was liking what he saw anyway. And he was in the mood.

"So, like, you want me to blow you now, while you're driving?" the kid asked.

"First, what's your name? I don't like just anyone sucking my cock. I like to know who they are. I'm Frank." Of course he wasn't Frank at all—in much of any sense of the word when he was working the street like this.

"Raul. My name is Raul. So, you want me to suck it now?"

"Be my guest. We're headed to a hotel up the road. I have a room there. But if you want to get a head start, go ahead."

The guy seemed to be anxious to get at it. He already had Hardesty unzipped and had a hand inside his pants. Others on the street must have told him to get right to it. That, if it was a cop, he'd have to back off at that point. Hardesty didn't play that game.

"Holy shit, Raul exclaimed when he'd unrolled the cock. It's big, really big."

"It'll get a lot bigger. And it's been needing attention. Take it in the face when it gets there."

Hardesty pulled over into a gas station that looked like it was closed forever, not just for the night, and pulled over by the pumps on the station side, the pumps blocking good observation from the street. He reclined his seat and put his hands on the back of Raul's head as the young guy bobbed his mouth up and down on the cock. He wasn't intending on taking it deeply, but Hardesty used his hands to make sure that the Hispanic did just that, gagging and gurgling as his lips tried to get to Hardesty's short hairs. Part of Hardesty's plan was for it to bother the guy.

"Now, pull off now," Hardesty commanded, releasing Raul's head, and the young guy managed to pull back up just in time to take a thick wad on his cheek and nose. He started to sit up, but Hardesty grabbed the back of his head and held him there to make sure he took the second, and third load as well.

"Do you always . . . ?" the guy said, with a voice of awe.

"Always. You're not bad. Here's a Kleenex," Hardesty said, reaching down between the seats to pull one out of a box. "Clean it off." It wasn't a bad blow job, but it wasn't anything close to the most professional one Hardesty had had, which was further evidence that he had caught the guy early.

He nosed the car back on the street and drove the three last block to the Downtowner hotel on 16th Street, in the close-in northwest of D.C., above Union Station. He pulled up in front of a dark clothing store front several doors down from the hotel's front entrance. "You get out first—yes, you can take the twenty that you've already earned. Go over and stand just inside that alley over there and wait for me. I'm going to repark the car."

The Hispanic docilely did as directed and Hardesty parked down the street where the curb was cleared in front of a fire hydrant. He walked back to the mouth of the alley, where Raul stood, hunched over on himself and looking very nervous.

"Down the alley," Hardesty said.

"Why?" Raul asked. "Thought we were going to the hotel."

"We are. But you don't want them to see you taking a john into the hotel, do you?"

"Suppose not."

Hardesty went back into the alley, followed, not too closely, by Raul. He opened a door and light tumbled out into the alley. "Come on then," Hardesty said, and Raul caught up with him to find they were entering a back hallway, some sort of employee's entrance. There was a service elevator too that took them up to inside a storage room on the fourteenth floor.

Down a narrow hallway, Hardesty turned at one of several doors along the corridor, used a key to open it, stood aside and ushered Raul inside.

It was a small room on the back of the hotel. A double bed, brass headboard and foot rail, covered in an off-white chenille bedspread. A threadbare gray carpet, a nightstand with a lamp with a torn shade on it, a scruffed-up dresser, and a writing desk, with a boudoir chair pushed into it. The bathroom, which had seen better days two decades earlier, opened off to the left. The one window, bordered by gauze curtains that probably wouldn't meet over the window, overlooked a blank brick wall across the alley. They must be close to the street front, as the on-off glow of a green neon sign filtered in from the right of the window.

"Strip and go down on your belly on the bed," Hardesty commanded.

While Raul did so, Hardesty stripped too. Out of the corner of his eyes, the young Hispanic saw Hardesty place a tube of lube and three condom packets on the nightstand.

"Hey, man," he started to say, and he sat up on the bed. But then he saw Hardesty put two fifties down on the top of the nightstand as well, and they choked off anything he had to say. But he did shudder. More evidence he was a neophyte.

"On your belly, on the bed," Hardesty growled again and with a low moan, Raul complied. He groaned as Hardesty saddled over his buttocks embracing the young man's thighs on either side with his knees. He murmured in surprise, though, when Hardesty began to massage his back muscles.

"You're tight. I don't want you tight," Hardesty said. "Relax."

The massage went on at length, and Raul did relax. In fact he was so relaxed and loose that he had nearly dozed off with the first snap of the belt awakened him in surprise and pain. Hardesty was up on his knees above Raul, still holding the young man's thighs between his knees. His thick leather belt was folded over and, whack, whack, whack, he was snapping it on the Hispanic's tender flesh—on his back and his arms. On his buttocks and his thighs. Again and again. Whack, whack, whack. Raul sobbed and writhed under the beating, but there was no competition between them. Hardesty had him by fifty pounds.

"Oh shit, oh fuck," Raul cried out as Hardesty let off with the flogging as fast as he had started it up. He was using the belt to tie Raul's wrists together over his head.

"Up on your knees," Hardesty commanded, not waiting for Raul to comply as he ran an arm under the young man's belly and jerked him up. Grabbing Raul's cock and balls in one hand and squeezing the balls while Raul squirmed and cried out for mercy, Hardesty buried his face in Raul's butt crack and ate his ass out, running his tongue deep into the young man's hole. No mercy was given.

In short order Hardesty had rolled a condom on his cock, mounted Raul's hips, worked his thick cock inside, grasped Raul's waist between his hands and, as Raul groaned and moaned and asked for patience and time to accommodate the dick that wasn't provided, Slap, slap, slapping his balls against the tender flesh of Raul's inner thighs, Hardesty fucked the shit out of him. Raul was hanging onto the brass rungs of the headboard for dear life as Hardesty rode his ass hard to an ejaculation. The bed groaned and shuddered at the intensity of the bouncing, the springs squealed, and Raul had to let loose of the brass rungs to keep his knuckles from being bruised by the headboard beating against the back wall.

When Hardesty had come, he went up on his knees, letting Raul collapse, sobbing to the bedspread. But he didn't leave him. He jerked off the spent condom, three-pointed it into a wastebasket beside the desk, and went back to massaging Raul's heaving back, running his fingers over the welts he'd raised with the belt.

When he was ready to go again, which was quicker than Raul was ready, he rolled on another of the condoms; thrust his cock inside Raul's channel again, to the sound of Raul howling; leaned down and put Raul into a full Nelson hold; and, arching Raul's torso up to his beefy chest, rocked back and forth vigorously, letting the rocking motion do the cock pumping for him.

Afterward Hardesty sat in the boudoir chair he'd pulled up to face the side of the bed, while Raul lay stretched out on his belly on the bed, panting and moaning low, exhausted, with his now-unbound arms radiating, uselessly from his torso, the one on Hardesty's side of the bed dangling down to the threadbare carpet. His eyes were big as saucers. His expression was one of surprise, shock, and incredible weariness. He was warily eyeing the service pistol Hardesty was holding in his lap.

"It's going to be like that here in D.C. if you choose this life. Every night, sometimes twice and three times a day if you want to make a living at it and don't have a sugar daddy. And you won't last long," Hardesty said. "Is that what you want?"

Raul said nothing. He obviously was scared stiff and hurting from the flogging and rough fuck.

"I'm a cop, see. A Vice cop. I could take you in for this. I should take you in for this. That's why I'm out on the beat tonight." He was flashing his "yes, I really am a D.C. cop badge" at Raul. Raul was impressed, but there wasn't much he could do about it.

"Oh, Christ," he did say. "Please, man."

"You have two choices from this point," Hardesty said. "I'm putting another hundred on the nightstand here. That's two hundred, plus the twenty you got in the car. I don't know where you came from, but that should be enough to put you on a bus to go back there and forget you ever came to D.C. to get killed doing this."

He slapped two more fifties on the nightstand. "The other choice is to stay at it. If you do, though, I have some words of advice that should keep you alive a little longer than the way you're going about it. First, don't approach a car by yourself like you did tonight. Get a buddy and cover each other's back. Have him stand there while you make the deal. Make sure the john in the car knows the other guy saw and memorized his license plate and can describe him. It could be a stolen car, but it, plus the ID, would be a start for the cops—and the john would know that. He's less likely to do more than fuck you as agreed. Also, if you want to get serious about it, get a cop for a boyfriend and protector. A Vice cop boyfriend and keep you from being constantly pulled off the street.

"Also, you charged too little. It's a dead giveaway that you aren't in full control and could be taken for a ride. Ask fifty for a blow job and be prepared to settle for forty. But have change for a hundred so he can't work you on not having the right money. Give the blow job through the window of the car, if you can. You're always in danger if you go someplace else with the john. I could have easily shivved you at the gas station or in the hotel room. Ask a hundred for an anal fuck but settle for seventy-five. Any cheaper and he'll know you're a newbie.

"Don't give your real name. You did, I think. I've looked through your wallet, and unless these are good forgeries, your name really is Raul. My name isn't Frank. A john won't give you a real name unless he's as much a rube as you've been tonight. Don't believe the bit about a cop can't carry through on the deal and still take you in. I could.

I have you recorded making the deal—but nothing beyond that. It would be your word against mine that I fucked you, and they'd believe me for court purposes, even if they knew I'd done it. Vice cops like me took it up for a reason. Most of us are randy for it ourselves. I've got regular snitches and I've got snitches I fuck. Most Vice cops will be the same. You stay in the business and I run across you again, I'll fuck you and not pay you. I won't protect you, though. No offense, but I'm partial to blonds.

"And don't let a guy bring you into a hotel like I did. Go through the front door. Don't let them get you into an alley and don't believe them when they say there's a back entrance that would be better. Make sure the doorman or someone else in reception sees you and the john real good. They don't give a fuck why you've come into a hotel like this. I could have fucked and offed you in the alley, or I could have brought you up here through the back, fucked you, and then offed you and walked away without anyone ever knowing I'd done you. I'd have all night to erase the evidence if I wanted to. Got that?"

"I said, got that?" Hardesty repeated when Raul didn't answer.

"Yes, sir," Raul said, his voice low and wavering.

"Last thing."

Hardesty paused, and Raul finally said, "What?"

"You do have a sweet ass, even though you're not blond. I wanted to fuck you. I want to fuck you again. But there's someone waiting for you wherever you came from who can love you properly. And you are a sweet fuck. Find love, not a john. I've got another condom on the nightstand and I've more than paid you for another round, so I'm going to do you the right way now. It isn't just the lesson. I want your ass again. And I have the power to take you whenever, and as many times, as I want. Remember that. I see you out on the street again, I'm bring you here and do you hard again. I won't pay for it, and you can't complain about it."

Hardesty moved to the bed and sat down next to Raul, coaxing Raul's face over into his lap. "You're going to suck me again now."

With a low moan, Raul opened his mouth over Hardesty's cock head. Hardesty twisted to where he could do the same with Raul's cock. After a few minutes, as they were both panting more heavily and were hard, Hardesty gently pushed Raul down on the bed on his back and moved his knees between Raul's bent and spread legs. He pushed his knees under Raul's buttocks, raising the young man's pelvis to him, and slowly entered the young man's channel again with his cock. the cock went in easier, as it had already reamed the channel twice that evening.

This time he took Raul slowly at first, in long, languid strokes, as he embraced the young man and covered him with kisses from his forehead down to his nipples. Raul lay in Hardesty's muscular embrace, open and in total, acknowledged surrender, and sighed at this version of the taking. As he heated up, he began to move his pelvis too, working with Hardesty, until the intensity of the fuck overtook both of them and they were pounding at each other and growling for the fuck, Raul taking the cock deep and hard and thrusting against it to take it deeper and harder. He was crying out, "Yes, yes, fuck me! Fuck me hard!"

And Hardesty *did* fuck him hard, the two of them moving in consort, not just a rent-boy and his john, but two well-tuned and toned lovers, getting as much as they could from each other—clawing at each other and thrusting their pelvises forward to get that last inch of depth. Once again, the headboard pounded against the wall and the bedsprings squealed, but now they both were so much into establishing and maintaining a coordinated rhythm that they were making music, not noise.

At the end, Hardesty rose and withdrew. He ripped the spent condom off, scored another three-pointer on the wastebasket with it, and creamed Raul's chest, while Raul, waiting for the multiple spoutings to finish, stroked his own cock with a hand, and arced his cum up onto his chest to mingle with Hardesty's. Hardesty lowered his face to tongue up the cum and then shared it with Raul in a kiss.

"Find someone at home who will do *that* with you," Hardesty said, as he jumped off the bed and headed for the bathroom.

At the door out to the corridor, showered and dressed, Hardesty turned and said, "If you can only remember one of the options I gave you, remember the first. It's what will keep you alive longer. I don't really want to see you on the street again. Remember, if I do, I can fuck you rough and not pay." And then he was gone.

Raul lay there for much longer, spread-eagled and one leg and arm dangling off the side of the bed. He was exhausted, but he had a small smile on his face. If this cop wanted to fuck him again that would be fine with him. And, no, he wouldn't have to pay for it. If anyone every asked him what a total fuck was, it was this.

* * * *

Raul gingerly climbed the seven stories of stairs to the one-bedroom apartment he shared with three other street rent-boys on 14th Street just a few blocks away from the corner he regularly stood to conduct his business. He was mulling in his mind what this "Frank" had said about pulling out and going home. Except the guy wasn't named Frank. He'd left a card, whether purposely or not, Raul didn't know, on top of the money on the hotel nightstand. It identified him as Hardesty, a D.C. Vice cop, and gave a telephone number.

He was going up to the apartment more to get the card out of his possession than for any other reason. If not that, he could have gone back to his corner. He'd heard the cop about the dangers of this work but he'd have to think about it. But even with the money Hardesty had given him, he'd still be tapped out. His share of the rent for the previous month was due. If he was going to cut and run home, he'd still need to turn tricks for a while to get relocation money.

He couldn't bring himself to toss this card, but he sure as hell couldn't let someone find it on him, and Raul couldn't predict who would be undressing him.

"What's happening?" he asked when he opened the door to the apartment. All three of them were there. That almost never happened. There were two sets of bunk beds crammed into the small bedroom, but they rarely were all occupied at the same time—nor was the rest of the apartment. But there they were, Jason stuffing crap into a suitcase and Drew prancing around just in his briefs mouthing off to Jason—and Lyle—tall, thin, black Lyle standing off to the side and taking it all in.

"Jason thinks he's throwing it over and leaving town. Going back to Allenton is Jason. Just like that. When we need to come up with the rent."

So much for me leaving now too, Raul thought, as he sat on the side of his lower bunk and slipped Hardesty's card into a pocket calendar in the nightstand drawer. "Why? What's happened?"

"You read the news—the national news?" Drew, a short blond who easily could be Jason's brother in looks, said.

"Drew," Jason exclaimed, stopping his packing and looking up. "Don't."

"News?" Raul asked.

102

"Yeah, a dude who's just been tapped to be vice president is a client of Jason's, and Jason, for some reason, thinks that makes life difficult for him in New York."

"Drew, shut your yap," Jason yelled. "You had to be there, dude. His goons were gonna off me. But I wouldn't have told you anything if I thought you were gonna broadcast it from the roof."

"Vice president?" Raul said.

"Yeah, vice president of the fucking United States. Gets it on with Jason. Whips him and beats him for his jollies. Gives him welts. You've seen them, haven't you, Raul? Well it's this possible fuckin' vice president of the United States that gives him those."

"Just fuckin' get out of the room—all of you," Jason said. "And keep your yaps shut. This is bigger than all of us."

Raul moved out into the living/dining space with Drew and Lyle.

"What're we gonna do?" Lyle said in a shaky voice.

"We're gonna let him go, if he wants," Drew answered. "He's been nothing but trouble anyway."

"No, I mean what're we gonna do about a big time politician beatin' up on call boys."

"I have my ideas," Drew answered. "Where the fuck you goin', Raul?" he growled, turning toward Raul, who had his hand on the door to the outer corridor.

"You said the rent's due," Raul said. "I don't know nothin' about this political crap, but I can see I have to get down on the street and rustle up some more rent money. Maybe you two better start thinking how you're going to throw more into the till until we get another roommate too." He'd put most of the money he'd gotten from Hardesty in the envelope taped to the underside of the nightstand drawer when Jason was getting all of the attention in the bedroom. But he'd kept some back. He

103

needed a drink—he needed a drink even before caging a drink off a john.

When he entered the gay bar near Logan Circle, the Purple Pig, he didn't make it all the way up to the bar before a big guy, who was bent low over the bar, nursing a drink, had seen him, swiveled toward him, given him a boozy smile, and opened his right arm out, waving with his hand for Raul to come into the space beside him.

"Want a drink?" the big guy, maybe six six and well over two hundred pounds asked, as Raul bellied up to the bar.

"In exchange for what?" Raul said, although that didn't keep him from bellying up to the bar, standing nearly a foot shorter than the big guy, and signaling to the bartender for a Corona.

"A bit of company, maybe leading to something more chummy. I've seen you standing the corner." The man put his hand on Raul's buttocks and Raul didn't flinch. He let his own left hand come down to rest on the thigh of the man's bent leg, with his foot raised to the bar rail. The man reached down, took Raul's hand, and slid it between the man's thighs, to his basket. Raul kept his hand there. The guy had a beauty of a bulge. The negotiations had begun.

"My name is Chaz. From out of town. And this is a lonely city."

"I'm . . . Julio"—Raul had remembered at least this of what Hardesty had said about survival in the business— "and no one with money need be lonely in New York."

The dude—the guy who said his name was Chaz, but it probably wasn't—dug his hand under the hem of Raul's T-shirt and was feeling up the young man's back, skin on skin. He stopped moving up abruptly and his fingers traced the edges of the welts Hardesty had raised there with his leather belt. The man gave a low whistled and looked directly into Raul's eyes.

"You do sessions?"

"Sessions? What do you mean?" Raul asked.

"You know, sessions. Bondage, whips, straps."

"Not usually," Raul said, shuddering.

"But you've done them. You did one very recently."

"Well—"

"$500 for a session. Now."

So much for negotiations. Raul very much needed money right now. Five bills was a mother lode.

"Money up front."

The money was produced and Raul flagged the bartender to come over and hold it for him. This was a regular service provided at this bar. the bartender would know what to do with the money if Raul didn't come back for it—he'd pocket it. But if Raul did come back, he'd return it less 5 percent.

The black SUV was parked in the alley behind the club. There was a driver. Chaz pushed Raul into the backseat, pulled a black hood over his head, and pushed him down to the floor. "Just security and your safety," Chaz said.

Raul already felt way the hell out of his element, but there wasn't anything he was going to do about it.

They drove for about fifteen minutes in city traffic. The hood was pulled off Raul's head as he was being pulled out of the back of the SUV. They were in another alley between two brownstones of four or five stories. Raul was hustled through a door and up three flights of the back, service area of whatever building they were in.

The bedroom was decked out in red satin, silk, and velvet—all very garish. It appealed to the Hispanic in Raul, though. The room was dominated by a four-poster bed, and Raul quickly learned that rest restraints dropped from the top corners of the canopies and restraint leads came out from the four bottom corners. Human cries of pain could be heard faintly from other parts of the building—both men and women.

He was stripped naked and hooked up at the foot of the bed, facing the bed, his arms raised, spread, and restrained and his legs spread and restrained.

Chaz fondled and felt Raul up intimately in that position—but not for long. Only long enough for Raul to hyperventilate and wonder why the hell he'd agreed to this.

The door opened and in walked a tall, slender man in black leather. His body was well-muscled but with the caveat that he probably was in his fifties. His body was well muscled for a guy in his fifties. He had a black leather cap mask that came down below his eyes and over the bridge of his nose. There was a matting of mostly gray hair on his chest and forearms. A black leather harness with a brass ring at his sternum caged his chest. He was wearing black leather leggings with the crotch and buttocks exposed. His pubic hair was salt and pepper. His cock was erect. His balls hung low in their sacs. He was carrying a hand whip.

It wasn't Chaz.

The whipping didn't last long, but it was hard enough to make Raul writhe and scream, adding to the cries elsewhere in the building that Raul still could hear. The tormentor seemed to enjoy this. It certainly enhanced his erection. The initial fuck, from behind, with the man cupping Raul's buttocks, raising his feet off the carpet, and setting his channel down on the man's cock, lasted longer and was relentless, the stroke strong and deep, with Raul, again, writhing and crying out.

There was a knock at the door before the man had come and he went over to open it and to talk with someone through the crack in the door. He raised his mask to talk and Raul, who had turned his head in that direction when the knock was heard, sucked in air.

He had, in fact, seen some news. He had no idea who this political guy was who was being touted as a running mate in the presidential race, but this clearly was the same guy they'd shown in the photos. He turned his head back in the other direction so the senator—he couldn't think of him with another name, although he didn't know his actual name—wouldn't know he'd been IDed.

When Senator Etheridge returned, he released Raul from the restraints, but only to force him onto his belly on the bed and to restrain him from the four bedpost corners again.

Whatever had transpired at the door had dampened the senator's ardor. He had to resort to the whip again, lashing Raul's back, arms, buttocks, and thighs repeatedly until he's worked his cock up. Then, mounting Raul's ass, and thrusting his cock deep, the senator started pounding his ass again as Raul cried out in pain mixed with a passion he couldn't deny and writhed as best he could within the limits of his bondage.

Chapter Two: Pumping Day One into the Next Day

Weary, Hardesty let himself into the fifteenth-floor apartment in Crystal City, across the Potomac from Washington, D.C., in Alexandria, Virginia. The apartment had spectacular views from all rooms across the Ronald Reagan Airport runways to the national memorials and the Mall. He was happy to see that the warning light by the door wasn't on. He needed some down time at home.

It hadn't been his decision to move across the river. Housing was expensive, to be sure, in D.C., but he'd inherited a small fifties-style rambler in the Northwest section that had done him well for a decade. But he couldn't argue with the view from here. It was a splashy apartment, which was the impression it was suppose to give and the service it was meant to provide. Two large bedrooms, each with their own bath, and a living-dining-kitchen great room sheathed on two sides by plate glass windows with an extraordinary view. He hadn't picked out the furniture either. He'd never feel like this was home, but he was weary enough tonight—after midnight—not to care about that. It was all part of an effort to keep his life together and not lose Toby.

If the warning light had been on, he'd have known that Toby was entertaining a client and that he should find someplace else to crash. Luckily, there was an old maid of a guy, Paul, down the hall in a smaller apartment who would be happy to take him in on short notice for the night in exchange for a cuddle and a quick fuck.

The apartment was part of Toby's escort service set up, with neither Hardesty nor Toby paying the whole fare. The service paid more than half the rent, but you can bet that the money came out of Toby's earnings. Except when he was an escort, he was Todd, not Toby. That's how Hardesty had first met him, as Todd, and it was the name under which he'd first fucked and fallen for him.

Even as Todd, though, he was Hardesty's ideal match—still young, at twenty-four, small, blond, fun to be with, movie-star handsome, with a channel that fit Hardesty's shaft like a glove, and fine with Hardesty's style that could get rough when he was unleashed. The two of them had been together for nearly four years now—if both of them having a separate, active fuck life could be considered "together." It was as close as Hardesty could demand, though, and there always was hope for something closer. Inevitably Todd would age out of the escort business, and Hardesty hoped to be there then to begin a new phase of their relationship. He would age out of the life of a Vice cop who could get whatever he wanted however he wanted in the not-too-far-distant future himself.

Hardesty went almost directly to the refrigerator for a cold beer. He applied the butt of the bottle to the back of his neck before opening it and walked around the living area, looking for someplace to light. Inevitably a headache was coming on. Nothing beckoned him, though. All of the furniture was sleek and modern—and covered with easily mopped-down leather. As usual, he wound up at the window, watching the Washington, D.C., skyline. The city at night—that's what he could relate to. Glittery, mysterious, the center of power—and imbued with every vice known to man. His gaze landed on the Washington Monument obelisk. A gigantic cock, overlooking the center of the city. A phallic symbol—a hugely erect one—always seemed such a natural one to him of the city in which he worked vice. another symbol of the power of the city.

The phone on the kitchen island rang. But it was Toby's work phone. He gave it a listen as the answering service switched over. "Tomorrow's 1:00 p.m. United flight to LaGuardia. A Brazilian, attending a meeting at the UN. Dinner at eight, clubbing afterward, and then whatever he wants. Aaron will meet you at security at the airport at eleven thirty with the packet."

So, Toby would be gone for the next couple of days. Hardesty would miss him. Nothing special on this weekend, so they could have done something together. Oh, well, as tired as he was, maybe it was for the best. And he had weekend duty anyway. Looking around the living room and deciding once more that it cold, not the least bit inviting to him, he retired to his bedroom, which was furnished with stuff he'd brought from his own house—stuff his parents had owned before him. So much more like home, down to the brass bed with the tired mattress and box springs.

He took a shower. As he was coming out of the shower, he heard the warning buzzer. They'd had that installed down in the lobby, by their mailbox. Toby—Todd now—was bringing a client up and had signaled Hardesty to disappear if he was in the apartment. Hardesty went over to his bedroom door and took a peek through the fish lens peephole that took in the full sweep of the living and dining area of the apartment.

They had been to the theater or some other formal occasion. They were both in tuxes and both looked good. Todd, of course, always looked like a million dollars. The other guy, though, older and Oriental, also looked good. He was probably older than Hardesty, in his late forties maybe. Elegantly dressed, though, with the flash of a diamond ring. He'd had to be wealthy or being treated by someone wealthy to afford Toby. He had black hair slicked back, and an inscrutable, slightly foxy, appearance to him. He was tall and slender. He looked confident and experienced and like he could be cruel. Hardesty would have to keep a check on the peephole. Knowing that, Toby wouldn't take the man into his bedroom until and unless he was sure of him.

They paused to kiss beside the kitchen island, and Toby must have said he'd fix drinks and then get into something more comfortable. In Toby's absence, the man walked around the room, swilling drink in hand, taking a good look at it, and winding up by the window. The view drew the attention of everyone who came into this apartment. Putting his drink down on a side table, he shrugged off his jacket and draped it over the back of a chair and loosened his bow tie, letting in dangle from his collar. But he didn't stop there. He undid the studs of his shirt, carefully pocketing the studs, and unbuckled and unzipped his trousers. Stepping out of them, he carefully deposited the folded trousers over his jacket. He paused, shirt hanging open, which, in the three-quarters profile he was giving Hardesty, revealed a slender but well-muscled, hairless torso. He had a gold chain around his neck, with some sort of green jade medallion nestled between his pecs. His legs were muscular. A puckered scar of a slash rose diagonally from below his navel to just below the bulge of the pectoral muscle on the opposite side of his chest. It gave him an aura of mystery and danger.

He was wearing what Hardesty recognized as expensive Ergo mini boxers, in black. They were the type of brief a rent-boy would splurge on to look sexy in. He looked sexy in them. They rode low on his hips and had a pronounced bulge at the crotch, designed to separate and project the crotch package. It took a well-hung man to wear them well. He did. His socks were black silk, knee high, held up on shapely calves by black garters just below his knees. The muscular thighs were those of a soccer player. He flipped his black pumps off by toeing the heels and deftly maneuvered them to beside the chair where his jacket and trousers were folded.

He obviously knew where this evening was headed, and he also obviously wasn't self-conscious about using what he had paid for and was an expert at it. Every move was deliberate, planned, and smooth. Cold blooded. There was no reticence or uncertainty of outcomes here or indication of time to be lost in getting his pleasure.

Toby could be in danger of a rough night here, Hardesty thought—not that he was one to talk about that.

Toby returned, wearing a red silk robe, loosely tied with a red sash, but showing his perfectly formed small body. He was wearing red silk bikini briefs.

It started with the Oriental guy sitting on an ottoman in full view of and in parallel to where Hardesty was watching through his bedroom door peephole. Toby handed the client his drink and then, at a murmured request—or command—of the Oriental guy, got right to business, kneeling between the man's spread thighs and mouthing his dick through the material of the Ergo boxers. After getting the guy's package wet enough that even Hardesty could see the shape of the glans through the material, the client raised his hips while Toby slowly slid the boxers off and down his legs. The client was hugely erect.

He was cool and nonchalant through the subsequent blow job, raising his knee sock-clad left leg to Toby's right shoulder, leaning back on the ottoman on his right elbow, and swigging from the glass held in his left hand while Toby's mouth went down on his long, thin, hard cock. It got a little more intense toward the end, with the client putting his drink down on the floor next to the ottoman, sitting up, and guiding a deep-throat suck with his hands on the back of Toby's head. There was a sense of the cruel again as, when it looked like Toby might gag at trying to swallow too much of the cock, the guy held his head trapped in place until Toby did, in fact, gag. Toby did a professional job of it, though. He was a good, neat deep-throater, and Hardesty didn't see a cum shot, so the young blond must have taken the load in his throat. It all came across as smooth and natural.

They then settled on a sofa with its too-low-slung back turned to Hardesty's bedroom door with their drinks. After they'd gone through a session of face kissing, the client's head disappeared, obviously down into Toby's lap. Toby stretched out his arms along the top of the sofa back and the movement of his shoulders indicated the client was taking thrusts of Toby's cock in his mouth. With a jerk, Toby's body relaxed, and it was evident that he'd come.

All seemed in order for a fuck session worth what the Oriental guy would be paying for it. He'd be paying by the day, not by the ejaculation, and it looked like the guy was a strong reloader and in shape, as was Toby. Hardesty turned, finished drying himself off with the towel, and puttered about, putting his dirty clothes in a hamper and picking out clothes for the next day. Although it had only been a few minutes, when he returned, naked, to the peephole, they had already stepped it up a notch and were going at it. This client didn't waste any time.

Toby was draped on his belly over the back of the sofa, his arms dangling down toward the carpet. Hardesty could see his red robe puddle by the front edge of the sofa. His red briefs were draped over the top of the sofa back beside him. His client was crouched behind him, his tux shirt flared and his fists holding the ends of Toby's sash, which was lassoed around Toby's throat, pulling his head up. Both of their bodies were jerking to the same rhythm, so Hardesty knew that Toby was being doggie fucked. He was looking right at Hardesty, a glassy-eyed look of the professional doing his job in his eyes. There was a hint too of the client being more demanding and better equipped than most.

He knew the Vice cop was on the other side of the bedroom door. This was a time when Hardesty gave the young blond comfort. Even as careful as the escort service was, who was to know that a client wouldn't go too far? And it would be quite possible in this position, with the red sash around Toby's throat, that the fuck could go too far. But Hardesty was here. And he could take care of any man Toby brought back to their apartment. The client needn't know the cop was here unless he went too far.

The client was athletic—and demanding. He raised Toby's legs to being hooked on his shoulders and raised himself up, wheelbarrow fucking Toby. The hands went to Toby's waist, though, to keep Toby from falling forward, and the red sash had fallen to the floor behind the sofa. This was safer even if the expression on Toby's face indicated that he was being challenged harder. Hardesty had his hand on his own cock, which was erect. Hardesty couldn't say that he didn't enjoy these voyeur sessions. He enjoyed fucking Toby—as Todd—more himself, but this wasn't bad. Hardesty got off on this voyeurism.

There was a roaring noise behind him and a flash of lights. He turned to see a plane coming in for a landing at Reagan Airport. They weren't supposed to land this late, but of course they did. This was Congress' airport. Congressmen's flights landed when Congress needed and wanted them to, not by FTA agreements. No matter how long they'd lived here, Hardesty had some sort of internal radar that could be surprised by a late-landing airplane but not by busier traffic during legitimate hours.

When he looked back into the room, the two had moved to being stretched out along the sofa cushion. The sofa was one with a low back that destroyed any chance of comfort in sitting in it. What it was according now, though, was a view of Toby's right leg hooked on the seat back, his left leg hooked on the client's right shoulder, their heads together in a kiss on the arm of the sofa, and the client's well-formed buttocks—tan lines showing he was partial to string bikinis—appearing above the level of the seatback and then thrusting down. Up and down, a strong-stroke fuck.

This guy should have been charged double, Hardesty thought. Still, he knew from personal experience that Toby enjoyed it and could handle it. Toby was using the usual encouraging words that male prostitutes used with their clients. In this case, praising the prowess of the client seemed to be in order.

When they weren't kissing, Toby's head lolled over to the side on the sofa arm, facing Hardesty. Hardesty could tell by the flash of his eyes and the way that he was panting that this client was more demanding than most of them—that he was fucking harder and deeper than most. There was a time when the Vice cop saw this reaction from Toby and thought about intervening, but now Hardesty knew it was what Toby wanted. Hardesty got off on watching it too. Indeed, it was what Hardesty gave Toby— what the young blond begged from Hardesty. By the next evening, Toby would be describing how expert and satisfying the client was—it was the intensity of fuck that Toby lived for. If Toby didn't have to be going to New York, the two of them might have been lying next to each other with Toby talking about this evening and both of them beating themselves off. Sometimes Hardesty thought Toby wanted rough, demanding sex more than the money lying on his back for a man brought.

They ended in a mutual ejaculation, Toby up the client's belly and the client standing over Toby and giving him a facial, on the ottoman, where Hardesty got the full visual of Toby on his back on the ottoman and the client standing on the floor, crouching between legs Toby had hooked on his hips, and finishing him in long strokes.

Hardesty finished with them, splattering his side of the bedroom door with cum.

The two moved back to sitting on the sofa, with Toby going to the kitchen to refresh their drinks. Hardesty then lost interest in anything going on of a prurient nature or a physical threat to Toby, went back in the bathroom and, having made himself all sweaty and bothered watching them, took another quick shower, brushed his teeth; shaved his thighs, chest, and forearms; and trimmed his pubes and facile hair. This ritual took maybe ten or fifteen minutes, as he tended to it pretty much every day to keep in form. He came out and looked through the peephole in time to see Toby ushering the client into his bedroom.

The client must have been someone really important. He could be Chinese or Japanese for all Hardesty knew. Either could be big money. He had a good body, though, and a cock that reached for his knees. They paused outside Toby's bedroom door for a standing deep kiss and the client stuffing much of his hand, the one with the big-rock ring on it, up Toby's ass, with Toby hooking a leg on the client's hip to give him deeper access with his fist. Hardesty could see Toby grimace, but he also knew Toby could take it. Hardesty himself drew the line at taking sex that far. Toby didn't. With this escort service, you got what you paid for, and you paid a lot.

Hardesty gave up and went to his bed, turning out all of the lights. The walls between his bedroom and Toby's weren't so thick that Hardesty didn't know that Toby was getting the shit fucked out of him on the bed. One thing—besides his looks—that made Toby a really good rent-boy was his stamina. He could take a dick all night long. He could take two dicks at once. He even could take a fist. And tonight it seemed like he was doing just that—taking a fist. That made Hardesty's sphincter clench and a shudder to go down his body, but it didn't stop him from masturbating to the sound as he drifted off to sleep.

He knew that most people wouldn't be able to understand how he could live with a guy who sold his body like Toby did, but Hardesty had no other choice if he wanted to be with Toby, and his own sex life separate from that with Toby was pretty fucked up too—and was tolerated by Toby. So, it was what it was.

* * * *

He thought he was moving into a nice wet dream, but he was close enough into consciousness to wake to Todd lying between his legs, sucking his cock. He must have been at it for a few minutes, because Hardesty was hard.

"Toby," he murmured.

"Hello, lover," Toby pulled off the cock long enough to answer. But then it was back to business.

"It's dark, dark. What the fuck time is it?" Hardesty looked over at the nightstand. It was pushing 4:00 a.m. "What the fuck. I've got to be up at six."

"And you weren't keyed up enough by Mr. Wang to want this?"

"I always want this, Toby, but—"

"Yes you do. That's why I keep you around. I can't get enough of cock. Yours in particular."

"After earlier, I wouldn't have thought—"

"Ah, so you *were* watching. Quite the cocksman, wasn't he, my Mr. Wang?" Toby moved up to straddle Hardesty's pelvis with his knees. He was facing Hardesty and put a hand behind him to keep Hardesty's cock inside his buttock crack. He was rising and falling on it. The older man groaned.

"Was? Is he gone now?"

"Yes, he left happy."

"And with his cock deflated and worn out, I hope. He really called Wang? He had one hell of a one."

"He did, didn't he? Opened me up for my lover. I don't know if his name was Wang or not. I called him

117

Sydney. That was the name on the form. Someone big here is entertaining him, though. I recognize him from the papers. A Hong Kong financier."

Toby was good about scrutinizing faces in the papers. It often saved him from making gaffes with clients he wasn't supposed to know.

"It's late, Toby. I've had a day and face a back-to-back shift. Looks like you've had quite a day too."

"You're hard for me."

"That's beside the point. We're both worn out, and did you check your voice mail? You're off to New York tomorrow."

"Today. It's today already. Yes, I've caught the voice mail. I should be gone for two days. I know who the Brazilian is. He'll give me a workout. But you being hard—me always being randy. That's the point. That's the only point here."

No, it wasn't the only point, Hardesty thought. It wasn't the only point in this strange relationship that needed to be examined and worked out. But, god, the delicious little piece was sexy and enticing. The images of the Wang guy pounding Toby in an athletic fuck—two toned bodies, two very different but equally sexy bodies fucking up a storm. He groaned as Toby went up on his knees, knowing what inevitably was coming next, being too tired for it, but aching for it.

"Toby, I know you've had a challenging day."

"And I know I want you. If you don't want me, it's OK, I understand."

"I want you," Hardesty croaked. Oh how I want you. Oh how many ways and how deeply I want you, he thought. He groaned again as, reversing himself on Hardesty's pelvis and drawing Hardesty's legs up into a bent position, Toby reached down, held Hardesty's cock in position, and sank on it.

"You. Do it. Fuck me," Toby cried out, raising a bit on his knees, coming up on the cock. Using the leverage of his feet, flat on the bed, Hardesty grabbed Toby's waist and started a counterpoint of thrusting his cock up into the channel and pulling Toby down on the cock. Toby grasped Hardesty's knees and started mouthing off. "Yes, yes, Christ I've want you all day. Fuck it. Getitgetitgetit."

The two of them had a secret. Toby had a tattoo on his lower belly at the side, of a gecko, a gecko whose long, thin red tongue went down to the base of Toby's cock and wrapped itself around the root. Men found the tattoo interesting and amusing. Hardesty knew it was more than that. Toby had an erogenous point that sent him into the stratosphere sexually. The tattoo had been inked on that point.

Involuntarily, almost without being aware of it, Hardesty did what he usually did to push the two lovers into an overdrive that made them the best match in sex that either promiscuous stud had with any other man. One of his hands went around to Toby's lower belly and rubbed the gecko tattoo.

"Oh, fuck! Shit, shit, shit, YES!" Toby cried out, and he took over the fuck, kicking up into overdrive, slamming himself up and down on Hardesty's cock.

And then the sounds started, the sounds that Hardesty loved to hear during his lovemaking, the reason he'd kept his parent's old brass bed. Toby was grasping the rungs of the footboard, cantilevered out over Hardesty's legs, pistoning his channel, which was conditioned to fit Hardesty like a glove, and the bed was shuddering, the springs groaning, the brass headboard doing a tattoo of rhythmic grinding against the bedroom wall.

The music Hardesty loved to hear. All telling Hardesty that he was getting the fuck of his life.

Chapter Three: The Next Day

Hardesty dragged into the Vice unit over an hour late, looking very much hung over.

Phil, his sometimes partner of several years, took a critical look at him from across the desks they had shoved against each other so that they could discuss cases and strategies face to face, and winked at him. "Quite a night between the sheets, I'm betting," he followed up with a popping of his tongue in his cheek and a laugh.

His partner scowled. "Pulled back-to-back shifts, which you damn well know. My turn on the street for a shift last night, and I'm expected to be at work for dayshift today."

"Oh, you're killin' me," Phil said, playing an invisible violin for him. The relations between the two were touch and go, based more on what they had on each other than respect. Several of the men in the unit were gay tops and predators. There were others that did the same on the straight road. It helped the unit, as it put the cops in a good position to work the worlds they were thrown into and to meld with the mindsets. Phil and Hardesty were both gay power tops and they both rode the other with innuendo and sarcasm and covered for the other in exercising their fetishes.

Phil was nearly ten years Hardesty's junior; better looking—which he flaunted—better cut, blond, tall, with a slender waist but a muscular chest, and soccer-player thighs. He was the nastier of the two in sex, albeit Hardesty was nastier than most. And he was the more ambitious of the two, working hard and not always on the up and up to get ahead and, as a consequence, not moving ahead too fast. He was in the third stint as Hardesty's partner, no one else in the unit wanting to be matched with him. He'd twice transferred with the thought that he'd move faster elsewhere, but elsewhere didn't tolerate his vices like Vice—and Hardesty—did.

He leaned in toward Hardesty's desk. "Tell me. Was it a nice piece last night? Did you fuck him good? Details. Give me details."

Before Hardesty could answer, the chief of the unit, Crane—who knew every vice anyone in his unit had—walked by the desks. "No arrest reports with your name on them, Hardesty. Are the reports late?"

"Not late, boss man. Nonexistent. I spent time convincing a fresh rent-boy that he wanted to go home instead of working the street."

"OK," Crane said. "Not being on the books either now or in the future is better than arrest processing, I guess."

He moved on, and Phil grinned and asked, "So, did he have a sweet ass?"

"Yes," Hardesty asked. "They both did." He was pulling his drawers open, not looking at Phil. "Where's the fucking Tylenol?" He upped the volume for the room. "Who's got the fuckin' Tylenol? I'm dying with terminal headache here."

"First time I've heard the clap referred to as a headache," a voice floated over the room, a remark that was met with a raised middle finger from Hardesty and laughter from the room.

Three bottles of pain killers came through the air and landed on his desk.

"Good, you're here," the unit admin assistant, Larry, said as he approached the desk. Phil leaned over and swatted him on the butt, and Larry shook his ass and turned around and gave Phil a smile. When the guys were hard up, Larry was their go-to lay. He was a miracle worker as an admin assistant too. "Three phone messages for you already this morning, Hardesty. Claims to be one of your informants. Says he has something juicy for you. Gave his name as Drew."

"Yes, that's one of mine," Hardesty said, warily, lifting his hand but keeping his head down. He was screwing off the lid of one of the pain killer bottles and tossing three, dry, down his throat.

"Here, I'll take that call," Phil said, sweeping in and taking the yellow slip from Larry. He didn't pull it away, though. He held Larry's hand long enough to say, "Later, Larry. I'll give it to you hard."

Larry pulled his hand away, smiled, said, "Later, lover," and flounced off.

"Here, give that to me, Phil," Hardesty said. "He's one of my special boys."

"Small, blond, pretty, and well reamed is he? One of your fuck snitches. Don't worry. I'll treat him special. You need to lose that headache. Take a walk down to the graveyard and don't come back until you can smile. I've got this."

Without waiting for Hardesty to claim jurisdiction again, he was standing, grabbing for his suit coat, and on his way toward the door.

"Yeah, he's small, blond, pretty, and well reamed," Hardesty muttered to thin air.

* * * *

Drew was on the floor, supported on his shoulders, his legs flung over his head, his toes digging into the floor in front of him—jackknifed. Phil was bent over him, toes digging into the carpet beyond Drew's, Phil's knuckles pressed into the carpet behind Drew's curved back. Drew was crying out, "Oh shit, fuck! Shitshitfuck! Pound me!" as,

122

pistoning in and out of Drew's ass channel, Phil was doing just that—pounding the rent-boy snitch's ass hard. Phil was a "take no prisoners" type of guy, and Drew had asked for it.

Phil had picked the rent-boy up at Dupont Circle. If Hardesty had pressed him on the matter, he would have said that he was quite willing to just take the information that the snitch had thought to be so important and let him back out of the car at Dupont Circle. But he'd go on to taunt Hardesty by saying that Drew had wanted more than that from him. He'd wanted more than Hardesty gave him. Phil could do more.

"Hardesty gives me attention—and a couple of bills. I think this information is worth five bills."

"You could get it from me. The attention you crave."

"A strapping god of a stud like you?" Drew had said and had flashed goo-goo eyes at Phil. Phil had grabbed the back of Drew's head, forced his face down into Phil's lap, and made Drew give him a gagging deep-throat suck as he drove through Georgetown, across Key Bridge, and to a motel in Rosslyn across from the Iwo Jima Marine memorial that was stuck in the 1950s in style and somewhere in the stratosphere for hourly rates.

Tiring of that position, Phil came off Drew and holding the whimpering young blond where he was, came around from behind him, crouched over his waving buttocks, sank his cock deep, and jackhammer fucked the shit out of the little blond.

Afterward, Drew lay on his belly on the floor, panting hard and moaning, while Phil pulled up a desk chair, reversed it and straddled it right next to where Drew lay.

"You called Hardesty three times this morning. You think you have some shit important enough to tell him that you'd bug him three times before 9:00 a.m. And you think it's worth five bills. What is it?"

"Maybe show me the five bills first."

"Maybe I just fuck your lights out again."

Drew smiled at that. Maybe not the best threat, Phil thought. "Maybe you just tell me what you think is worth five bills and I let you leave this room alive." He put on his mean face and took his gun out of the holster that had been draped over the back corner of the desk chair. It must have been convincing.

"It's all over the news."

"What's all over the news?" Phil hissed. "I don't want to play twenty questions here."

"That senator from Pennsylvania. The one who has just been named as a vice president running mate. Hal Etheridge."

"Yeah? What about it?"

"He's gay and he's kinky?"

"And what makes you think that?"

"He does one of my roommates. I live with three other call boys. The senator does one of them. Whips and beats and then fucks him."

"Rent-boys, I think, not call boys," Phil said. "You work the streets. You don't get called. You get picked up off the street. A call boy would make big bucks and live in the Watergate."

"Whatever. The guy I'm talking about gets done by a fuckin' U.S. senator. That's as good as living in the Watergate. You want to hear the rest of my news or not?"

"Yeah sure, but the short version. I don't have the whole day to fuck around here."

"One of my roommates has this Senator Etheridge as a client. The senator is into leather and bondage and whips. And now that he's been tapped to maybe be the vice president, he isn't too fond of my roommate. He tried to have him offed last night. So, the senator's into murder too.

My roommate rushed back home, packed and already is out of town."

"Offed? Isn't that a bit farfetched?"

"My roommate put one of his attackers down for the count. On the 12th floor of the Downtowner Hotel. You can look for it in the police reports when you go back to the station."

"I will. What's your roommate's name? And where has he gone?"

"I think I should tell Hardesty that. I'm Hardesty's informant."

"And I'm Hardesty's partner. That makes you my snitch too."

"I think maybe I should tell Hardesty."

"That's the way you want it?"

"Yeah, I think so."

Phil gave him a long, hard look. Then he rammed the gun back into its holster, abruptly stood, leaned down, and scooped Drew's body up like it was light as a feather. He tossed the slight rent-boy on the bed, belly at the foot of the bed. Grabbing the young blond's legs, he jerked them wide, causing Drew to cry out in surprise and pain. Mounting Drew's ass and striking his cock home in a long, vicious slide that caused Drew to cry out again, Phil began pounding his ass hard. He reached over and retrieved the belt from his trousers, which he looped around Drew's neck, pulling it taut. Pulling on the end of the belt, he arched Drew's torso up to him, grabbed the blond mop of hair on top of Drew's head, and jerked the young man's head back to him as well. He pounded on with his cock deep in Drew's ass.

Gurgling and gagging, Drew clawed at the belt drawn tight around his throat. His eyes were popping out.

Phil released the tension and leaned over and whispered in Drew's ear. "The roommate's name and where, exactly, has he gone?"

Drew was still gagging a struggling for breath. Phil didn't give him time to recover and answer. Putting him back in the choke hold, he gave him another minute of the cock and then pulled out a thick rubber dildo shaped like a cock, with thick veins on it, and cruelly screwed that into Drew's ass and twisted. Even while chocking, Drew was trying to scream from the demanding penetration of the dildo, larger even than Phil's cock had been.

This time when he released the tension, Drew held up his hands in supplication, signaling he'd talk. When he was able to, he croaked, "His name is Jason Stuart. He has a sugar daddy in Allentown, Pennsylvania, from his old days named Ben or Benton something."

Phil tightened the leash and Drew clawed at his neck. When Phil released the pressure, and Drew could talk. "Benton Clark. He owns some stores or something there."

"Is that all?"

"That's all, I swear. Now let me—" The sentence ended in a gagging sound. Phil was cruelly pulling back on the leash again and jerking Drew's head back with a fist in his hair. His cock was going to town, pistoning Drew's channel.

* * * *

Hardesty woke, groggy, but not as drained as when he'd barely gotten to the lower bunk in the graveyard room before he passed out. The headache was gone too. He might have slept on but for the cop who had come in to sack out on the other lower bunk that was foot to head with his and had kicked Hardesty's bed in the process.

It took him a couple of minutes to figure out where he was during which his brain was telling him there was something he should be doing. He finally figured out that he needed to tell Phil he'd take the meet up with his informant, Drew, himself. He was pretty possessive of his snitches—especially the ones he gave special attention to. And he particularly didn't like the idea of letting Phil get at them.

He lifted his arm, looked at his watch, and groaned. He'd been out, what? Three, four hours. That wasn't surprising really. Toby had ridden his cock for more than an hour and then had left him, telling him that the he'd lied, that the Oriental guy, his client that night, was still in his bed and would be waking up for more attention.

When Hardesty had gotten up that morning, the signal light by his door wasn't on. That meant Toby and his client were both gone. Either his "date" with the Oriental guy wasn't over yet or Toby had some shopping to do before he flew up to New York. He's said the client was more than a little rough when they'd gotten into the bedroom, but that Toby could handle him. Hardesty didn't really want to hear what they'd done, even though he'd heard what they were doing through the shared wall of the bedrooms. Toby wasn't going to stop doing it, whatever it was.

Now he felt guilty about Drew and about leaving him to Phil. Phil could be rough too. And it wasn't like Drew to be so insistent about having information to pass. Hardesty usually had to run him down and fuck the information out of him.

He fretted all the way back upstairs to the Vice bullring. He shouldn't have left Drew to Phil. Phil's desk wasn't occupied, though, when Hardesty got upstairs.

"Where's Phil? Anyone seen Phil around?" he asked to the room in general.

"Thankfully no," came the answer from one direction.

"Thought he left with you," said another.

"Who cares?" rang out a third.

Phil wasn't the favorite cop in the unit. Everyone there thought Hardesty was a martyr for taking him back as a partner each time he tried to bolt only to find that no other unit wanted him either. But all of the other cops were just glad it wasn't them Phil was hooked up with. It wasn't his vice—that he dipped in the goods himself—that put them off. Hardesty did that and the others liked him just fine. It was that he had proved again and again that he was totally without scruples in getting what he wanted and was a schemer on a grand order to boot—and that he grabbed at all of the pats on the back given for group effort.

Hardesty was about to check down in the motor pool for him—there was a mechanic down there who liked Phil's cock well enough—when Crane came out of his cubicle.

"Who's up? We got a body across the river that Arlington Vice says is one of our boys from over here."

"Where and what's the description?" one of the other cops asked.

"Laid out on a Civil War grave in Arlington National Cemetery, all nice and arms crossed. Strangled. Young, blond, the usual cute for that type. Wallet left with him. Someone wanted us to find this one."

Hardesty's antenna went up and his heart sank to his stomach. His mind went directly to Toby—in the guise of Todd. He spent half of his life warning Toby about his chosen profession and the other half worrying that Toby would wind up as a good many of them with that description did. National Cemetery was within sight of their apartment in Crystal City.

"I'll take it," he said. "Maybe Dan can go with me. Phil doesn't seem to be around."

The scene was on the western side of the cemetery—it was a very large cemetery—not the eastern side near where Hardesty's apartment was. The gate they went to to reach the dip in the landscape where lower-ranked Union soldiers from the Civil War were buried, the generals being planted up the hill around Arlington House, which had been grabbed from Robert E. Lee for commanding the southern army, was reached by a drive off the circle around the Iwo Jima memorial, the distinctive, flag-raising Marine group statue memorial from World War Two.

Still, Hardesty's heart didn't return to place until he'd hopped out of the Impala sedan even as the engine was turned off and rushed over to the grave where other cops were standing around watching a medical examiner do his work and Hardesty saw that it wasn't Toby.

It was, however the rent-boy snitch who Hardesty knew as Drew Dunston.

An Arlington Vice detective Hardesty knew came out to meet Hardesty several yards from the grave. One of the oldest burial sections, the marble tombstones here were grayer and not as uniformly spaced as they were in the sections for soldiers from wars in the twentieth and twenty-first centuries.

"Think this must be one of yours," he said when he'd reached Hardesty. "The ID is for a Washington, D.C., address. The name's Drew Dunston. Your card was in his wallet."

"Yeah, he's a D.C. rent-boy," Hardesty said. "Works out of the Logan Circle area. How did you guess he was a prostitute, though?"

"Other than your card, with your specialty, being naked, being a pretty boy of the type, and having a dildo stuck in his ass when we found him, the ME said his ass was built for sex and he'd had sex before he died—or, more likely, while he was dying. No semen though. His last trick wore a rubber."

"He was coming to see me," Hardesty said, his voice a little distant, sad. "He said he had something explosive to tell me."

"He's not going to be telling you whatever that was now," the Arlington detective said.

"No, he's not, Hardesty agreed." But maybe Phil had gotten to him first and gotten the information. And maybe he hadn't been blowing smoke. Maybe his information *was* explosive—explosive enough to get him killed.

Which raised the question—where the fuck was Phil?

"Any other bodies found around on graves?" he asked.

"No, but we didn't look for them. Should we?"

"It's just a 'maybe might' thought," Hardesty answered.

* * * *

"There you are, Hardesty. You have a visitor upstairs. Gotta be one of your rent-boy snitches and he's hyperventilated. Won't see or talk to anyone but you. He's got your card in his hot little hand. And I must say he's pretty hot himself."

"Is Phil back yet?"

"Nope."

The cop had seen Hardesty arriving back at police headquarters from a window in the Vice unit and had come downstairs to hustle Hardesty back to the unit.

Raul, the Hispanic rent-boy Hardesty had tried to scare off the street the day before and a roommate of the dead Drew Dunston Hardesty had just watched being zipped into a body bag in Arlington, was standing just inside the unit and hyperventilating.

"He's dead. Someone broke in. I came back to the apartment. Wasn't gone for more than an hour and he was just laying there on the floor, dead."

"Who's dead, Raul?" Hardesty asked, putting his hands on Raul's arms with the thought that he'd have to hold the young man up. "It's OK, you're safe. Show me."

130

He gestured to some of the others who already were rising from their desks and pulling their jackets on.

The outer door of the seventh-floor walk up on 14th Street had been busted open. The body of Lyle, the black rent-boy who lived with Raul, Drew, and Jason, was lying on the floor between the two sets of buck beds in the small bedroom. His legs were spread and bent and his head was lolled over to the side, his eyes were bugged out, his tongue was hanging out of his mouth, and there was a cord pulled tight around his throat. There were bruises on his naked body, but there was no telling how long ago he'd received those.

While soothing Raul off to the side as other cops looked around the apartment and the medical examiner examined the body, Hardesty murmured, "I told you there was a danger of this happening, Raul. This isn't the life for you. It wasn't the life for your friend here either."

"I don't think it was a john," Raul murmured.

"It's pretty obvious that he was killed during sex, Raul. It's a rough trade."

"No, I think it's bigger than that. Not that he hasn't been killed during sex—but I think it was someone wanting to find Jason. Someone who didn't want something being told. But Jason did tell. He told Lyle and Drew and me."

"Drew?"

"Yeah. One of my roommates is Drew. Drew Dunston."

"Shit," Hardesty exclaimed. "OK, you'd better tell me. What does this Jason know and who's trying to silence him? And where the fuck is he?"

"That's just it. Jason's gone. He was so scared that he took off for home yesterday."

"Where's home for Jason and why was he scared?"

"Pennsylvania. Allentown. Jason's from there. He said he had a sugar daddy to go back to. Some guy who owned a store. The guy who initiated and took care of Jason before he moved here."

"What was he scared of?"

"One of Jason's regulars—a kinky guy, Jason said, keeps coming up on TV. A senator or someone. He's up for some important office. Vice president or something."

"Etheridge? Halburton Etheridge?" Hardesty asked?

"Yeah, that was the name."

"Christ almighty," Hardesty exclaimed.

"Yeah. Jason sometimes comes home with welts on him. Some guy—this Etheridge, apparently—likes to whip and fuck him. Jason always said the john paid him real well and that he kinda got off on it himself. Anyway, last night—he was the same hotel you took me too . . ."

"The Downtowner?"

"Yes. Two of this senator's goons took Jason there, with Jason thinking they were taking him to the senator, and they fucked him up and he said they were going to kill him to keep him quiet about the senator now that there was a big job at stake. But he got one of them down and got away. Came right here, packed, and left. He told the rest of us what happened while he was packing, though."

Hardesty knew about the body of a private cop that had been found in one of the rooms of the Downtowner.

"Shit, Raul, we've got to get you out of here. Somewhere safe."

"And Drew too. I don't know where Drew is, but he heard the same thing Lyle and I did."

"Drew's safe now, Raul. Ain't nobody who's going to hurt him now. It's you we need to worry about. Give me a minute with the guys here and I'll take you somewhere. We'll keep you safe."

* * * *

132

"Shit, this is some place," Raul said when they entered the apartment. "Whose place is this?"

"This is my apartment," Hardesty said. "You can spend the night here. We'll figure out what to do with you tomorrow."

"Spend the night here? With you?"

"If you want. If it will give you comfort."

"I want. Hey look, you can see all the important shit in Washington from here. The Washington Monument too." He gave a little laugh, the first time Raul had been anything but close to tears since Hardesty had returned to police headquarters and found him, shaking and scared, waiting for him there.

"Yeah, it's quite a view," he said, pulling off his jacket and undoing the harness for his gun holster.

"You know I can't look at the Washington Monument without thinking of—" Raul started to say.

"A hard dick," Hardesty finished for him. "Yeah, me neither."

"Your hard dick," Raul said. "I can't forget you fucking me yesterday. Fucking me good, with a huge dick." He had turned from the window and come back to where Hardesty was standing. "Fucking me rough. I didn't know I wanted it that rough. And when I was sucking it . . ."

"Is that what you want, Raul? Will that help you calm down? Do you want to suck it again. Being fucked by it again?"

"Yeah, that's what I want," Raul said, sinking to his knees in front of Hardesty. "What do you want?"

"That's what I want too, Raul." Hardesty unzipped his trousers, and Raul did the rest—pulling the cock out, which of course was erect, opening his mouth to it, sucking it.

It occurred to Hardesty what he was mimicking while he fucked Raul, and he almost laughed. The only difference is that Raul was bound—because he said he wanted to be—at the wrists by his belt and at the ankles by Hardesty's belt. Otherwise it was the same position on the sofa that Hardesty had watched the Oriental client fucking Toby the previous night. Raul's knees were pushed into where the sofa cushion met the sofa back and he was bent over the back of the sofa, his bound arms dangling toward the carpet behind the sofa, his legs bound together, and Hardesty, feet up on the sofa cushion, crouched over Raul's back, mounted on him and fucking him from a high position while grasping the hair on the back of the young Hispanic's head and arching his head back.

Pounding, pounding, pounding the young Hispanic, just as they both wanted to avoid thinking about the power of the man out there who was searching for Raul and Jason—the two survivors left—and to assuage their own carnal lust.

Afterward, Raul wanted Hardesty to take him into Hardesty's bedroom and continue fucking him, but Hardesty said, "No, not until later. You'll find what you need in the refrigerator and then you can shower and sit and contemplate the similarities between the Washington Monument and my dick if you want to. I have someplace to go before the government closes down and then I have to make better arrangements for you for the next few days than here."

He made it up to Capitol Hill just before the congressional offices were closing for the evening. He got a surprise from the receptionist in Senator Etheridge's office.

"Someone from the police has already been here this afternoon," she said. "I told him that the senator went back to his home state to meet with constituents earlier today. Didn't the other policeman tell you that?"

"The other policeman? What did he look like."

"Tall, blond, handsome, but with a smart mouth," she said.

Phil. So that's where he went. Drew had told him the story. He was following up on it on his own.

"What state is the senator from? Where has he gone?"

"He represents Pennsylvania. He left for Allentown this morning, I think."

Allentown? The same place the guy he wants to smother went? "Shit," Hardesty said, as he whirled around and left the office.

"Another smart mouth," the receptionist said to no one in particular as she returned to closing up the office for the day. "But sexy as hell. As sexy as the other one, but in a different way."

Hardesty put in a call to Crane at Vice while he drove back across the river to Crystal City.

"Sure, you can go up to Allentown if you want tonight—to be there tomorrow," Crane said. "I'll make connections. You'll have to leave it to the police there, and, being as how it's a senator, they'll probably have to get some ducks in line politically. You can fill them in when you get there. So you think Phil has gone over to the dark side?"

"I think he's been mostly there for some time, Captain. I'm sorry to say that both of the strangled rent-boys look like his work. I wouldn't be surprised if he's trying to eliminate the competition in being able to blackmail the senator."

"So, when are you starting out?" Crane asked.

"Later. I have to put this witness to bed first."

Crane didn't ask what putting a witness to bed meant. It first meant Hardesty knocking on the door of the man down the hall in the Crystal City apartment who put Hardesty up when Toby needed the entire use of the apartment—in exchange for favors.

"Hardesty," Paul said when he opened the door. A big grin went across his face. He was in his mid fifties, but

135

he'd kept in shape and was a handsome man. He also could be a very lonely man. He'd been a real player in his day—a male model—and still did some catalog work when they needed an older man. He didn't get his itch scratched much these days, though. "You need a place to stay tonight?"

"I need a favor," Paul. "And I have an itch. Haven't been here in a while."

Paul had a support belt he liked to use—a thick, black leather strap with hand holds at both ends, a doggie sex strap. Hardesty fucked him with the strap supporting Paul's stomach, and Paul suspended in air out beyond the foot of his bed. The tops of his feet were on the bed, Hardesty was standing between his legs, and Paul's torso was arched back, his hands locked behind Hardesty's neck. Paul worked out a lot. He liked the athletic, testing fuck positions. He particularly liked sex with Hardesty, because the Vice cop was strong enough to support Paul's body suspended with the belt.

Paul was doing the splits on his dresser, his hands pressed on the dresser top in front of him, and his buttocks suspended beyond the front of the dresser with Hardesty gripping his waist and plowing his ass when Paul asked him what the favor was.

"As I remember, you like to go both ways. Is that right?" Hardesty asked.

"Yes, but you don't, so I don't usually—"

"I've got a real honey of a rent-boy you can use for a few days if you'll put him up and keep him a secret. I've got to go out of town for a few days, and he needs to be hidden. But he can be used hard."

Hardesty made some calls before returning to his apartment. He found Raul, naked on his bed, and asleep. A few snaps on the young man's back and buttocks with Hardesty's belt brought him awake, after which Hardesty use the belt to bind Raul's wrists behind his back, mounted his ass, and rode him hard while slapping his butt. Raul loved the attention.

After feeding him dinner, Hardesty fucked Raul again, this time reclining on the ottoman in the living room and having Raul crouched between his spread legs, facing away from him, backed into his cock, while Hardesty grabbed the young man's wrists and pulled them back toward his shoulders. Raul fucked himself in this position.

When Hardesty delivered him to Paul's apartment, He was met with a smiling Paul, who already was ready, naked, and fisting the handles of the doggie sex strap he'd introduced Raul to for the next two days.

Chapter Four: Subsequent Days

Barely into the new day, 2:30 in the morning, and Paul is taking Raul again in his bedroom. Raul is suspended in air, his belly supported by the doggie sex strap, his arms extended and spread, his hands clutching the front edge of a dresser, his legs hooked on Paul's hips, and his ankles pressed into Paul's upper calves below his knees, while Paul grips the strap hand holds, crouches between Raul's thighs, and pulls the small Hispanic on and off his cock. Raul is making the usual "Yes, yes, fuck me; fuck me deep, daddy," murmurs and panting that can be expected of a rent-boy, but he, in fact, is amazed that the old boy can keep going on with this—and, indeed, Raul is feeling stuffed and well worked.

This is the third taking with the doggie sex strap and by 3:00 a.m., the two will be stretched out on Paul's bed, Raul still panting and Paul sighing, astonished at the present Hardesty has brought him. He rarely gets sex these days and even more rarely as a top with a bottom as luscious and sweet as Raul is. He will do what he can to pace himself, but he has no idea how long his good fortune will last, how long Hardesty will leave Raul with him. Subsequently, through tonight at least, each time he wakes and feels strong, he'll roll over on top of Raul. And each time Raul, also marking his good fortune of being hidden and protected by Hardesty, will open and spread his legs, rise off the leverage of his feet to put his pelvis in ideal position, and take the long, thick slide inside him with an intake of breath and a "Yes, yes, again" whisper, putting his own pelvis into motion as the pump begins, going with the rhythm of the fuck.

At 2:30 a.m., 200 miles away, in Allentown, Pennsylvania, Raul's erstwhile roommate, Jason, is hanging around—literally.

A film is being shot, the view now zooms in to Jason's left nipple and the sound of his groan as a tit clamp at one end of a metal chain the other end of which is already clamped on Jason's right nipple is attached. "Shit, yes, punish me," the camera makes sure to record from Jason's reaction to establish that Jason is good with the action. The camera pulls out as an electric zapper is raised to the clamp and touched, and with a scream, Jason writhes, his feet barely touching the floor, as he hangs from a ceiling beam by his wrists.

"You came back to me," Benton Clark murmurs, giving the young man he's tormenting an affectionate smile.

"Yes, yes, I came back to you," Jason answers through gritted teeth. "I couldn't stay away. Give it to me; give it to me good." He cries out again as the tip of the electric zapper, its motion followed by the camera being held by Benton's houseboy, the black, muscular Tre, as Benton zaps Jason's exposed ball sack. The zap pulls Jason's legs up into his stomach before they drop again. "Shit, shit. Do me!" he cries.

"Because you want what I have to give you."

"Yes, daddy, because I want what you give me. Fuck me, daddy, please, fuck me now. Split me with that nasty dick of yours."

"You went away from me. You need to be punished."

"Yes, I was bad. Punish me, daddy." He screams as Benton zaps him on the balls again. Benton is already tired of the game, however, and has needs of his own. When the pain in the balls causes Jason to pull his knees up into his stomach again, Benton drops the zapper, runs his arms

139

under Jason's knees, spreads the young man's thighs, and moves in between them. His cock is hard and erect and easily finds Jason's hole. The hole is gaping; this isn't the first time this evening Benton's cock has been in there.

Benton slides his cock up into the hole, deep. "Yes, daddy, yes. Fuck me. Fuck me hard, rip me apart," Jason murmurs in an exhausted voice. Benton proceeds to do so, with Tre moving around him, getting it all on video. Suspending his thrusts, holding still other than little twitches in his body, letting it build up inside him, with a jerk and a final deep thrust inside Jason's channel to the tune of Jason crying out, "Yes, yes, YES!" Benton explodes in an ejaculation.

Nobody has been able to pull it out of Benton as Jason has. That's why when Jason appeared at the front door of his stucco and wood-sided house on S. Glenwood Street in a quiet, upscale residential area of Allentown, babbling nonsense about being on the run and needing a place to hide, Benton had let him in.

"You know what you'll get here," he'd said before he stepped aside for Jason to enter.

"Yes, I know. I want it. I want you again," Jason had said. He was in a panic. He had no idea where else he could turn. He had no other choice that he could see.

Benton pulls out of Jason and lets the young man just collapse, hanging there, spent, his head hanging down, the tops of his feet dragging on the floor, his arms completely numb from supporting the dead weight of his body. He jerks and groans as Benton picks up the zapper and gives him another charge on his nipple, but he just hangs there.

"You can use him and then put him to bed," Benton says to the muscular black houseboy operating the camera as he wipes his dick off with a moist washcloth and heads for the stairs to the first floor. No one other than young men in training like Jason in Benton's acquaintance has had any idea he had a secret sex torture chamber in his basement. Jason had been like the rest, trainees for a service Benton ran for a club of men who liked to punish and fuck young men. Jason was different, though. He'd acquired a patron and left Allentown. Benton hadn't continued to make money off Jason, and for that Jason would continue to need to be punished. Not too badly, though, because Jason also was the best fuck Benton had ever enjoyed. There was always a good chance that Jason could be reintroduced to the club as well.

He stops at his library on the first floor before going to his bedroom, taking a shower, and getting some shut eye to be able to appear all chipper and wholesome smiles at his store in downtown Allentown later in the morning. Does he have anything unusual on for today, he wonders, as he looks at his calendar.

Ah, yes, his friend Senator Hal Etheridge is in town today and they are set up for lunch. He has a word or two to say to his old friend too, Benton thinks, as he heads for the stairs to the bedroom level. It had been Hal Etheridge who had enticed Jason to leave him, to leave Allentown, to go to Washington, D.C.

In the torture chamber, Tre releases Jason's body, and the young man just collapses into his arms with a sigh. Tre carried him over to a sling hanging from the ceiling in the corner of the room, drops Jason into the sling, binds his wrists and ankles to the four chains hanging from the corner chains, unzips himself, penetrates Jason's hole with his hard, thick cock, and begins to pump.

Between the manhandled Raul in Arlington, Virginia, and the tortured Jason in Allentown, Pennsylvania, at 2:30 a.m. Hardesty has cleared the Capital Beltway on I-95 and is headed north, approaching Baltimore. He's keyed up, not just on a pressing quest to get to Allentown, coordinate with the police there, and try to find a key witness, Jason, to possibly the biggest vice crime story to hit the country in a decade, but he's also sexually charged. All of this charges him sexually.

He's thinking of Raul—not just about his luscious, fuckable body but also about what draws young men like him to the danger of doing what they did. Look what it did to Drew and Lyle—what it may even now being doing to Jason. Why couldn't Raul see that and back away? Hardesty had tried to shock him into leaving the life, and that hadn't been working. It hadn't worked with Hardesty either, he had to admit. It hadn't kept him away from Raul.

He pulls into the rest stop off I-95 near Columbia, Maryland. It's going to be a long drive to Allentown. He has a motel room booked there, but he's only going to get a few hours of sleep and a gobbled meal before meeting with the Vice unit in Allentown. It has taken a lot of effort from Crane to get Allentown Vice involved in this at all—to take up an investigation of one of their own U.S. senators. Hardesty has to be firing on all cylinders at 9:00 a.m. If he just wasn't so keyed up.

The rest stop is pretty much deserted and when he enters the men's room and bellies up to a urinal, there's only one other guy in there—a young blond. The guy looks nervous. He's down the line of urinals, already set up when Hardesty unzips. A small, young guy—of "the" type, Hardesty's type.

He's still there when Hardesty finishes pissing. Hardesty just holds there, and sure enough, the guy moves up to the urinal beside Hardesty and gives him a meaningful look. Hardesty turns his body three quarters toward the guy to give him a good look, if that's what he wants. The guy wants, and Hardesty hears the guy's intake of breath and uttered "Holy fuck" when he sees what Hardesty is packing. The guy tentatively reaches over with a hand, and Hardesty doesn't stop him from touching his cock and then, as it responds by engorging, grasping it and giving it strokes.

Hardesty is keyed up. He has his needs. He's angry that this is just another guy getting hooked on the life. Hardesty has his own way of trying to get these guys to back away from it. And the young blond is his type, his weakness.

"In one of the stalls," he growls. The guy follows him down the line to the last stall in the double row.

Hardesty sits on the toilet, his trousers and briefs folded up and sitting on the tank top behind him, as the young man kneels between his open thighs and gives him head.

What Hardesty does then is half this, half that. He has his need and he gets that itched, but he also is on campaign to get these guys to stop it, to back away from the life. His way of doing it is to show them how rough it will be for them. He gets the young blond, sans pants and briefs, bent over the toilet, hands on the back wall, legs spread. Hardesty is crouched over his back, palming the young guy's belly with one hand and yanking his head back, arching his torso back, cruelly, with his hand buried in the guy's blond curls. He's humping the guy to beat the band, thrusting hard and deep, ignoring the guy's pleas for mercy, for him to go slow. He fucks the shit out of him and leaves him, sinking to his knees and hugging the toilet tank with his arms, moaning and groaning, close to sobbing.

"It's going to be a rough life of that, son, if you don't just back away from it and turn your life around," Hardesty says, as he reaches into the back pocket of his trousers and pulls out his badge. He flashes it the guy enough for him to see it's a fancy badge but not enough for him to see it's from D.C. and didn't mean all that much in Maryland, where they now were crowded into a rest stop toilet stall.

"You know I could run you in," he says menacingly.

"Please, sir," the guy says, voice quaking, not all from fear of his position, crumpled on the floor with a cop standing over him with a dick out he'd just blown and sheathed; some because of the pain of the fuck.

Hardesty rummages around in the pockets of the young guy's pants, comes up with a wallet, takes out a driver's license, showily looks from it to the cowering young man to show that the face in the photo on the man matches, and pockets the license.

"I may or may not turn this in for action," he says. "Maybe if I don't hear in the wind that you're out here anywhere doing this again, I won't. Like I said, walk away from this life, son. Now."

He pulls his trousers on, zips up, and returns to the Impala from the bathroom, dumping the license in the garbage bin outside the restroom door when he passes by it.

He doesn't really think his rough fuck is going to cure the guy, but the guy asked for it and getting his rocks off has settled Hardesty, so it isn't a complete waste of his time.

* * * *

Benton Clark was arriving late to work, but since he was the boss and wasn't the one who opened the store, that didn't bother him too much. If he hadn't dallied with Jason, though, he would have been on time. Luckily, he saw a parking space just a few doors down from the store. The car coming from the other side did a U-turn, though, and obviously was headed for the same space. As the car, an Impala, zeroed in on the space, Clark said "Shit" out loud. He'd had his turning signal on, signaling his intention to park there. The space was on his side of the street. The fucker knew he intended to park there. He drove up next to the car and stopped, turning an evil eye on the driver of the Impala.

He might have done more, but the guy looked mean and was muscled up. A real thug—or maybe a cop. He thought the latter, because, not paying a bit of attention to Clark's glare, the guy got out of the Impala and jaywalked across the street right along the front of Clark's car. Clark resisted the urge to run him down just to see the surprised look in the fucker's face but, instead, sat there and watched him walk up the stairs of the police station across the street.

That's when Clark noticed he'd left home in such a hurry that he hadn't brought his briefcase. There was stuff in there he needed. With a sigh, he put the car in gear to drive back home to pick up the stuff he needed.

* * * *

Phil, the arrant Vice cop, was mounted on Jason's ass, fucking him hard when he heard the buzzer down at the door. Ignoring it, he kept on thrusting. Jason, moaning and grunting, was spread-eagled on his belly on the bed, his wrists and ankles tied off at the four corners of the bed. Pillows were stuffed under his belly, lifting his ass to a deep approach angle, first for Benton Clark an hour earlier, Tre after Clark left for work, then for another guy, and now for Phil. Jason's ass was taking a progression of men, which in itself didn't upset him all that much. It was what was interrupting the fucks.

The buzzer had gone off earlier while Tre was fucking Jason. He had seen Clark's briefcase in the foyer after the man had left and before Tre came up here to take over the plowing of Jason's ass. Maybe he'd left his keys too. Maybe, Tre thought, it was Clark trying to get it. He headed pulled out of Jason's ass, rolled off the bed, pulled on his jeans, and headed downstairs.

It wasn't Clark at the door, a glass fronted door. It was one of the bodyguards for one of Clark's friends. Clark opened the door to him.

A few minutes later, Chaz, the cleanup thug for Senator Etheridge, entered the bedroom, walked over and stood over Jason's bound body, smiled, leaned down and wiped off his knife blade on the edge of the bedspread, and unzipped his trousers.

"Hello, Jason, long time no see."

Jason turned his head. His eyes went large. "Oh, fuck," he exclaimed. The last time he'd seen Chaz was when he escaped him at the Downtowner hotel in D.C., with Chaz' sidekick Fred being wiped out in the process.

"Fuck, indeed," Chaz said, with a laugh. He mounted Jason's ass and began bringing reality to the word "fuck." He plowed Jason's spread-eagled and bound body to an ejaculation and then pulled out the rent-boy' ass. The tip of his knife went to the opening his dick had just vacated.

"Too bad," he murmured. "You're a great lay, but orders are orders."

The roar of a gunshot caused Chaz' eyes to go big in total surprise and he toppled over on his side on the bed.

Phil was standing in the doorway, holding a smoking gun. "Who the fuck are you?" Jason asked, with a trembling voice. That's all he had time to be asking, though. Phil had pushed Chaz' body off onto the floor and was on top of Jason, choking and fucking him. He made quick work of his taking, rammed the barrel of his gun up Jason's well-worked ass, and muttered, "Bye, bye, fucker."

The resultant gunshot blew Phil away and he, in his turn, rolled off the bed on top of Chaz' body. Benton Clark was standing in the doorway, holding a shotgun. "Who the hell is he?" he asked no one in particular. "He left Tre a mess downstairs in the foyer." Then it was, "Oh, shit, who the hell is that?" as he saw Chaz' body under Phil's. And the room was suddenly full of cops, among them the bruiser who had stolen Clark's parking spot downtown not much more than a half hour earlier.

* * * *

146

Hardesty was helping, but Jason was doing most of the work. He'd been so grateful for being saved—not just from Chaz but then from Benton too—that he'd been all over Hardesty since the Vice cop had brought him back to D.C., and, ultimately into his own bed at the Crystal City apartment. Raul was still off having a demanding but also grateful time under Paul down the hall.

Hardesty was using his feet as leverage to fuck up into Jason's channel as the young blond straddled his pelvis and leaned over him, his hands pressing Hardesty's arms down on the mattress above his head while Jason dipped in from time to time for a kiss or a bite on Hardesty's nipples.

The Vice cop could take this only for so long, though. He rolled over to the side, taking Jason with him, turned Jason facing away from him, and pulled Jason into his body. Turning the young man's buttocks away from him, he reached over for the strap he'd been using before, that Jason had begged for, saying that it was what increased his pleasure. Jason's buttocks were already rosy red from the attention of the strap. Hardesty gave the tender skin two more lashes, and Jason groaned, his cock lurching and going harder. "Fuck me hard, daddy," he cried out. Hardesty fucked him in a side split, punctuated by lashes at his buttocks and Jason's cries of passion. "Yes, yes. You're so nasty and so huge. Rip me apart!"

God, it was a miracle the guy was still alive, Hardesty thought, considering what he egged a man to do to him. This must be from that Clark guy's training.

"Split me with that big dick! Strap me, punish me, punch me! You're a stud; you're a brute!" Angry and consumed by lust Hardesty gave him the lash again and then shoved a thumb in his mouth and grabbed his throat with the other hand. Jason settled down, sucked on the thumb, and they finished the fuck in a calmer, more deliberate thrust and counterthrust pumping rhythm to a mutual coming.

Coming out of the shower, Hardesty found Jason still lying on the bed, on his back, his legs spread and bent, and masturbating himself.

"Come back to bed," he mewed. "Do me nasty again. You're a thug. I want you again."

"Not now. You're too wild even for me. Gotta go to work. Gotta wrap up the paperwork on this and get you and Raul into witness protection."

"You have it in you to give me all I want. I can tell. And I thought you had a heart-to-heart talk with the senator last night," Jason said.

Hardesty shuddered at the thought of Jason seeing in him the capability to tear a guy a new one. His fear was that Jason might be right. He had been sorely tempted to do Jason harder, nastier when he was begging for it. Hardesty was afraid of himself and his own desires and impulses.

"I did, but I don't know if he's going to take the deal or not. He may have someone else to throw at you and Raul. Maybe even at me. The stakes are big here and he's a big-time player. You didn't tell any of this to Benton Clark, I hope. The cops in Allentown haven't come up with anything to charge him with. They're just trying to hush it all up. They weren't much help to me with the senator either. Said they couldn't link whatever one of his employees did to him directly. He's too important."

"No, I didn't tell Clark why I'd come back to Allentown," Jason said. "He thinks I find him irresistible."

"I think you find him irresistible too to voluntarily go back to what he did with you."

"You're the one I find irresistible," Jason cooed. "Shit have you got a cock, and you're nasty. Come back to bed."

"Later. Hang tough here. There's food in the frig. If a great-looking great—looking a bit like you and older—comes in, be nice to him. It's his apartment. But don't expect any action from him. He's a bottom too."

"A good one?"

"The best."

When Hardesty had gotten to the Vice unit; reported in to Crane, which took a while as it had to cover the attempt by the unit's own rogue cop, Phil, to cut down the competition in a blackmail scheme against the senator from Pennsylvania; and walked back out to the bullpen, a TV was blaring.

"Turn that fucker off," he called out. "It's giving me a headache."

"I think you'll want to hear this," one of the guys piped up. And indeed he did.

"In a surprise announcement this morning," a TV commentator was saying, "Republican senator Halburton Etheridge of Pennsylvania has removed his name from consideration as vice president on the Republican presidential election this November. In a further surprise move, he has said he had decided he needed to give more time to his wife and two children, so he was resigning from Congress as well."

"Well, shit, it worked," Hardesty said out loud. And suddenly he didn't have as much work to do today as he thought he did. Raul and Jason wouldn't be needing witness protection services. And maybe it would be just him and Toby at the apartment when Toby got back from New York, none the wise on what had transpired since he'd left.

It was a good thing that his work had been cut down, because at the end of the TV announcement, there was a small blond guy at the door to the unit, asking for him. It was Craig, a street-working rent-boy who was one of his snitches—one of his special snitches who was another unsuccessful attempt of his to get off the streets.

"I have something I think you need to hear," Craig said to Hardesty when he reached the door.

"Want to come on over to my desk and—?"

"Uh, I'd rather give it to you somewhere else," Craig said, reaching out and touching Hardesty's arm.

"Where? Down in front of the office? At a coffee shop?"

"You know."

"In a hotel room?"

Craig didn't answer directly. He just dipped his head and gave a little smile, the universal signal of a submissive. "You know what I want."

Hardesty's cock went hard. He knew he shouldn't, but he also knew he would. "Well, let's go," he said, and as they turned to the door, he put his hand possessively on Craig's butt. Back to business as usual.

He ignored the cat call that accompanied their departure.

Retribution

Chapter One: Christmas Present for Himself

Jan heard his voice in the foyer and glided away from the man who was circling in on him and went to the front foyer. The big Slavic bear of a guy, who had been introduced to him as Victor, had been pursuing him for nearly an hour and Jan was running out of ploys to politely elude him. That couldn't last long, because a customer was a customer, and Victor and his master were regulars of Jan's. It wouldn't be long before Justine noticed the man's dance of "want" and signaled for Jan to take him upstairs. Something in the man's eyes told Jan he didn't want to go upstairs with him tonight. The front door out onto the short lawn of the townhouse in the fashionable embassy section of Kalomara in northwest Washington, D.C., was open, and Jan could see that it was snowing. Not bad for Christmas Eve, he thought.

Justine was at the door, towering over the man who was entering even though the guy wasn't all that short himself. Justine was in full drag. The man entering and pounding the snow off his black leather coat was much as Jan had seen him before—a lot of black leather pulled tight across the well-toned muscles, an aura of danger, yes, but also of authority and self-confidence. Sexy, but clearly in a fully masculine way. The bow to Christmas was that the tight T under the coat was red rather than the usual black. He still looked the borderline thug. He still made Jan go hard just looking at him.

Jan knew Hardesty had pushed hard past forty—that showed in the gray struggling with the black of his buzz cut and in the close-cropped mustache and beard. And he'd had a hard life, as evidenced in rugged features and a nose beaten slightly off kilter. But he was one sexy dude and could, as Jan knew, deliver. He could deliver right to the edge and then do it again ten minutes later. The challenge was surviving the delivery—but once having done that, there was a need to do it again.

Hardesty's eyes moved briefly from Justine, whose stature and over-the-top look tonight was arresting, to Jan. His steely gray eyes slitted, and Jan shuddered at the sensation of being stripped down to naked and manhandled. This, even though Jan was wearing only a silk, Christmas-festive slip over filmy panties like all of the rest of the "girls" were on this party night, so there wouldn't be much stripping required. Jan knew from that look that he wasn't being rejected for the night; he was in the running for Hardesty's pick.

"Good you could come, Hardesty," Justine said, stepping back so that the man could enter the all-male brothel. "We couldn't celebrate or feel well protected without you. Here, let me take your coat. Leslie," the madam called out, his fingers snapping and his voice turning to the harsh whiplash that so easily followed not being fast enough to do Justine's bidding. Another of the "girls" in a slip then stepped forward to take the man's black leather coat.

Leslie, Jan thought. Of course Leslie would be there jolly on the spot. Well, he better not try to mess with Jan's plans tonight. Now that Hardesty was here, Jan had every intention of maneuvering to be the one he took upstairs.

"Oh, my, you seem to have come armed," Justine said, and let out a harsh hoot of laughter.

Jan looked to where Justine was gesturing and almost hyperventilated. Hardesty had stretchy bands hanging out of the side pockets of his black leather trousers—a red one from one pocket and a green one from the other. The Christmas mood. Jan recognized them to be restraints, Velcroed restraints at either end of a short lead. Hardesty had come armed for nasty business. The brothel was fully equipped for such fun, but Hardesty had brought his own toys. Jan shuddered again, his mind racing with the possibilities, his determination to be Hardesty's for the night burgeoning. He knew that, though Hardesty was rough, he was controlled and would never go too far. Jan couldn't say that about all of the clients here. He looked around to see where Victor was lurking.

"Well, it's Christmas," Hardesty said, with a smile on his face and a twinkle in his eye. "And I find the best Christmas presents are ones I give myself."

With a shiver, Jan retreated back into the parlor and went roving around the room, which was decorated for Christmas, complete with ornament-laden tree, some of the ornaments being festive-colored condoms and others dangling ball gags and ball weights. Justine's was an extreme services brothel and didn't mind advertising that fact. A roaring fireplace with sheer net stockings hanging from the mantle completed the picture.

It was Christmas Eve, so the number of "guests" was sparse and there were more young men in slips in the room than there were older men being pampered. It was a closed party, something special Justine provided for a select number of important men who helped keep the operation unhampered. The ratio of guests to rent-boys helped Jan remain largely unencumbered while he circled the room, always keeping within the scope of Hardesty, while never making a direct move. He knew that Hardesty wanted to control and make the choice. Leslie was throwing himself at Hardesty, but Jan wasn't worried. He knew that didn't work with the thuggish hunk. Hardesty made his own decisions, and he preferred to have to pursue his quarry a bit. He valued a bit of resistance and tease.

He kept moving about until he knew that Hardesty was following him with his eyes. The Victor guy was tracking Jan again too, and Jan knew that he had to work a little faster on who he wanted to go upstairs with. Then two of the players got swept off the board, leaving Jan with a free path to his goal. The hulking Victor had gone to stalking Leslie, another one of his regulars, and it wasn't long before Jan saw the big brute cornering the competition and herding Leslie toward the staircase in the foyer to the upper rooms. The path clear, Jan posed and flirted with his eyes and body position until both he and Hardesty had made the unvoiced deal. Then he moved toward the stairs, stopping at the bottom of the steps, where Justine had taken up position.

"The blue room," Justine murmured, "Whatever he wants for as long as he wants."

Jan smiled at the madam and continued up the stairs as Hardesty came out into the foyer, nodded to Justine, and started mounting the stairs. Whatever he wanted as long as he wanted was exactly what Jan had in mind.

* * * *

Just inside the doorway to the Green Room, Victor slammed the door shut with one hand and backhanded Leslie to the carpet with the other. Leslie went down on all fours and Victor was on his back immediately, making short work of tearing away the silk shift and panties and getting himself unzipped and freed. Leslie didn't cry out, and even if he had, the reinforced walls and hidden peek passageways between the rooms of the brothel's bedrooms would have absorbed the sound. This was a special needs brothel—both clients and rent-boys understood that. Just about anything short of wet work went in these bedrooms. For a special party like this, run for those who enabled Justine's to exist, even wet work might be tolerated and covered up. There was no evidence it ever had happened, but there was no evidence that it hadn't either.

Leslie's "little extra" apparel for the evening had been a colorful scarf tied around his neck. Victor made use of it, fisting it, pulling it tight, arching Leslie's head and torso back as Leslie gagged and scrabbled at the scarf to try, vainly, to relieve the pressure on his throat. Victor made quick work of him, mounting his hips, penetrating him hard and thick, and pumping him furiously. Having Leslie fully under his control, Victor released the scarf and let Leslie's head drop, cheek to carpet and his glassy-eyed stare focused on the Green silk covering of the wall, as Victor rode him to an ejaculation.

In the time out following the eruption, while both were breathing heavily, but Victor not moving off Leslie's back—a sure signal he wasn't finished yet—the Slavic brute lowered his thick lips to Leslie's ear and whispered, "When I am done with you, you will leave here with me. Another important client requires his present tonight. I will arrange it. The house will allow it."

"Yes, Victor," Leslie responded in a low whine. The Russian didn't have to say who the client was—or that there may be others there to service as well. How had Leslie gotten this involved in this business, he wondered. It had been a slow process working into a dangerous and untenable situation. Perhaps it was time he told someone. His mind went to Hardesty, who he had teased and lost downstairs. Then his thoughts went to his sore ass, as the brute, hard and insistent once more, thrust inside him and commenced pumping his channel again.

* * * *

Entering the Blue Room, which, of course, was decorated almost entirely in cobalt blue to distinguish it from the Red, White, Green, and Gold rooms, Jan went directly to one of the nightstands beside the king-sized tester bed, retrieved a tube of lubricant and a handful of condom disks, and moved back to and sat down, primly, on the foot of the bed.

Neither of them said anything when Hardesty entered the room. They'd both been here before—they'd both been here together before. Hardesty pulled the T-shirt over his head. His torso and biceps were hard-worked muscular, with veins prominently standing out because they had no fat to run through. The torso was marked with scars from knife slashes and a few pock marks from encounters with bullets luckily placed. This enhanced the image of the man as a thug but also increased the danger of him and Jan's arousal. His pecs were bulging, his nipples rock hard. Jan was one of his favorite lays, and Jan knew it.

This was a special party; Hardesty could demand and receive special attention.

Hardesty was horse hung and would be fully erect already. Jan knew that too, and he could see the stressed tenting at the man's crotch. What he didn't know was how he would be taken this time. Hardesty's heights of pleasure hinged on invention. Sometimes Hardesty took him fast and hard; sometimes he took his time and made Jan suffer deliciously. The restraint leashes hanging out of his pockets indicated he would take his time tonight, Christmas Eve. Jan trembled. He was going to be taken to heaven for Christmas—but on a very rough road.

He moaned softly when he saw Hardesty take other toys—a ball gag, tit clamps connected by a gold chain, and a string of graduated balls—out of his pockets and lay them on the bed on the other side of Jan from where the young rent-boy had placed the tube of lube and the condom packets.

Without further ado, Hardesty, standing close to Jan, moved his hands up Jan's trim and shaved thighs, grasped the waistband of the young man's panties, and slowly pulled them down and off his legs, caressing Jan's flesh as he did so. He'd didn't rip them, as Victor had done with Leslie in the Green Room. Hardesty's technique was a breath-taking combination of velvet hardening into steel.

Jan lifted his butt off the bed, in total submission, to aid the lowering of his panties. Hardesty then ran his hands into the hair on the back of the strawberry blond's head, gripped hard enough to make Jan give a little cry of surprise, and pulled Jan's face to his chest. Jan licked and kissed Hardesty's torso as Hardesty forced the head lower. By the time Jan reached the man's crotch, Hardesty was unzipped and his cock was out and proudly raised in a hard erection. Jan opened his mouth over the cock and, gagging slightly, took it deep into his throat.

It was the perfect pairing—the demanding dominant and the yielding submissive.

* * * *

Jan clinched the ball gag in his mouth hard with his teeth. His eyes were watering; he was grunting, groaning, and moaning; his legs were cramping and going to sleep from the restraints, the red one on his right side trapping his wrist close to his ankle as he was positioned on the bed, chest and knees pressed to the mattress, and tail in the air. The green one was on the left doing the same with the other wrist and ankle. He was concentrating hard on remaining open—and opening further—to the baseball bat of a cock that was deep inside him; he was being rocked back and forth on his chest on the bed by the powerful, rhythmic thrusts of Hardesty's cock; Hardesty had a painful grip on the hair on the back of Jan's head and was arching the young rent-boy's torso back toward the thuggish man's chest; He was slapping Jan's butt cheeks red with the other hand.

The young rent-boy was in ninth heaven, being taken to the edge again and again. Whenever Hardesty sensed that he or Jan was going to come, he held until the danger passed, but then he'd let Jan come and he'd done so himself, only to start the process all over again. Nobody did this better to Jan than Hardesty did. He didn't want it this roughly from anyone else. But, from Hardesty, he wanted it constantly. He'd gotten it again and again from the hard-bodied hunk. He'd taken it from Christmas Eve into Christmas morning.

Exhausted, the young man zoned out. When he woke again, he was draped on Hardesty's body, his arms raised over his head, secured to the headboard of the bed with the red and green restraints. Hardesty was under him, stretched out on his back, his arms embracing Jan's chest, his fingers gently pulling on the rings in Jan's nipples even as the older man slept—and lightly snored. Hardesty's cock was flaccid, but it was still inside Jan's channel, long and thick enough to maintain purchase there without becoming dislodged.

Hardesty was slowly awakening, though. Jan could feel that in the increased strength of the pull on his nipple rings, which made him want to cry out and moan at the pain-pleasure of it through the confining ball gag still in his mouth. And he could feel it in the hardening of the cock inside him. Hardesty stirred enough for Jan to know he was awake—and that the man was going to fuck him again with renewed energy. Hardesty widened the stance of his legs under Jan's, thus spreading and lifting Jan's legs. Jan did cry out through the gag and clinch down on it with his teeth, as Hardesty set his pelvis in motion, thrusting deep again.

Thrusting faster and faster, until both men collapsed, as Hardesty shot another load.

Neither man had time to recover before there was a rap on the door. Without being answered, the door opened and Justine was filling up the space inside the door frame. He didn't look pleased.

"You are needed downstairs, Hardesty," he said, with a disapproving scowl on his face. "There's a police detective who says he needs to take you away. He's outside on the doorstep. I didn't let him in. It's still snowing."

"Shit," Hardesty said, reaching up to undo the restraints on Jan's wrists. "It's Christmas. I was just beginning to enjoy my present." The reprove that someone who wasn't privy to the brothel's existence and secrets might know Hardesty was here was clear in Justine's demeanor.

The ball gag and wrists restraints off, Jan moaned. It was a satisfied moan, though.

Hardesty sat up and shuffled down to the foot of the bed on his bare buttocks, having gently rolled Jan off to the side. But once there, his hand brushed on the string of graduated balls he'd brought. They were in two alternating shiny colors—red and green.

"No, dammit," he said. "It's Christmas and I haven't used all of my presents yet. Tell the guy on the stoop to give you an address and I'll turn myself in there in an hour or so. Don't want him getting cold on your doorstep waiting for me to shower and dress."

"I don't want a cop standing on my doorstep at all," Justine hissed. He turned and left, slamming the door behind him. It was enough to establish that Justine wasn't pleased. He wouldn't go further with Hardesty, though. For some other man, it might mean banishment, but not for a man like Hardesty.

Taking the string of graduated balls in his hand, Hardesty moved back up the bed. Jan whimpered as

159

Hardesty moved up to him, but he made no move to get off the bed or resist in any other way. Hardesty pulled two fluffy pillows from below the headboard, moved the slim, boyish figure of Jan onto his back, his pelvis raised on the pillows, and, sitting up beside the young man's right side, he grasped Jan's right leg. The older man hooked the trembling rent-boy's ankle on his shoulder.

Jan raised, spread, and bent the other leg, placing his left foot flat on the surface of the bed. Knowing what was to come, he rolled his pelvis up and emitted a deep moan.

Hardesty ran his left hand into the strawberry curls on the back of Jan's head. Jan winced, as Hardesty gripped his hair hard and held his head flat on the bed. Hovering over Jan's face with his own, Hardesty locked his gray eyes onto Jan's baby blues. He took in the slight fear and aroused anticipation in the young man's eyes—and watched as the expression turned to slightly more fear, pain blending into pleasure, and slitted lust as, with his right hand, Hardesty pressed the first of the graduated balls into Jan's ass.

Jan gasped, indicated an inclination to struggle, but settling down as he realized that struggle against such as Hardesty was useless, and whimpered as the second, larger ball, went in. He was panting heavily, their eyes locked, Hardesty's mouth set in a small, slightly cruel smile as the third, larger ball went in. Then the fourth.

"Merry Christmas to me," Hardesty murmured as Jan emitted a deep moan.

Jan was stroking his own cock with his left hand. His right hand was trapped behind Hardesty's back, where the younger man clutched at one of the older man's butt cheeks. He dug his nails into the cheek each time a ball was pressed inside him, sending the earlier balls deeper up his channel, but Hardesty just laughed. The rent-boy periodically took his hand off his own cock to brush against Hardesty's. The older man was rock hard again. Jan knew that it wouldn't be anywhere near just an hour before Hardesty was anywhere else. He knew Hardesty would fuck him again—maybe with the balls still inside him. The male whore trembled and whimpered at the thought, but it made him go harder still under the stroking of his hand. Whatever Hardesty did to him, that was all right with Jan. The rent-boy trusted Hardesty not to take it over the edge.

Jan yelped as the balls were pulled out of his ass in one quick jerk. Hardesty rolled over on top of him and entered, entered, entered him. He immediately began to pump, hard and deep. Jan turned his head to the side, his mouth slack, his eyes flashing, loving each killing stroke of Hardesty's cock as Hardesty lowered his face to Jan's chest, took a nipple ring between his teeth, and pulled on it. Jan winced and emitted a little yelp, which Hardesty marked with a cruel thrust of his hips.

The pleasure flowed over Jan through the pain—almost because of the pain and the total taking of the sex. He remembered now why whenever Hardesty showed up here he wanted to be the one chosen. Jan was a whore. Not yet twenty-one, he already felt used up and callous toward what had once been so arousing and fulfilling for him—the delicious, illicit thrill of being fucked in the backseat of a Ford by a coach or his best friend's father when he already was out past curfew. He sometimes lay under three men a day now, in a luxuriously appointed room, taken by men of power and prestige who Jan could pick out in the pages of the *Washington Post*. Justine's was a first-class, full-service brothel. But it was nearly all impersonal now. Once sex had been very important to him. It's why he'd been sucked into this business, what had brought him to Justine and the male brothel in Kalomara. But most of them had become just johns to him—dicks for him to suck and sheath for a half hour. Hardesty was different. With Hardesty, he still remembered why he liked to be fucked. Hardesty fucked him totally. He made Jan feel the fuck—made him

161

remember how it felt to be totally fucked. Made him feel alive while he was killing him.

After Hardesty was gone, having taken his time showering, Jan remained lying on his back on the bed, his pelvis elevated by the pillows, his legs spread and bent, rocking himself slightly with the leverage of his feet—unable yet to close his legs, his channel gaping and sore. Humming to himself. Fully satiated and thinking ahead to Hardesty's next visit to Justine's.

Chapter Two: Under the Ice

"What gives?" Hardesty asked the new partner he'd been given in the D.C. Homicide Vice Unit, Glen Whitehall. When Hardesty stepped out of the taxi into the parking lot of the Georgetown University boat house on the Potomac River, Glen was there, taking charge of a gaggle of beat cops who were standing around with their hands in their armpits to keep them from turning to ice and wisecracking with each other. Cold air was coming off the river and Hardesty pulled his leather jacket closer around his neck.

Whitehall was a strapping young, athletic, and all-American-looking blond who was on his first detective assignment. He'd been a beat cop up until a couple of months previously and was being drummed out of the service when the Homicide Vice unit chief, Crane, plucked him out of the discard pile. There wasn't anything wrong with his copping ability. It was more that he'd been found cavorting with prostitutes too much and had a penchant for being rough with them. But Crane's outfit was made up of detectives who could cavort with, rough up, and use prostitutes, which was why Hardesty was in the unit. The difference was that Whitehall's vice was with females and Hardesty's was with young males. So far, though, although the two did a bit of dancing around each other, Hardesty's seniority and quicker wits were recognized by the young blond, and they were doing OK with each other. Whitehall was sufficiently happy to still have a job he liked and was smart enough to know he could learn from Hardesty.

Hardesty had his own vice but he was known to be a straight arrow on seeking and almost always getting justice.

It probably helped too that neither saw the other as competition in their own vices.

Hardesty's weakness was for young blond men, but he liked them of slight build and a bit more androgynous than Glen Whitehall, who was well over six foot and of linebacker build. Besides, both men were power tops. They both sought out submissives.

"Stiff in a car," Whitehall answered to Hardesty's "what's up?" question. "Merry Christmas."

Hardesty looked around the parking lot, which wasn't large. Space was at a premium here. This was a high-priced-spread section of the city on the line along the waterfront between the federal city and the preexisting river town of Georgetown. To the east of the boathouse along the shore of the river was the infamous and ultraexpensive Watergate complex, the first act scene of the undoing of President Richard Nixon. To the west the Gothic buildings of Georgetown University, a venerable and prestigious Catholic institution, rose on a hill. It wasn't hard to pick out what car Glen was talking about. There was one civilian car in the lot—a sleek, black Mercedes S550 coupe. The rest of the cars in the lot were cop cars. The Mercedes was isolated from the rest of the world with yellow crime scene tape. Even from here Hardesty could make out the vanity plate on the Merc: It was a D.C. plate, CURTIS1.

"A stiff that required Homicide Vice to be called in on Christmas morning?" Hardesty asked.

"Come on over," Glen said. "Judge for yourself."

The body was in the backseat of the Mercedes, leaning toward the center of the seat. The cause of death was obvious. There was a bullet hole in the guy's temple. It hadn't bled much. He was young and blond and naked.

"Why Vice Homicide, because he was young and naked?" Hardesty asked Glen. The half dozen uniformed

164

cops who were standing around were looking very interested in what was going on. Some looked slightly embarrassed, but a few were nudging each other and looked like they were just busting out to make a crack or two.

"Because he is naked and young and probably not the owner of this car," Glen said, "but also because, you can't see it from here, but I have it on good authority that he has a dildo up his ass and something else too, something special. The guess is a rent-boy who was popped during sex."

"Something special?" Hardesty asked.

Glen drew Hardesty's attention to the body's dick.

"Holy fuck," Hardesty said. "That's a sounding rod sticking out of his dick. This was a serious backseat ride, interrupted in faglio delecto."

"I think the term is in flagrante delicto—in the act," Glen said with a straight face. Hardesty was ever needling Glen about his college education and pushing him to say something Hardesty could claim was queer baiting, but Glen never bit. He had a tight little smile on his face, though.

"I think my version fits this case better," Hardesty said. "Who does the chariot belong to?"

"It's been called in. It's a slow day for research though. Christmas and all."

"I doubt this is Curtis. He doesn't look like money. I guess prints will take even longer."

"They've been scanned, yes, and sent in," Glen answered. "Not much else we can do here for a while, though. With the holidays it will take extra time."

"Not much else to be done than post a couple of beat walkers and find a Starbucks nearby that's open."

"There will always be a Starbucks open nearby," Glen said, "even on Christmas Day."

"Ain't that the truth." Hardesty's eyes went to a cop who was walking quickly and with determination in their direction from the boat launch area on the river.

"You the guys from Vice Homicide?" he was asking as he approached.

"Yo," Hardesty asked, "And you are?"

"Thomas of the Fifth Precinct. Found something. You're going to want to see this. Over by the river."

"Where? What?" Hardesty asked as he followed the policeman over to the edge of the water. The river was iced up a good fifteen feet out. There were skid marks on the ice from a kayak that had been pushed out into the river—or Hardesty assumed it had been a kayak. There was a rack of them over against the wall of the boathouse and one of the slots was empty.

"So, someone's gone into the river?" Glen said as he walked up beside Hardesty and Patrolman Thomas.

"Yeah, but that's not the point. Can you see him?"

"Him who . . . oh shit," Hardesty said. Whitehall had joined in the "Oh, shit" part. They were looking down into the ice at the edge of the boat launch. A face was staring up at them from under the ice. It was a man. His eyes were bugging out and his mouth was open in a silent scream. There was a bullet hole between his eyes.

"Well, fuck," Hardesty said, his voice disgusted.

"What the hell?" was Glen's contribution. "Suppose it's Curtis Whoever?"

"Afraid not. I know him," Hardesty said. "He's Russian. His name's Victor. At least that's the name I heard he goes by. I don't know a last name. But he's a bad ass." What he didn't want to say was that he'd seen the man a couple of hours previously—at Justine's. He was one of Justine's special clients. This was getting dicey. Glen knew about Justine's, but he didn't know everything there was to know about Justine's. Hardesty's chief, Crane, and the department certainly didn't know about Justine's—

Hardesty hoped. Crane knew Hardesty could tap most of the male prostitutes in town—but Crane didn't know the depths of his relationships with their pimps and houses. How was he going to handle this, and . . . "I want to see the stiff in the car again," he suddenly said, turning and moving back to the parking lot.

The passenger door was open and the front seat was pushed forward. He leaned into the car, grasped the dead young man's chin, and turned the face to him.

"Shit."

It was Leslie from Justine's.

He stood up from the car and took a long look out toward the river, at the Key Bridge, which spanned the river from Georgetown to the near-skyscraper business center of Rosslyn on the Virginia shore.

"What is it?" Whitehall said. "You recognize this one too?"

"His name—his professional name—is Leslie," Hardesty said, a bit of sadness in his voice. Leslie had been a fun and willing lay. He could take it. Well, short of a bullet in the temple. "It's right that we were called. He's a high-stakes rent-boy. Guess it's our case after all."

They both turned their heads at the sound of the siren-blazing arrival of another cop car and watched their captain, Crane, climb out.

"Hey, hey, the gang's all here now," Hardesty said, as the captain approached. He didn't look the least bit happy. "What brings you out on Christmas Day, Captain?"

"Beats me," Crane answered. "I got a call from topside to get my ass over here pronto. And it looks like it's not a moment too soon," he said, as they all watched the arrival of another vehicle—a black Cadillac Escalade, the jittery blue and red lights going bananas behind its grill. Two formidable-looking men in black suits hopped out of the back of the SUV and strode over to the Mercedes.

They looked inside. "Fuck," one of them said. "The boss knew this could get messy."

The boss? Hardesty wondered.

The other one turned to Crane, recognizing him as the senior on duty. At the same time he flashed a badge, which they all recognized. Secret Service. "This the only one?" he asked.

Crane shrugged. "I just got here."

"There's another one under the ice over by the boat ramp," Whitehall answered.

"Shit," the man said. "Maurice, over by the boat ramp, the cop said. Another one over there."

All five of them, the agents in front, with Whitehall leading them, trooped over to the side of the river and looked down into the face under the ice.

"Isn't him," one of the agents said.

"Isn't who?" Hardesty asked. They didn't answer.

"Looks like he'll keep until the team gets here," the other agent said, and they turned and trooped back to the Mercedes.

"What team?" Hardesty asked, a bit more belligerently. Again, neither agent answered him. He was about to say something else, but Crane put a restraining hand on his arm and gave him the Pig Latin "ixnay" look. Fine, Hardesty told himself. Two can play the silence game. Let them find out who these guys are on their own. They went back to the car and the agents approached the vehicle from different sides and leaned into the car.

"Fuck," one of the agents said, standing up from where he'd been feeling around in the car. He'd come up with a gun. Hardesty immediately recognized it as a Glock G30S, military issue. A compact pistol for easy concealment but with a big .45 payoff.

"Where'd you get—?" he started to say.

"Doesn't matter," the agent answered in a monotone. "Kid was shot with a .22, it looks like. This would have taken his face off. Same with the face under the ice." He looked sternly at the three Vice Homicide unit detectives. "So, you guys didn't see this pistol. And you can fuck off now."

The other agent produced a plastic bag and the first agent put the pistol in it, took the bag back to the Escalade, tossed it in the backseat, and returned.

"That's part of the crime scene," Hardesty said. "Shouldn't that have stayed in the Mercedes?"

"What? I didn't see anything," said the agent who had taken it to the Escalade.

"I told you the kid wasn't shot with it. It's government issues, like this one," the first agent, the one evidently taking the lead, said. He patted a holster under his armpit. "We wouldn't want to muddy up the issue with an official-issue piece, would we?" His chin was jutting out like he was daring Hardesty to disagree with that, and then, when Hardesty, with a look he shared with Crane, wasn't quick to do so, he went on giving instructions. "Two of the uniforms should stay until our team can get in here. An ME been here yet?"

Crane looked at Hardesty, who looked at Whitehall, who said, "No, sir. Not yet."

"Good. You can call yours off. Our team will handle everything from here. You sure no one has seen another man around here?"

Well, there's that at least, Hardesty thought. These guys have lost someone—a man—and he's of more concern to them than these two dead guys are—these guys who I have some idea about who they are and the Secret Service probably doesn't yet. Maybe the guy they were looking for had something to do with a license plate that read "Curtis." He set his jaw. Leslie was a rent-boy, and someone he knew—that meant he'd be damned if he lost interest in this case. And he, at least, had someplace to start. Leslie wouldn't have made it out of Justine's this morning

169

without Justine's permission and, more likely, without Justine sending him to someone.

"Nobody I've talked to has seen evidence of anyone else," Whitehall said to the agents. "It looks like someone might have taken a kayak out into the water, though. The rack by the boat launch is unlocked, there's an empty space, and there are drag marks on the ice, going into the water."

"Fuck," one of the agents said.

"Yeah, we were told he takes a kayak out on the Potomac nearly every day," muttered the other agent. The two of them turned and walked back toward the boat launch. Whitehall made to follow them, but Crane stopped him.

"You heard them. They're taking over," Crane said. "It would be a good time for us to leave."

Hardesty dug in his heels. He looked to see that the two Secret Service agents were far enough away that they couldn't hear him. "I know the young man in the Merc," he then said. He couldn't bear to call him a stiff or a vic. "He's a high-end rent-boy."

"One of yours?" Crane asked. "One you've been laying or one you've been using as an informer?"

Whitehall gave them an embarrassed look and went over and stood next to an unmarked car from the unit.

"Yes," Hardesty answered, not separating the two actions. "We're as good for this case as those monkeys are with what we know so far."

"I said we might as well leave here now, Hardesty," Crane responded in a low voice. "I didn't say we had to roll over on investigating the case. The kid in the car being a rent-boy is good enough for me for us to do some of our own investigation. You want this, or are you too close?"

"I laid him, Cap; I didn't love him. But I liked him well enough to want to do right by him. Yes, I want to follow this until upstairs takes it away from us."

"OK. You can ride back to the unit with me. We'll discuss what we've got while we're riding."

Hardesty turned a hard look toward the two Secret Service agents who were milling around the drag marks on the ice. Something big was going on here. He could smell it. These goons could worry about some bigwig all they wanted. He was worried for justice for Leslie. And he knew where he had to start—back at Justine's where he'd last seen both Leslie and the guy under the ice.

Chapter Three: Case Not Closed

It was Jim, not Justine, who met Hardesty at the door of the male brothel in the exclusive Kalomara section of Washington, D.C. Out of makeup and the flamboyant dress, he was just any other balding late-middle-age man of commanding height and beer belly.

"Hardesty," he said with a mixed response to having the Vice detective on his doorstep in the cold sunshine of late morning Christmas Day. Hardesty was necessary to him—and he even liked the man—but he was wearing on Justine's rent-boys and he'd brought a cop to the brothel's door the previous night. "Back so soon? None of the young men are here today. I gave them Christmas Day off."

"When was the last time you saw Leslie?" Hardesty asked.

"I don't know. Sometime last night. What—?"

"I think we'd best discuss this inside," Hardesty said, and he didn't wait for an invitation to brush past Jim and move into the downstairs parlor. He sat in a wingchair and motioned for the brothel's madam to sit in the one facing it at the fireplace. The fire was out and the stockings had been taken down. Leslie's stocking? Had all of the guys opened their stockings that morning before leaving and Justine knew then that Leslie wasn't there?

The Christmas tree was still behind the chair where Jim sat, albeit not as impressive unlit and in the daylight as it had been the night before. Hardesty now saw that it wasn't a real tree but was an artificial one that had seen better days. Jim had seen better days too. In the daylight, so had the wingchair he was sitting in and the carpet on the

172

floor. Paid for sex always was more tawdry in the daylight than at night, Hardesty had learned.

"I haven't come here for pleasure, Justine." Even when he was out of drag, Hardesty would maintain the name pretense for the madam. "I won't hold back. I've just come from a crime scene in Georgetown. Leslie has been found in the back of a swank automobile with a bullet in his head."

Hardesty gave the madam a moment to absorb that, but he looked carefully into the man's face, gauging the reactions as they went from shock to pain to concern to a wariness about the eyes.

"I'm sure you knew he wasn't here this morning."

"Yes, I did," the madam answered quick enough. "He was checked out for the night. I wasn't expecting him back before this afternoon."

"You knew who he was with, didn't you?"

"Victor paid to take him out for the night. A Russian businessman took him for the night. You saw him here last night. He has a client. For the money they pay me, I haven't shown a lot of interest who that client is. The best I can do is set it up so you can connect with Victor— without him knowing I set it up, I hope. He has rough friends. Ones you probably don't want to make enemies of either. You have to help keep my operation out of this. Leslie. He can't be traced back to here. That's what we need you for."

Interesting that this would be the madam's priority concern, Hardesty thought. And he didn't believe for a nanosecond that Justine had no idea who Victor was pimping for. But then, perhaps sensing how callous and revealing he'd been, Jim doubled back, shielded his eyes with a hand, squeezed them shut in search of tears that didn't quite come, and murmured, "Poor Leslie. Poor, poor Leslie."

"That's not what I've come about," Hardesty said. "I covered that for you before I got here." Hardesty was as aware as Justine was what was expected of him to maintain his privileges here. "I've contacted a pimp who will acknowledge Leslie was his. If you come up with $12,000 in cash, he'll even cover the burial. It needn't come back to you if you can keep your men in line and on the same page."

"I can handle them," Jim said, looking up, not a trace of "thanks" or gratefulness in his face. He knew how valuable the services here were for Hardesty. Hardesty could pick up any rent-boy on the street he wanted, of course, but he couldn't get one as high class as the ones he got here—other than the one Jim knew he had in his Crystal City apartment—nor could he easily get one who would go as far as Hardesty sometimes wanted to go. "Then why did you come here? You could have told me this over the phone."

"I think not," Hardesty said. "I believe I've told you not to do business like this over the telephone. I don't control all aspects of police work in the district."

"Point taken," Jim answered icily.

"I've come because I'm going to investigate the crime and I have competition in that. I want to know whatever you do about who Leslie was entertaining regularly and the circumstances under which he left here last night. The Russian, Victor, is dead too. I last saw him circling Leslie in this room last night."

"Victor? Victor's dead too? Shit."

"Leslie couldn't have gone out of the house without your permission. You say he went with Victor?"

"Yes," Jim answered.

"Why? Victor could have had him here."

"Victor did have him here. But, as I indicated, he does pimping duties for another client. He said that other

174

client wanted Leslie for the night. Victor paid me for the service. This isn't unusual."

"And who is the other client? Don't try to tell me you have no idea who it is?"

"I just know him as Mr. T. He's someone with power and influence, though—even for Washington—I can tell you that. He first came to us on referral. High-level referral and a lot of cash."

"Referral from who?" And then when Jim didn't answer, Hardesty leaned over and put a vice grip on the man's forearm. "Referral from who, Jim? There is a limit to what I'll do for you for privileges here, and I could get you shut down in an hour and take one of the men for my own use. There's only so much I need from you."

"It was the mafia—the Russian Mafia. I knew the connection, but nothing more specific. I don't say no to people like that."

Hardesty sat back in his chair. "But the man, this Mr. T, comes here sometimes? He doesn't always order out?"

"Yes, he's been here."

"Does he have a favorite fetish?"

"Yes. Sounding. We don't have much demand for that."

This was interesting and connected with how they'd found Leslie in the backseat of the Mercedes. But would a man leave a sounding rod in a rent-boys dick and go off kayaking? Wouldn't he finish with the sounding game first?

"And you'd recognize him if you saw a photo of him?"

Jim didn't answer immediately, and Hardesty repeated the question, somewhat more forcefully, adding, "None of this need be official; none of this need trace back to you. I just want you to provide a yes or no if I end up with a photo of a suspect."

"Yes, I'd recognize him."

"You say Victor did Leslie here himself last night."

"Yes."

"Upstairs?"

"Yes, the Green Room."

"Were they the last to use the Green Room last night?"

"Yes."

"Has the room been cleaned yet?"

"It's Christmas and we're closed tonight. No it hasn't."

"I want to go up there and look around."

"You can do as you want," Jim answered in a tired voice. "You will anyway."

"But I'd think better of you if you gave me what I needed with a smile," Hardesty retorted.

The detective did a pretty thorough search of the room, coming up with two used wine glasses, which he handled carefully and wrapped in hand towels. He wanted to steal a march on the feds, if he could. They'd have fingerprints of both Leslie and Victor and should be able to come up with real names. But they'd work through channels. Hardesty could cut corners and had friends in the labs. If Leslie's and Victor's fingerprints were on these glasses, and they were in the system, he'd know before the feds did who the victims really were. He'd go right back to the office from here. Larry, the unit's clerk, had pulled Christmas duty. He also had the hots for Hardesty. It was a desire that hadn't been satisfied yet, although Hardesty had a reputation for spiking any of the male unit clerks who were interested. Hardesty could get IDs rolling today. The feds would wait until tomorrow to push the "go" button. They obviously were worried about someone who wasn't found at the scene more than they were interested in Leslie or Victor.

When he came downstairs, a sweet-looking mulatto rent-boy he knew as Sean, but who he hadn't known

176

intimately, was coming in the front door. The madam had come to the foyer.

"I suppose now that Sean is back, you'll want to take him upstairs," Jim said to Hardesty. Sean looked quite willing to go upstairs with Hardesty.

"Thanks, but I have someplace to go and night's better than day for fucking a nice piece like Sean. I'll take a night check on that."

Neither Jim nor Sean had the foggiest notion what Hardesty meant by that, but both stood by the door as Hardesty left. Sean looked happy and hopeful, as Hardesty had paused to kiss him on the mouth and give him a bit of tongue. "Later," he'd whispered to the young man. "Count on it." Jim was just relieved to see Hardesty off and having given more support than grief.

* * * *

Larry was belly to wooden desktop in the dimly lit Vice Homicide squad room, where he and Hardesty were alone on the afternoon of Christmas Day. A fluorescent tube light in the ceiling over the desk was the only artificial lighting going, and it was flickering in a repeated off-beat pattern.

The gangly twenty-something desk clerk still had his T-shirt and sneakers on, but otherwise was naked. He was gripping the far side of the desk, his arms stretched over his head and spread. His legs were spread too, his toes touching the floor in front of the desk. He wasn't a handsome young man, but he wasn't ugly. He just hadn't survived the acne phase yet and when he did, he'd have to endure facial scarring. He was more "willowy" than muscular, but not fat by any means—rather the opposite. What had held Hardesty back from what obviously had been offered was that Larry was flamboyantly gay and flounced around and made goo-goo eyes a lot. But he had a cock and a hole and he had needs. He had fantasized a need for Hardesty since the day he'd come on duty in the squad. Indeed, he had sought duty in the same squad Hardesty was in, having heard the gossip of how Hardesty took good care of seeking desk clerks so that he'd receive good support services.

Although he hadn't given Larry a second look, while being neutrally pleasant to him, Hardesty had increasingly become aware of Larry's infatuation, and he needed help today in expediting the fingerprints from the wine glasses in the Green Room through the system.

And it was Christmas. Hardesty was giving Larry his Christmas present. The squad clerk was a valuable asset. Vice cops who wanted good services from them gave them presents.

The detective was crouched on the floor between Larry's legs. He was keeping his clothes on, but he had his fly open and his dong out and encased in one hand. The young man had a nice, long cock, a pleasant surprise, and Hardesty had pulled it back between his legs and was stroking and sucking it while intermittently tonguing Larry's hole, which blossomed right open to him. Larry's channel was well known to men, Hardesty realized. He played with rubbing the glans of Larry's cock against the young man's own hole and laughed when the hole puckered up and tried to pull it in. Larry moaned, pleading, "Yes, yes, do me, please fuck me." He came pressed up to his own hole.

And so Hardesty did, crowning himself with a condom, climbing up on the desk with his feet, crouching down and grabbing Larry's slim waist between his hands. He thrust his dick up inside Larry's channel through the lubricant of the young man's own cum. The hole and passageway spread right open to receive him.

Quickly Hardesty had achieved a synchronization of the pattern of his thrusts with the flickering of the defective fluorescent tube overhead.

"Merry Christmas, Larry," he murmured. Larry answered with seventh-heaven moans and groans.

Needless to say, arrangements were made for Hardesty to have his fingerprint IDs from the lab by the next day.

* * * *

Hardesty always tried to be home for twilight. He didn't always make it, but he did often enough and it was special to be here on Christmas Day to watch the sun go down, while he was looking past the runaways of the Ronald Reagan Airport across the Potomac from Washington, D.C., where he had a good view of the Washington Monument and the Lincoln Memorial.

The apartment had been Toby's demand when the two of them had decided to move in together nearly five years earlier—that and Toby had insisted that he wasn't going to give up his life as a high-class male hooker until age, and the ravishes of time on the body, dictated that. Toby thought he'd have about four more years of that high-paid life and then he could retire before thirty. Hardesty thought Toby was underestimating how much time he had left. He was a gorgeous, small-stature blond with a perfectly formed body, great submissive bottom technique, endurance, and little evidence of aging.

Hardesty believed Toby could pass as nineteen or twenty for ten more years. Hardesty didn't like it, but, although he dominated Toby in bed, the young man called the shots elsewhere in their life together. "You screw whoever you want and I don't complain, and I'll let whoever I want screw me," was Toby's closing statement the few times they fought over the issue. He'd follow up with the kicker, "We both know we are best with each other."

This apartment was a case in point in Toby's control of their lives. When they'd come together, Hardesty picking Toby—whose professional name was Todd—up for solicitation, screwing his lights out rather than taking him in, and then taking him home, Hardesty had been comfortably, if a bit shabbily, living in a fifties rambler in Northwest Washington that he'd inherited from his parents. Toby had been living around with various high spender sugar daddies who wanted someone legal who looked like he was sixteen.

Toby had refused to live in Hardesty's house, even though prices in D.C. had made it a gold mine. Toby wanted to live someplace expensive and flashy and he wanted to have it available for his work. So, here they were, high up in a high rise in Crystal City, overlooking the airport and federal Washington, D.C., with a two-bedroom, two-and-a-half-bath apartment sporting a floor-to-ceiling glass wall spanning the living area. The furniture was sleek modern, with white leather that was easy to clean. You never could tell when any of the pieces of furniture would be splattered with spunk. The furniture was also designed to provide interesting surfaces for fucking.

Toby frequently brought his johns back here. One of the bedrooms, both of which had a bath attached, was set up for Toby's business, complete with furniture welcoming to sex position angles. They called this bedroom the "show" room, and both of them tended to use it when they brought men other than each other home for sex. The other bedroom was set up with furniture Hardesty liked and had brought from his family home. Both men slept in Hardesty's bedroom. Hardesty spent most of his time in his own bedroom or the kitchen alcove off the living area, or here at the window, in the twilight, and at night, watching planes land and take off and the lights on Washington.

The only element the two bedrooms shared were the restraints on and over the beds. Toby delivered demanding, kinky sex for clients in the "show" bedroom and to Hardesty in the Vice detective's bedroom. They had come to an agreement that Hardesty couldn't complain about what Toby gave his clients if Toby gave that and more to Hardesty.

Toby happily gave it all to Hardesty, and, in appreciation, Hardesty tolerated whatever else Toby did, although he worried about him out on the street, even though his clients these days were all high rollers.

In order for the apartment to serve them both, it had an elaborate warning and protection system. If Toby was bringing a john back to the apartment, there was a button he could push near the apartment's mailbox off the lobby before they came up. This would activate a red light and buzzer in the apartment's kitchen, and Hardesty could then barricade himself in his bedroom, where he usually stayed anyway. There was a red light next to the entry door that could be activated if Toby was entertaining when Hardesty came home.

They had a friend down the hall in his late middle age, but who was still a player, Paul, who was happy to let Hardesty hang out—or even bunk—there with him if the apartment was in use. They didn't mess around with each other, but Hardesty provided Paul with a male hooker occasionally when the deal was that otherwise Hardesty would have to take the rent-boy in to the station. The rent-boys never left Paul's apartment unhappy. Despite his age, Paul was a looker, having been a model, and Paul could go all day and night. When young men left him, they were exhausted, but humming, and they told Hardesty afterward that Paul was a lover, not a john.

The city didn't encourage vice arrests and turned a blind eye to some of Hardesty's ideas of alternative punishment and recompense. There wasn't enough cell space to handle all of the hookers in the political town and a low vice crime rate statistic was better than a high arrest

181

stat. And this *was* a political town. Everything and everyone was for sale anyway.

If the rent-boy was sturdy and of a type Hardesty liked, with the ability and willingness to take what Hardesty liked to provide, making favorable conditions a bit rare, Hardesty dispensed control and justice himself. Otherwise, if they met Paul's interests, which centered on his use of a plow belt, he often was enlisted to do the honors. In return, Paul watched out for his unusual-couple neighbors.

In the protection department, there was a wide-angle fish-lens peephole in Hardesty's bedroom door. This wasn't strictly for voyeur purposes when Hardesty was home when Toby was entertaining in the living area, although he *did* enjoy watching the action; it also accorded Toby some protection in case a client got out of hand. Toby didn't take johns to his bedroom unless he fully trusted them. When they did their business in the living room, Hardesty could monitor it and provide assistance, as necessary. Toby had made sure that there were sufficient interesting-shaped pieces of furniture in the living room to accommodate almost any position fetish a client might have.

So it was that the evening of Christmas Day, at the back edge of twilight, while Hardesty was standing at the full glass wall, beer in hand, and enjoying not just the view across the Potomac but also the reflection of the multicolored lights of the Christmas tree behind him reflecting off the window that the buzzer and red light in the kitchen went off. Looking around for any evidence of untidiness and not seeing any, Hardesty retreated to his bedroom, shut the door, and stationed himself at the peephole.

Hardesty recognized the two guys entering the apartment with Toby immediately. They towered over Toby's five foot six frame. Both of them were NBA players measuring out at six foot eight or nine. Now that he thought about it, Hardesty remembered that Toby had said he was going to show a couple of players from the Chicago Bulls around before they played a game here with the Washington Wizzards. Hardesty hadn't thought much about the guys being johns, but, of course they were if Toby was "showing" them around. They were team stars. Malcolm Howard and DeAndre Brewer. They were both forwards on the team, each weighing in close to either side of 200 pounds—compared to probably 140 pounds wet for Toby. And they both lived up to the team name. They were black bulls, hung like bulls, as they quickly evidenced.

They both went down to their briefs while Toby fixed them beers and then they pawed and undressed Toby, with the three of them standing in the center of the living area while they drank their beers and talked too low for Hardesty to hear them. They obviously had come to the apartment for immediate servicing, as they wasted no time. They had enormous erections on that were obvious despite the briefs they still wore. When Toby, naked now, went on his knees in front of them as they linked arms, the briefs came down and off, and Toby gave both of their cocks suck play together. The guys were definitely a team.

Hardesty could see through the peephole that they weren't going to get to the bedroom. The scene was going to be right there in the living area, according him a good view. The oversized white leather ottoman was one of the favorite stages of Toby's serving, and it would prove to be so now. Both men were super hung; both had brought their own Trojan Magnum XLs. Toby went down on the small of his back on the ottoman. He flared his shapely legs up and out, grabbing his ankles with his fists. DeAndre crouched between his legs, grunted through the penetration, while Toby fluidly waved his buttocks about, responding as any good rent-boy would to the size of any cock invading him, although Hardesty doubted the pain-pleasure of it had to be feigned for the hung DeAndre, and he started a slow pump.

Toby arched his head back over the side of the ottoman and opened his throat to Malcolm's cock. Malcolm's big hands went to Toby's small, perfectly mounded pecs and worried his nipples. In a surprise move, though, after a few minutes, Malcolm pulled his cock out of Toby's throat, came around to behind DeAndre, and saddled up on him. Holding DeAndre's hips in his hands, Malcolm mounted and penetrated DeAndre's ass, and it was DeAndre fucking Toby and Malcolm fucking DeAndre.

Quite chummy teammates, Hardesty thought, with a bit of a smile. He had the brief urge to go out there and mount Malcolm and make it a real train, but he fought the urge. He'd probably be beaten to a pulp. The image of two black bulls working a small, beautiful white guy caused Hardesty's fluids to flow, though and he unzipped himself and worked his cock while he watched the three fucking on the Ottoman.

* * * *

"Wait, I don't think you want to do that." The voice, a rich baritone, had come from farther down the corridor from Toby's apartment door. Jan, from Justine's, turned to see a man in a short robe and bare legs standing outside an open door into another apartment. He was old in Jan's eyes, probably in his fifties, Jan assessed, but he was unusually handsome and trim. He had a healthy head of hair, graying at the temples, which made him look all the more presentable. The silk robe only went to below his knees. Jan, always speculating and having accommodated more than his share of older men, in a wide range of acceptability, immediately assessed this man as top drawer and wondered what he had on underneath the robe and how big he was.

"Look at the light. It's red. That means they aren't ready for company."

184

"Oh," Jan said, taking his hand away for the door buzzer like it was a hot stove. "I guess I should . . . I, um . . ." He backed off from the door.

"If you're a friend of Toby's, you'll know what he's busy doing," the man said, giving Jan a speculative look and then, when Jan didn't indicate that he wouldn't know why Toby would have a red light like this out, he smiled and continued. "You don't need to leave or wait out in the corridor. Toby and Hardesty are friends of mine. You're welcome to come inside my apartment and wait until they aren't busy. I have a light in my apartment that is connected to theirs."

"You have a light in your apartment connected to theirs?" Jan didn't know if he had heard correctly or not.

"Yes. As I said, we're friends and watch out for each other. I know why that red light is on. We don't have any secrets. Come on in." He stood aside and Jan walked into a small apartment living room, which, nonetheless, was nicely furnished. The man entered the apartment, closed the door, and gestured for Jan to sit in an arm chair facing a small sofa. Everything looked natural in the apartment except for a black leather wide strap slung over the back of the sofa. Jan knew what that was. He could see one handle at the end of the strap and knew there was another handle on the side hanging down the back of the sofa.

He looked up at the man with surprise in his eyes. Jan could see now that the man, although slim, was muscular and no ancient weakling. It took strength to use a plow belt, and this man looked capable of supporting a man's body on it, especially someone as small as Jan. The man smiled at him and undid the sash of his robe, letting the robe flare open. He was naked under the robe. His cock was magnificent. Not thick, but long. His physique was, indeed, quite good for a man his age. Black, curly hair, smattered with gray swirled around on his pecs and

185

descended in a line down his sternum and belly to his tightly trimmed pubes.

"Am I embarrassing you?" the man asked. "My impression is that you're in the same profession as Toby is."

"No, you're not embarrassing me at all," Jan answered, unable to take his eyes off the man's dick. He was being forward, but Jan thought he had every reason to be proud in displaying himself. Jan knew that he himself clearly signaled who and what he was.

"My name is Paul," the man said. "If you know Toby and look and dress as you do, I'm guessing you're a rent-boy too—one of his professional friends."

"Umm," was all Jan could come up with. But he hadn't denied it.

"Have you come to see Toby or Hardesty?"

"Toby's a friend of mine, but it's probably Hardesty I've come to see."

"Did he send for you? Are you to be his Christmas evening delight?"

"No, I need to talk to him about something."

"But you do fuck for money, don't you?"

"Yes."

"Hardesty has laid you before, hasn't he? You are just what he can't resist."

Jan didn't respond to that, and Paul went on as if he'd answered in the affirmative. From the look on Jan's face, it was obvious that Hardesty had worked him over a time or two. "What can I get you while we wait for Toby to finishing servicing his client? Ice water, Coke, beer, wine, milk, an aphrodisiac? A cock up your ass?"

"Excuse me?"

"You're looking at this," Paul said, lifting the leather strap. "Do you know what this is for?"

"Yes," Jan answered. "It's a plow belt."

"Has it been used with you before?"

186

"Yes."

"Did you enjoy it? Would you enjoy it with me for, say, two hundred dollars? I've been bored tonight, and it's Christmas. It may be a while before Toby or Hardesty are available. There should be some pleasurable and profitable way we could use the time." He took a small wad of bills out of the pocket of his robe and laid it down on the seat of the sofa next to where the plow belt had been.

Jan began to undress. Paul watched appreciatively for a moment and then helped him, slowing down the process as bit as they fondled and groped each other.

* * * *

Malcolm was sprawled out on his back on the ottoman in Toby and Hardesty's apartment. From Hardesty's vantage point, he looked like a spider that had been turned over on its back. His gangling legs and arms were draped off the sides of the ottoman. His knuckles were scraping on the white carpet. His feet were on the floor, and he was using them for leverage to fuck up into Toby's passage rapidly and with much force. Toby was saddled on the basketball player's pelvis, riding his cock cowboy style, facing him, riding him like he was a bucking bull, which in all functional purposes he was. DeAndre approached from behind, encircled Toby's waist with one arm and pressed the center of the smaller man's back, lowering Toby's chest onto Malcolm's. Malcolm and Toby both settled down. DeAndre took his arm from around Toby's waist and guided the bulb of his cock to Toby's hole, above the root of Malcolm's buried cock and started working his shaft inside Toby above Malcolm's cock.

Toby cried out and flopped around a bit while DeAndre was skewering him. Hardesty took his breath in, but he knew Toby wasn't really in distress—that he could take both cocks. He was mostly doing what would be expected when someone was being double penetrated. The cocks were fat and long, though, so it wasn't a cake walk.

DeAndre began to pump and, with a whimper, deep moaning, and heavy panting, Toby settled down to docilely letting the black bulls have their way with him.

In high heat himself from watching the performance, Hardesty stripped, went over to the nightstand to retrieve a Fleshlight, and returned to the peephole, working his cock with the Fleshlight as he watched the two black professional basketball players working Toby. He discerned when they were both shooting off, pulled the Fleshlight off his cock, took matters into his own hands, and shot his load against the bedroom door.

* * * *

He was getting in deep. He was good, very good. He wore being over fifty well. And he was strong, hard bodied. Jan was draped over the plow belt sling on his belly, his arms and legs hanging down. Paul was standing behind him, gripping the handles of the plow belt. He was holding Jan off the floor. His cock was buried deep inside Jan's ass, and he was using the strength of his sinewy legs to support the young man's weight and the strength of his arm muscles to raise and lower the plow belt, causing his cock to dig and release, dig and release, inside Jan's passage.

"Shit. Fuck. Plow me!" Jan cried out.

Paul continued doing so.

* * * *

Hardesty answered the apartment door after looking through the peephole and ascertaining who it was.

"Jan," he said, after opening the door to him. "What are you doing here? Have you come to see Toby? He's taking a shower."

"I think it's actually you I've come to see," Jan said, giving him a sheepish look. "I'm sorry how late it is, but—"

"No, no. Come on in. You say you think it's me you've come to see? You don't know whether it is or isn't?"

"I don't know if it's anything to worry about," Jan said.

"Have a seat. We have some wine open. I'll pour us a glass. What are you worried about?"

"It's Leslie. I know he's dead. Justine told me. And Victor too. I never liked him—Victor that is."

"Yes, I'm afraid it's true about both of them. But—"

"Justine told me you were asking about Mr. T. Leslie went with him. But I have too—a couple of times. Justine thought maybe Leslie servicing him might have been what got Leslie killed. Mr. T is always so secretive and there is something about him that makes me think of danger and evil. I'm afraid . . . I'm wondering . . ."

"If you are in danger too?" Hardesty walked over and handed him the glass of wine, but Jan put it down on the coffee table in front of him immediately, as he was shaking too much to hold it. Hardesty was standing close to him, exuding the scent of musk. He was in a silk robe, just as Paul had been just now. Jan imagined Hardesty was wearing nothing under it, and then didn't imagine any more as the robe fell open a bit and Jan could see that Hardesty was naked under the robe and half hard.

As always, Jan wanted this sexy man. But he had several opportunities to be with him. Being taken with the plow belt by Paul had been fully satisfying and something new. That had been something different and yet so normal—just a long, attentive screwing by a cock that could reach up into his gut and make caressing love to every inch of his channel on its journey up to the quick of him, while he was secured in place by and fully captive to the man's powerful control. Paul had told him that he'd been a male model, but he'd also obviously done a lot of strength training. He made a straightforward fuck something special. Could Jan just come back at any time and let Paul plow him?

"Yes. I probably shouldn't feel like I'm in danger, but—" he started to say.

"Until we figure out what's going on—and I'm working on it—you probably are right to worry about it. If this Mr. T is fucking you regularly I assume you could pick him out of a lineup."

"Not too regular. He was one of Leslie's regulars. But, yes, I'm sure I could recognize him in a lineup."

"Where are you taken to be with this Mr. T? Can you remember? A hotel room? Someplace different each time."

"Mostly one place. He sometimes has Victor bring me to a park and he does me in the backseat of his car. But usually it's a small townhouse in Georgetown. On P Street. Very expensive furnishings; lots of books on shelves. I don't know the address, but it's painted sort of a dark yellow. The only one around that is. Victor always parks in back and hustles me through a garage and up to Mr. T's bedroom on the third floor. I only know what the townhouse looks like on the front because I was walking down there one day and picked the house out. The man's got money to be living in a place like that."

"Is there anyone else there when you are with him—other than Leslie or Victor?"

"There is someone named Kim who I think lives there. Leslie and I are not there at the same time. Leslie and I have just talked about being fucked the same way there. Mr. T's bed's got all the trimmings. He likes spread-eagle restraining, and he's got as many toys as you do."

"Anyone else from Justine's other than you or Leslie taken to Mr. T?"

"No, I don't think so. Just Leslie and me. Justine knows about it. It's all arranged with Justine."

"This Kim is there, when you were having sex with Mr. T?"

"Yes. Mr. T likes threesomes—and more. Kim is included, and Victor too. Mr. T likes to watch Victor fuck me or Kim."

"And this Mr. T wants demanding sex? himself."

"Yes. He has these metal rods. He ties me up so that I can't move and he takes these rods, one bigger than the next, and he pushes them down into my cock head and spins them. He does this until I come and then he fucks me. And then he watches Victor fuck me too."

"Does Victor use the metal rods?"

"No, Victor is very basic and rough. He likes—he liked—to fuck me on all fours on the floor, like a dog. And Victor is—was—a choker."

"Mr. T screws your dick with something like these?" Hardesty asked, taking a wooden box from the bottom shelf of a side table and opening it to display a set of graduated sounding rods.

"Yes, like those," Jan answered in a hushed tone. "You have them too."

"Yes, I have them too, Jan. I use them too." He didn't complete that thought, but went on with his questioning of Jan. This was dovetailing into his investigation of Leslie's death. "Sounding rods. That's what they're called, Jan. This Mr. T likes to sound you? And do you like it, Jan?"

"It's different," Jan said, turning his head away, not looking directly into Hardesty's face. "It's not as demanding as what some other men do to me, including you. You know what services Justine's provides. Mr. T isn't as demanding with fetishes as some of the men he makes me service are. But this shit with the rods is dangerous. It's got a high all its own because of that."

"He shares you with other men?"

191

"Yes, Victor, and there's a Russian he meets with. The Russian brings bodyguards with him, and Mr. T lets them fuck me while he's meeting with their boss. They— Mr. T and the Russian—sit and watch from across the room while they're talking in low voices to each other. And there are a few other men, secretive, catlike and cruel. One of those, a guy from where Mr. T used to work, he said, uses the sounding rods and is impatient and hurts me with them—and laughs." He turned his head back and gave Hardesty an eyelash fluttery look—to make clear that he didn't mind what Hardesty did with him, though.

"Does it make you come? Having the sounding wands used on you?" Hardesty asked, ignoring the come-hither look. "You said it does. Do you come more than once while Mr. T is doing this to you?"

"Yes," Jan answered in a low voice. "I come more than once. Mr. T comes too. He likes it. He's old and sometimes has trouble going hard. But this makes him go hard every time. The other, more cruel man, is younger and in a lot better shape. He has no trouble going hard—or coming more than once or making me come more than once."

"If you come more than once, then you enjoy it. Would you like me to use the sounding rods on you?"

"If you wish," Jan said, looking away again. But Hardesty could see that the young man was trembling. He suspected Jan very much would like him to use the sounding rods on him. and maybe . . . when this was all cleared up and Jan could return to Justine's . . . just maybe . . .

"Now? Would you like me to use the sounding rods with you now? Here? Me sitting on the ottoman over there, you sitting on my cock, and me holding you close and spinning sounding rods down into your dick?"

Jan looked up and into Hardesty's eyes with defiance. "Yes, I want you to use them with me now," he

192

said. "If that's what you want," he added. "You know you can have anything you want from me."

"Well, we'll have to wait on that, I think" Hardesty said, snapping the box shut and sliding it back onto the bottom shelf of the side table. "It's nice to know we have something new to look forward to, though. We need to concentrate on finding this Mr. T now. We'll have to see if we can find that house, and Mr. T, and Kim. Maybe we should stash you someplace safe until we figure out what's going on. I can handle it with Justine. And I have a few places I could—"

"Paul, from across the hall, has said I could stay with him."

Hardesty laughed. Paul certainly was a fast worker. "Stay with him and sleep with him? You've met Paul?"

"Yes."

"He's fucked you already, has he? Probably with that plow belt of his?"

"Yes."

"And you enjoyed it? You don't have to answer that."

"Yes, I enjoyed it."

"Well, OK, Paul it is for the time being, if he's willing to put you up. I strongly suspect he'll be happy to."

He went to the kitchen bar and rang Paul. Paul, in his silk robe and nothing else, was standing at his door, smiling as Jan left the apartment and moved toward him. Hardesty was smiling when he closed the door. Toby was coming out of the show bedroom, wearing a robe similar to the one that Paul was wearing in the hall but no doubt no longer was wearing, and toweling off his hair.

"Who was that?"

"Jan. He's going to be spending some time with Paul."

"Lucky Jan," Toby said. "I wouldn't mind going a round with Paul."

"Yes, lucky Jan—and I realize you've been antsy about what Paul might do with you. And lucky me. I watched your performance with the basketball black bulls tonight. Impressive."

"I'm glad you enjoyed it."

"It put me in heat. I want to fuck you too." He dug into both of his robe pockets, coming with a set of wrist restraints from one side and a nasty looking dildo from the other.

Toby looked at him and laughed. "Of course you do."

"On the ottoman, like they did."

"Of course. Afterward there's something else I'd like for tonight."

Toby was only panting heavily as he was belly down on the ottoman, wrists tied over his head and dragging on the floor on one side and legs bent and draped over two of the other sides, his eyes glued to the lights of the Christmas tree, while Hardesty rode his ass. He didn't start crying out in passion until Hardesty started driving the dildo inside his channel underneath his already buried cock. Neither of them was worrying if Toby could take it; he'd been opened up wide by the two black bulls. He often was horny as hell still after a session like he'd had with the basketball players.

* * * *

"You're trembling," Paul leaned over and whispered in Jan's ear. They were stretched out on Paul's bed, Jan on his belly and Paul's body running alongside him, on his side, propped up on his elbow. He was running the fingers of his free hand over Jan's back, buttocks, and thighs, running circles around the curve of the young man's butt cheeks, letting his fingers trail down through the crack between the cheeks and on down the perineum and along the line of the young man's cock. He had run it along this line again and again. Jan, hard and throbbing, had opened the stance of his thighs and was sighing with contentment.

Paul paused, his fingers at Jan's rim and pressed in, ready to start. But the young man jerked and tensed up. Jan was a rent-boy. Paul could take him now and Jan would manage him. But Paul wanted this to be special for Jan— and thus for he himself as well. When it came to entering him, he wanted Jan to be begging for it and for him to slide in up to the hilt with no resistance whatsoever. Paul left off fingering the hole to massage and caress Jan's muscles, but he returned to it, pressing a finger into Jan's channel again, testing again if Jan was open to receive him. He didn't want to force it. He wanted the young man to want the cock. Jan jerked and tensed up again.

"What is it, Jan? Did I hurt you with the plow belt? Was it too much? I know I have length and like to put all in."

Jan gave a dry little laugh. "Where I work, we don't think about what is too much. You can put it in anytime you want. I'll take it."

"I don't want you just to take it. I want you to feel it—to go with me in the ride."

"Yes, you're longer than most," Jan whispered, "but I like what you do with it while you're digging it in. Most men don't give me that attention."

"Does Hardesty give you that attention?"

"Everything Hardesty does commands attention."

"So you didn't enjoy the plow belt. As far as I know, Hardesty doesn't use a plow belt."

"Yes, I enjoyed it. It was fine. But . . ."

"But what, Jan? I know you're worried about something you are working with Hardesty on, but there's something else. You don't want me to fuck you again? You just want to sleep now?"

"No, it's not that. What you're doing now . . . this is nice."

195

"But what?"

"I'm afraid of what this is leading to. Men are cruel to me. You are unusually long and you are surprisingly vigorous. I didn't think you'd ever be finished with the plow belt. I finished a long time before you did. Men are always cruel to me. I don't know what you want tonight."

"You want me to make love to you? Without penetration?"

"No, I want to take it all, but, yes, it would be nice if you could make love to me—not just conquer me."

"Oh, Jan," Paul murmured. He leaned over and kissed Jan on the back of his neck and then between his shoulder blades, then the small of his back. Paul repositioned his body and kissed along the curves of the buttocks. With a sigh, Jan was spreading his thighs more and going up slightly on his knees. He moaned as Paul's tongue ran down his crack and then again and yet again, stopping at Jan's hole. Paul was holding Jan's cock and gently stroking it. This time when Paul's fingers went into Jan's hole, alternating with attention by his tongue, Jan was sighing and moaning, not jerking. And he was relaxed. The muscles of his entrance pulled Paul's finger inside and clutched it.

He was ready. "Fuck me, daddy. Be good to me," he murmured. Jan was begging for it. He wasn't just a rent-boy now; he was a young man begging for what Paul could give him. Paul moved his leg over Jan's thighs, saddled himself over Jan's pelvis and slowly, ever so slowly, started the long journey of his cock up the young man's channel. With deep moans, Jan opened his channel to the cock as it slid up inside him.

"Oh, god, you're deep," Jan murmured. He let out a long moan as Paul slowly started to move inside him in long strokes. "Yes, yes. There, like that. Yesss!"

"Yes, you're taking it deep. Take it. Can you take deeper? Yes," Paul whispered. "You're so beautiful. You're so sweet."

"And you're hitting all the spots. Every place most other men pay no attention to. Only Hardesty can fuck me rough and still give attention to all the places."

"I feel you caressing me and rippling over me," Paul whispered in response. "You're so good."

Twenty minutes later, Paul was still riding him in slow, languid, deep strokes. He slowly rolled over to his side, taking Jan with him. He stayed deeply sheathed, though, thanks to his length, and continued the slow, long stroking.

"You can do this forever."

"Yes, that's my talent. I can bring us together too." And then he did. They were in a close embrace, kissing, so deep in the kissing that there was nothing to be heard but the moans in harmony and the slow slapping of groin on butt cheeks when the telephone rang.

After ringing off, Paul went to the door into his apartment to make sure it was triple locked and then, before coming back into the bed and holding Jan close, checked his nightstand shelf to make sure his revolver was still there—and loaded.

The telephone rang again. Paul answered it, listened, and then turned over and shook a nearly asleep Jan. "He's changed his mind. We need to go," Paul said.

Chapter Four: Up the River without a Paddle

Somewhere Hardesty was hearing buzzing. It increased in intensity and insistence. He forced his eyes open. They were focusing on the nightstand in the show bedroom, where a cell phone was vibrating and complaining. It wasn't just that there was buzzing. It felt like he was on a rocking boat. He reached his hand across Jan, who was spooned into his body, sheathing his cock, and made a grab for the cell phone. He missed as Jan, awake, turned his face to him and took his mouth in a kiss. Jan's hand grabbed the one Hardesty was reaching out toward the phone and pulled it down to his crotch, encouraging the detective to latch on to his cock, which Hardesty did. He was hard inside Jan and, when the phone stopped ringing, he gave in to his needs and started deep pumping the rent-boy. He grabbed Jan's hips and forced him back hard into his crotch as he thrust forward. Jan was jerking and giving a little cry of "Yes, shit yes" each time Hardesty slammed him hard with the thick, long cock.

The bed was still rocking gently in a counter move to Hardesty's bed shaking. It was moving horizontally and vertically at the same time. Hardesty didn't think it was all in what he was doing with his yelp-inducing thrusts up inside Jan. He turned his head enough to see that Paul was beside him, crouched over Toby's prone body, Toby on his belly, his tail raised, and his wrists tied off at the headboard over his head. Paul was the one rocking the bed in counter movement as, in a straight-bodied pushup stance, he rose and fell on Toby's body in long, languid strokes, fucking him vigorously in the ass. How long had the man been at it?

How long could the old man go? From the glazed look in the eyes of Toby, a professional bottom, it had been for some time and it had been very, very good.

This is what Toby had wanted—to take Paul and Jan into their bed that night—not their bed, actually, but the show bed, which was larger. And he wanted to be fucked by Paul with the plow belt, which happened as soon as they had invited Paul and Jan over. Toby had never been taken this way before by Paul. He wanted it and he got it. And Hardesty and Jan watched. Paul performed with the belt and Paul performed in the bed with Jan and now he was performing with Toby. Who would have known the old man could stay hard so long and had so much cum in him, Hardesty wondered.

When Jan had come and Hardesty had finished, the bed was still rocking. Paul was still riding Toby's ass, murmuring how sweet Toby was, how he could go on forever. And he was going on forever. Jan rolled out of the bed and headed for the bathroom, Hardesty turned to Toby and the two went into a deep kiss, as Toby hummed and Paul pumped on.

The cell phone buzzed again and this time Hardesty grabbed it and turned it on. "Speak."

"Hardesty?"

"Yes, didn't I say not to use the phone?"

"Would you prefer I visited you at the police department in all my finery?" Jim or Justine, depending on what was being worn at the time, answered.

"I'm not at the department now."

"Then you must be fucking Jan now. I know he went to see you and he isn't here."

"I'm not fucking him at the moment, no."

"But will you fuck me again after I'm done in here?" Jan called from the bathroom.

"No," Hardesty yelled back, and then turned back to the phone. "Jan won't be back with you until we get a handle on this Leslie and Victor business, Justine. You won't want a target in the house. Why have you called?"

"Have you seen the morning paper? The *Washington Post?*"

"No, I've been busy fucking Jan."

"The obits. It's in the obits."

"What is?"

"Mr. T. A photo of him. There's an obituary. His name was really Curtis Talmadge. And, fuck, Hardesty . . ."

"What?"

"He was CIA. Retired, but the paper said he was a senior CIA official. It says he had a heart attack. He's fuckin' CIA, Hardesty, and he had the Russian—"

"The phone, Jim. Don't say it. I get the point."

"Then you wouldn't want to hear about the fierce-looking man who showed up at the door, a black Cadillac van idling at the street, and asked for Jan."

"What did you tell him, Justine?"

"That it was Christmas and everyone had the day off. That he should come back tomorrow. He didn't look happy, but he left."

"Did he look like government?"

"Walked like it; talked like it; smelled like it too. Fucker had a hand on his holster; if I hadn't answered the door with my own piece showing, it might have gotten ugly."

"Shit. OK, keep telling him Jan isn't there and that you don't know where Jan is. That's going to be the truth, so you won't be lying to him. Jan's not going to be here in my apartment. But thanks for calling. I'll track it down from here. Hold tight—and stop using the damn telephone."

When he disconnected, he already was sitting up on the side of the bed, which was still rocking. He reached for a packet of cigarettes. He didn't smoke anymore. Except for times like this.

He lit up as Jan was returning.

"Fuck me again," Jan said, nearly cooing the words.

"Not now, Jan. There's too much going on and it's getting shitty. And you need to stay hidden for a while—and not in this apartment."

He rose from the bed and headed for the bathroom. Paul was still languidly doing pushups on Toby's ass, and the small blond, his tail elevated to the effort and salt-and-pepper pubic hair mashing into the curly blonds with each slide of the nearly foot long, wasn't complaining a bit. Jan rolled back into the bed and lowered his face to Toby's. Their lips met in a deep kiss as Jan's hand reached for Toby's cock.

Hardesty had gulped down a cup of coffee and was about to leave the apartment when Jan floated out of the show bedroom, all grace and perfect Michelangelo's David statuesque. It was all Hardesty could do not to reach out for him.

"There's something I just remembered," Jan said, looking sheepish. "Something about Mr. T and Kim."

"Yes?" Hardesty said. What he was thinking, though, was, just thought, my ass; just now decided to trust me enough to tell me.

"The last time Mr. T sent for me—three days before Christmas—he and Kim had a great row."

"A row? Over what? Do you know?"

"I suspect it was about Mr. T bringing Leslie and me in. Kim is the jealous type—and has a temper."

"How bad of a temper?"

"Kim had a gun that day and was threatening Mr. T with it. Victor took it away and pistol whipped Kim before he took me back to Justine's. I just thought you should know that."

"Yes, thanks, very good to know, Jan." Hardesty said. What he really wanted to do was pistol whip Jan with the pistol he kept on a shelf under the kitchen island, by the sink. The little turd surely knew that was important

201

information for Hardesty to know. But he had other instincts too, including a reengorging cock, seeing Jan standing there, naked, highly desirable. Using his better judgment, though, he turned and walked out of the apartment.

"Triple lock the door behind me," he growled as he exited.

* * * *

The first desk to be encountered when one entered the Vice Homicide unit at D.C. police headquarters was that of the unit clerk. It's where the detectives picked up the results of records research before passing by the coffee bar and then on to their own desks.

Larry was on duty, his eyes going big and soft and his tongue darting out of his mouth and running over his parted lips, when Hardesty approached the desk. "Captain wants to see you first thing, Detective. And I have these results for you," he said. His eyes darted around the large room and, not seeing anyone watching them, he moved his hand over Hardesty's. "I loved every thrust of it yesterday," he whispered, the statement coming out in breathy tones. "Anytime, anywhere."

"I was afraid I might have been too rough," Hardesty answered, knowing for a fact that Larry had loved every second of it.

"I've never had it like that," Larry whispered. "Anytime, anywhere."

Hardesty felt his balls tighten—and not in arousal— but he didn't take his hand away. Other than screaming what he was in every move he made, Larry didn't really repel Hardesty. He just wasn't, in any way, a type who turned Hardesty on. But the young man was so needy and so worshipful. And he was basically a good egg. He would do anything for Hardesty that Hardesty wanted. He had made that clear. It wasn't taking advantage of him if it was his job anyway and all was in pursuit of getting Hardesty's cases closed. Or that, at least, was what Hardesty told himself. He didn't think about how it sometimes worked out when Hardesty wasn't paying attention to the man anymore. Some of these guys were certifiably needy. Larry showed every indication of being one of those.

"What are these reports going to tell me?" Hardesty asked, keeping Larry's hand in his, folding his thumb under Larry's palm and rubbing rhythmically there. Larry was trembling and there was a danger of him hyperventilating on the spot. Hardesty was playing the young man's need to the hilt.

"The owner of the car from the Georgetown boathouse case."

"Curtis Talmadge, a retired CIA big wig," Hardesty said. "Does the report give an address?"

Larry raised his eyebrows at providing information he'd worked hard to get that Hardesty already knew, but he went on. "Talmadge has a wife. Lives in Wesley Heights. The address is in the report. Thought you would like to know as well about gun permits."

"Yeah that would be good to know."

"Talmadge has two registered. One's a Glock G30S. A military man's pistol. I think you said one like that was found at the scene. The registration on that one says it was issued to him by the government. The issuing agency isn't given. But he has another one registered privately, a .22. You said the secret agents thought that was the caliber that was used on the two vics. Talmadge has a Ruger SR22, with a silencer. Pretty serious toys for a D.C. retiree. You don't need a silencer for protection."

"He was a pretty serious retiree—CIA," Hardesty said. "Interesting information, though."

Larry continued, "The younger vic's name is Leyland Larson. From Tulsa Oklahoma. Run by a local pimp."

"Yes, by Tony Fielder."

Larry gave him a startled look, but one that wasn't anything like the look and shudder he produced when Hardesty added. "I didn't know Larson's real name, but, between you and me, I knew him biblically. He was a great lay." He knew he was giving the clerk a sexual charge, but he needed Larry to give him priority attention, and he knew the young man was going hard for him.

"The guy under the ice was one Pietr Stanislov, an immigrant visa. He's—"

"Russian mafia, I'll bet," Hardesty said. So that was who Victor was—and who his friends were. A retired CIA top honcho palling around with the Russian mafia. No wonder the feds were taking an interest.

"You already knew," Larry said, putting on a pout. His emotions were volatile and his piques were a little bitchy. He made to take his hand back, obviously disappointed that his research hadn't resulted in revelation for the man he worshipped. Hardesty didn't release his hand, though. He squeezed it hard, forced his index finger between two of Larry's fingers, and moved it in and out between the fingers, an unmistakable signal in Larry's circles, Hardesty knew, although his own circle took more direct routes of signaling. Larry nearly melted on the spot.

"I didn't know all of what you had to report, and you have confirmed what little I had found out on my own. Great work, Larry. You were first in with what you had. I'm very grateful to you."

Larry mumbled something, clearly mollified, pleased, and preening now.

"When is your morning break?" Hardesty asked, leaning in to Larry, his voice lowered.

"What do you mean?" Larry was trembling again.

"You know what I mean. I want to show my gratitude. I want to fuck you again. When is your morning break?" It came out in a commanding growl.

204

"Whenever you want it to be." The answer came in total submission, with Larry lowering his head, a signal of surrender in both of their circles.

"I have to go in and see Crane. After that, though, before I settle in to work, we'll meet and I'll do you well. You're the supply clerk. You have a key to the supply room in the basement?"

"Yes, of course." Larry could hardly contain his excitement.

"Move in that direction as soon as you spy me leaving Crane's office. I'll stop at the men's room to make use of a rubber packet and then meet you in the supply room." Then and only then, he let loose of Larry's hand, lowering it to the desk and patting it.

Larry, speechless and shuddering, watched Hardesty walk, reports in hand, to Crane's office. He had been to the drugstore that morning himself to buy Trojan Magnum XLs to be prepared for what he dreamed about. That the man walked around with his own supply made Larry hyperventilate.

Crane waved Hardesty into his office and gestured for him to sit down in a chair facing the desk. Hardesty was relieved. If this was a dressing down, he'd have had to stand in front of the desk, tail between his legs.

"Miracle of miracles, Larry has passed me some reports on the Georgetown boathouse case," the captain said, lowering his face and looking at Hardesty over the top of his reading glasses. "Fast work for Christmas Day. You pumping your sources for information? So to speak," he added, giving Hardesty a little smile.

Hardesty had hinted he had sources to pump. He doubted that Crane knew he was pumping his unit clerk too, and Hardesty wasn't wild about that getting around—if for no other reason than he wanted to keep his reputation intact on his taste in young men.

"We can credit Larry with most of that," Hardesty answered. "He humped his ass doing research yesterday."

"And I gather you humped *his* ass in getting the work done," Crane said, dryly. "He's floating around above the ground today, and I know what he wanted for Christmas. Everyone in the squad knew. Larry's not very good at keeping his wants secret."

Couldn't get much by Captain Crane. It was a good thing he was so forgiving and flexible on these matters. There was no indication that he himself was anything but a straight arrow on sex. That's what made him so effective as a buffer between the unit and upstairs.

"Well, the bad news is that the feds have already closed the case on this Talmadge guy," Crane said, turning to business. "Died of a heart attack, they say. All so natural. The body was found under an overturned kayak not more than a 100 yards upriver from the boathouse. Over in a swampy area on the Virginia side. What they didn't tell me, but a friend of a friend in the Intell Community's medical examiner's office told me, was that he had a bullet in his back."

".22 caliber?" Hardesty asked.

"Right. Probably the same gun that got the rent-boy and the Russian. So, the feds are satisfied and there's no federal case."

"Well, then, that's it, I guess," Hardesty said, making like he was about to get up.

"Don't play me, Hardesty," Crane said, but he attached a laugh to make clear that he was in on the game. "You don't plan on leaving it there, do you?"

"Nope," Hardesty said, settling in his chair again.

"Well, you don't have to. Because the good news is that this leaves us free and clear to make our own case. We can ignore the stiff up the river without a paddle. Two men were killed on our turf—your rent-boy and the Russian."

"He wasn't really my rent-boy," Hardesty said.

"You fucked him, didn't you? More than once, I'll wager. And he was one of your informants, wasn't he? Therefore a secret asset of this office."

Hardesty had never used Leslie—or Leyland, he guessed—as an informant, but if the captain wanted to believe that—or pretend to believe that—that was OK with Hardesty. He could tell that Crane didn't want to let loose of this case any more than he did. He couldn't say he hadn't fucked the young piece more than once, though. So, he answered, "Yes, by extension, he was useful to the unit."

"So. Go, go, go." Crane was waving a hand toward the door. "It's your case. Yours and Whitehall's. Bring me the murderer of"—he looked down at one of the reports— "Larson and Stanislov. We'll just assume that takes care of the CIA guy too."

Hardesty was at the door when Crane spoke up again, "Oh, and go easy on Larry. It won't be the first unit clerk you've ruined for us. He's a sensitive guy and he's good at his work. Make him happy, but don't leave him unhappy. Don't break the heart and ass of another one, Hardesty."

"Got it, Captain," Hardesty said, turning and nodding to Larry, who immediately got up from his desk and headed for the steps to the basement.

"Strip," Hardesty commanded, as he closed the storage room door behind him and locked it. He turned the overhead lights off. There was an emergency light next to the door that gave enough light for him to work with. He could do Larry better in the dark—he could think of him as more desirable and give him the good time he deserved.

The young man was all arms and legs—gangly, but not a bad torso and face, at least in the dark. His cock, now rock hard and jutting up toward his flat belly in anxious anticipation, wasn't bad, either. He probably had someone fucking him, but it would be vanilla and probably amateur. No excitement. No one who could work him to the max.

Hardesty excited him, and Larry's moans, grunts, and groans and the distance he reached when he shot off showed that he, indeed, was sufficiently excited by what Hardesty had to give him. Hardesty found a large roll of cloth tape and used it to tape Larry's wrists and feet to one of the supply shelves—a sturdy one that, nonetheless banged against the cinderblock wall—luckily an outside wall of the building—while Hardesty was banging him.

Arms raised and spread and taped to the front edge of a shelf overhead, and legs spread, and bent, with feet and ankles taped to the second shelf from the floor. Larry's body jutted out from the shelf, his bare tail waving in the air. His briefs stuffed in his mouth completed the ensemble.

He'd quite willingly worked up Hardesty's cock before he was bound. He was an expert at blow jobs, Hardesty found. This, he decided, was Larry's primary talent among his friends. Hardesty made him a nice bottom that morning too, though, crouching behind him, grasping his hips, thrusting up inside him, and slamming the young man's ass up and down on a thick, long, throbbing cock until Larry got fully into it himself, and then Hardesty just stood there, arching Larry's torso back with one hand buried in his head hair and jerking back and snaking the other hand around Larry's waist to stroke his cock, while Larry used the leverage of his bound feet against the thumping shelf section to bounce up and down on Hardesty's staff until both of them had come.

There was no doubt now that Larry was Hardesty's willing and enslaved bitch, tool, and servant whenever Hardesty wanted him—or needed something from him. Hardesty didn't feel guilty. Larry wasn't getting slighted in the deal.

And he'd gotten his own rocks off again. Something he needed to do a couple of times a day, at least, as highly sexed as he was, to keep his balls from aching to evacuate cum. It meant one fewer self-service hand jobs needed.

Chapter Five: The Candidates

All of the eyes in the room were on Hardesty as he walked back into the squad room. They didn't waver in their stare when Larry came in behind him and slipped, gingerly, but with a grin he couldn't control on his face, back behind his desk.

Glen Whitehall was at his desk, which was facing and touching Hardesty's, leaning back in the chair and with his feet on the desk. He too had a grin on his face.

"Your hair is wet, Hardesty," he said. "How'd your hair get wet?"

"I gymed downstairs before coming up," Hardesty said as he dropped the reports on the Georgetown boathouse case on Glen's desk. He'd picked them up from Larry's desk as he'd passed. "Here, read these; we're still on the case and we're going for a ride."

"You sure about that?"

"About going for a ride?"

"No, about the case still being open. But, first, about Larry. You don't gym. I don't know how you get away without gyming and still being muscled up like you are."

"I do gym. Just not with you. We go to different gyms. We have different lifestyles, if you haven't noticed."

"Which brings us back to your hair being wet and Larry's hair being wet. Did you shower together? Is he a good lay?"

Hardesty took a deep breath, ending in a sigh. Did all the guys in the squad have to be so fast on the uptake? They were all still looking at him. "Any guy with a hole is a good lay in the dark, Glen, if you are healthy and need it regularly. Or any woman, in your case."

"Three reports here and we got the case only yesterday morning. And it was Christmas. You've been a busy beaver," Whitehall said, fingering the reports Hardesty had dropped on his desk. "And you started without me."

"It was your day off and Christmas. You told me you were going to get laid. I assume you accomplished that."

"Oh, yes. But I worked the evening shift. Out on the street."

"So the lay you got would be professional, cost free, and ever so accommodating that you didn't run her in?"

"You know me so well, Hardesty," Whitehall said, with a grin. "Her name was Claudia, and you're right on the money. She was ever so grateful not to be hauled in on a Christmas night. Thoroughly professional. A great blow job and a cunt that pulled your dick right in and worked it hard."

"I'm so pleased you had a nice Christmas present," Hardesty said. "Now get your butt out of that chair and let's go for a ride up to Wesley Heights."

"I don't think so; not quite yet," Glen said. "Crane will want to see you in his office. I'm sure it's about the boathouse case. I wouldn't be surprised if a kibosh was going to be laid on the case."

Hardesty turned his head. He could see all the way into Crane's office. The door was open. Nearly everyone else could see into the office too, and now he knew that he might have been mistaken about the looks he'd been getting from the guys and gals in the squad room. One of the Secret Service hunks he'd met—without a name—at the boathouse murder scene was talking with Crane. Crane saw Hardesty and motioned him into the office.

"The agent here,"—Crane didn't give a name—"wants to assure us of something, Hardesty," he said when the detective entered the room.

"It's a good case," Hardesty said defensively. "It's a good case for us with or without Talmadge."

"That's what I want to assure you of," the agent said. His delivery was smooth. He was used to impressing people and having his way. Hardesty was thinking that, if he were a bottom, the agent was just the sort of guy he'd let have his way with him. But, as it was, he was competition, and thus someone to be wary of. "We're happy to have you run the case on the two vics you've seen."

"The Russian mafia guy too?" Hardesty asked.

The agent raised an eyebrow. So, he hadn't figured them as knowing Victor—or Pietr, his real name—was Russian mafia. But the agent took it well, quickly regained control, and said, "The Russian too. He's not official. The Russian mafia here isn't the same as Moscow. So, investigate those deaths. Just leave Talmadge out of it. We're confident that if you find the shooter for them, you'll be doing justice for Talmadge too. It just isn't something for the public to know. And don't go considering the CIA as being responsible. Talmadge was doing their bidding still; they didn't want him dead."

It was Hardesty's turn to do a double take but to try not to show it. It hadn't occurred to him that this was a CIA retribution hit—presumably for one of theirs being in bed with the Russians. He'd have to consider that now. He wasn't fooled by the agent's attempt to put him off that scent.

But Crane must have read him. He broke in and said, "No consideration of the Agency, Hardesty. Upstairs has vetted that. We're to believe that—because we're assured it's true—and stay away from that path. We're told that if we break this case, it will be someone else. And if we don't approach it with that understanding, we'll lose the case."

The agent stood up from his chair. "Do we have an understanding here?"

"Yes, we have an understanding," Crane said. "Hardesty, tell the man we have an understanding and get on with the investigation."

The instruction was clear. Either Hardesty said it, or there was no investigation. The special agent had come all the way down here to tell Hardesty not to pursue a possibility that he hadn't even considered before the special agent mentioned it.

"We have an understanding," he said. But, whether or not he'd said it, he was determined to pin the murders on the right shooter. He stood and walked back into the squad room. All eyes followed him, this time Larry's eyes, which were dazed and worshipful, were the most noticeable. At least, Hardesty thought, they weren't watching him because he'd spiked yet another one of the unit clerks who revolved through that job here.

* * * *

"Don't look now," Hardesty said, "but check out the Black Escalade that pulled in a block behind us at the same time we parked . . . I said don't look."

"How can I see what you're talking about if I don't look?" Whitehall asked. "Yeah, I see it. Feds tailing us, do you think?"

"That would be my guess. The feds do love their black Escalades. Nice digs." The two detectives looked up a short hill that ended in a Tudor façade that spread a good distance between one lot line and the next. It was the address for Curtis Talmadge the records research had surfaced. Hardesty was thinking, though, that it was more the residence of Mrs. Talmadge—Maria—than it was for

Curtis. He chose to believe Jan's description that the P Street townhouse in Georgetown that looked lived in by a man of academic pursuits—and kinky gay male sex interests—was where Curtis spent more of his time. And without a Mrs. Talmadge around.

Hardesty's perception that a man didn't spend much time in this house was heightened when a battle ax of a maid let them in, showed them into a frilly living room, and disappeared. The blowsy blonde who then appeared—Maria Talmadge—was a bit of a surprise. First, she was foreign looking and had an accent. Hardesty thought Russian, which he then thought was a fascinating fact. Second, she was voluptuous, albeit well into her forties—Hardesty had expected older, considering that her husband was retired from the government—and she had an unapologetic eye for the two men. She also was discerning. Although both of the detectives were hunks in their own, separate ways, Maria Talmadge latched immediately onto Glen Whitehall, the heterosexual of the two. And she didn't let go.

At the first opportunity, Hardesty leaned into Glen and whispered, "Yours."

"Ahead of you there, good buddy," Whitehall answered. He was sitting with an open-legged stance, as if it would be too painful on his dick and balls to bring his legs together—and maybe it was—and he'd unbuttoned enough of his shirt to show her blond curls at his neckline. She didn't miss a beat. In a blink of an eye—faster than the eye could discern—she was showing more deep cleavage herself. Later Hardesty decided she'd even seen Glen readjust himself and, rightfully, had taken it as signaling. She certainly steamed straight ahead into declaring that she wanted him inside her.

After introductions, turning down an assortment of drinks because they were on duty, passing on condolences on the passing of her husband, telling her how nice her place was, and having it established that they could have a tour of the house, if they liked—with Whitehall showing interest and Hardesty not—Hardesty asked a few innocuous questions: Did she have any idea who might have been upset with her husband? No, certainly not. Was he active in any businesses, sports, or clubs in his retirement where he might have come in contact with the wrong elements? He was heavily involved in the stock market, but no businesses where he'd come into conflict with anyone; he kayaked, going out nearly every day on the Potomac, but kayaking was a solitary sport; and just clubs involved with his government career. She didn't offer that his government career had been as a master spy tracking down and exposing other spies.

"How about home life?" Glen asked. "Were you and your husband on good domestic terms?"

"Do you mean did we satisfy each other sexually?" She asked, turning her attention solely to Whitehall and jumping into the question as if she'd anticipated it and was dying to talk about it. "My husband was older than I am," she told Glen, laying a manicured hand on his knee. "Considerably older than I am." This undoubtedly was true, but hardly with the gap she was inferring. "We were a modern couple. He went his way. I am heavily sexed . . ." She let that swirl there for a few more seconds than necessary for Whitehall to get the clear invitation. ". . . and, no, he didn't completely satisfy me. But he was tolerant of me. I went my way as well."

She shifted in her chair, posing to drive home the notion that her way could be a lot of fun.

"Is this your only home? Yours and your husband's?" Hardesty asked. Maria turned and looked at him as if she only now realized Hardesty was in the room—and wasn't all that happy that he was.

"We have a flat in Paris, of course," she said. Hardesty wondered if that sounded as evasive to her as it did to him.

"Two pistols are registered to your husband," Hardesty said. "We think we have one of them, but do you know where the other pistol is?"

"What would I know of guns, or at least that kind of gun?" she asked. She was looking directly into Whitehall's basket. Truth be told, he was a little excited from her attentions—her innuendo and her hand on his knee—and he was noticeably on the rise within his trousers.

Hardesty decided that she was being too evasive on the questions and that they were unlikely to find out what they wanted to know through direct questioning. It was time to get inventive. "You offered a tour of your house, Mrs. Talmadge," he said, rising from the chair he'd been sitting in. "My partner here loves looking at old houses, and I should make some notes on this visit while everything is fresh in my mind. How about I go out to our car and work on the notes, while you give Detective Whitehall here a house tour?"

"Splendid idea," she said, popping up from her chair and sending her pendulous breasts to jiggling within her tight blouse. She obviously wasn't wearing a bra.

Hardesty noted that the black Escalade, with smoked windows so he couldn't see how many were in the front seat was still parked a block behind him when he went out to the car.

And Glen Whitehall noted that Maria Talmadge had a beauty mark high up on one of her inner thighs when he was knelt between her spread legs as she lay back on the foot of her frilly-coverleted bed, and sucked on her clit and raised his arms to weigh and squeeze her breasts and thumb her nipples.

It wasn't long at all before she was pulling at his bare biceps, encouraging him to kiss up her belly and breasts and cover her and, as she moaned and rubbed her heels against the back of his thighs, enter and start to pump her. As he fucked her—and she energetically fucked the young stud back—they whispered to each other. Most of what they whispered about were favorable comparisons of Glen's length, girth, vigor, and virility against an assortment of other lovers, but, in between the sex talk, Glen managed to pull out some of the other information they wanted.

A bit more than a half hour after Hardesty had gone to the car, Whitehall appeared at the passenger window. He was disheveled, but he looked fairly happy.

"Her husband's townhouse on P Street in Georgetown. Here's the address." He handed Hardesty a piece of paper through the window.

"OK, get in, and we'll go over there."

"Can't. I'm not finished with her. Or she's not finished with me, more to the point. We don't have all our questions answered."

"And you want to shag her some more," Hardesty said.

"She's got a bottomless cunt and her beef flaps have a mind and sucking technique all their own. You're damn right I want to shag her some more. She's starving for it. And she's every bit as good at it as Claudia was last night."

"But is she a natural blonde?"

"Alas not. Her curlies are brown, but I just bypassed that and went for the gold."

"OK," Hardesty said, with a deep sigh. "I'll go in and call a blue top to come out here and wait for you to be done. Pull more information out of her, if you can. And remember that she isn't just a honey pot; she's a suspect."

Whitehall hightailed it back to the house like he was running the Kentucky Derby.

As he pulled away from the curb, Hardesty's thought was, I wonder what the Escalade will do. Do they follow me or stick with Romeo?

216

They followed Hardesty.

* * * *

Even without the address, the house he sought on P Street, just a couple of blocks off Wisconsin Avenue in Georgetown, an area of eighteenth-century, mostly small, townhouses at sky-high prices was recognizable. Jan had gotten it spot on. It was a mustard yellow-painted brickwork. That fit in here, but almost everything else was faced with genuine mellow-red antique brick or was wood painted in muted colors. The house was narrow and three stories on top of an English basement. It couldn't be more than two bedrooms, as Jan had told him that most of the ground floor was a garage entered from the alley running along the back of the row of townhouses.

Whereas the house wasn't a surprise to him, the one who answered the door and gave him a look moving from appraising to "I could eat you with a spoon" gave him a jolt. He hadn't given a thought to the possibility that the name "Kim" was for a young man, rather than a woman. But of course he should have, considering what Jan had told him about what went on in this house. He was young, blond, a bit obviously gay—certainly clearly a submissive, and, from the look he gave the detective despite being shown a badge, ready and willing—and small of stature, but perfectly formed. Pretty much Hardesty's menu of choice. Hardesty knew immediately that he was going to fuck him. Kim seemed to know that too and to approve of the idea.

He was dressed all in black—a shiny silk lounge suit. Hardesty decided that he must know that Curtis Talmadge was dead. Otherwise he'd be outfitted in flashy colors. Hardesty's eyes began to assess how he was going to go about undressing the young man quickly and efficiently and decided there wouldn't be a problem.

The young man confirmed the assumption that he knew Curtis Talmadge was dead. "You must have come about Mr. T's death," he said. "Please come in—the living area is upstairs." And then, fluttering his eyelashes at Hardesty, he added, "The bedrooms are above the living area. I'm here all alone. And I'm very, very bored."

What Hardesty zeroed in on was that Kim called Talmadge Mr. T. That dovetailed into the information that Jan had given. He had matched up Justine's special client with the dead man in the kayak. He wondered how close behind him the Secret Service was in figuring that out.

"Yes, I do have a few questions about Mr. Talmadge. May I come in?"

"You may come anyway you like. Yes, by all means come up. The men in black have already been here, turned the place upside down, taken a bunch of stuff away, and given me a deadline to be out. But I've got a lawyer, and I'm betting when the will is opened, this house will be mine. But enough of my troubles, I—"

"Men in black? There have already been men here going through Talmadge's stuff?" They were going up a narrow set of stairs from a small foyer at the entrance level that ran back through a wide, arched doorway, through a formal dining room, with a kitchen beyond that. "Who were they?"

"Who were any of the men Mr. T was cavorting with? There were his secret friends and then the Russians. The Russians came in rumpled brown and some of Mr. T's former friends from work came in black and slinked in through the garage in back."

"The Russians?"

"Yeah. Coming in at all hours of the day and night—disturbing our play time."

"So, which were the men in black who've been here going through the house? I've just started with this case. The house really should have been locked down by the police. Were they these secret friends you mention or Russians?"

"Yes, both. First the spooks and then the Russians. The Russians were mad they got sloppy seconds, but they were more fun than the spooks. I was bored, and a couple of them wanted to play. Big brutes they were. And by big—"

They had reached the next level, which was one long living space, divided by an archway. Very expensive furniture and loaded bookshelves taking up most of the wall space. "What was going on here?" Hardesty broke in. "Did you know that Talmadge was a retired CIA officer—a senior one?"

"He never said and I never asked. It was enough that he paid the bills and took care of my needs. And I have very special needs."

They had seated themselves on two close-facing leather loveseats. Kim leaned forward and put his hand on Hardesty's knee. "I have a confession, Mr. Hardesty. I know your name. And I know you by reputation. We have mutual friends—Leslie and Jan. Do you remember them? You're every inch the mean-looking, sexy hunk they said you were. I am highly sexed, and I like special treatment— the sort of play Mr. T also liked. I'm upset that Mr. T is dead—mainly because I don't know where I'm going to find a playmate now who is challenging. I've been bored out of my mind the last two days. Leslie and Jan told me that no one does them better than a cop named Hardesty does. I'm sure you have more questions for me, and I have answers. But I have needs. Let me be blunt. I want you to fuck the answers out of me. I understand you have certain skills."

"Like what?" Hardesty said. As Kim had spoken, he'd gone down on his knees in front of Hardesty. He'd run his hands between the detective's thighs, and Hardesty had widened his stance, letting Kim rub his inner thighs with his

219

hands. If Hardesty didn't stop him, he was going to get a blow job right there and then.

Hardesty didn't stop him. He got the blow job and a quite expert one it was. He lay back in the sofa, with his arms running across the top of the back, while, with the exclamation of "God, they were right; you're hung like a horse," Kim fished Hardesty's cock out and sucked him to a throbbing erection.

"What special way do you want it?" Hardesty murmured when it was getting close to where the choices were to ride or blow.

"I hear you're great with restraints. And what do you know about using these?" Hardesty lowered his face to see what Kim was talking about. The young man was holding a box of sounding wands open for Hardesty to see.

"I know quite a lot about using those, actually," Hardesty answered.

They did it in what had been Talmadge's bedroom. Kim said it would give him a thrill to do it there. Hardesty was sitting on the foot of the bed, legs spread a bit, and feet on the floor. Kim was in his lap, facing away from him, and imprisoned, under Hardesty's total control. The young man's arms were wrapped around Hardesty's torso and bound at the wrists behind the detective's back. His ankles were bound to Hardesty's ankles. His channel was fully possessed by Hardesty's cock, which wasn't pumping. He was just holding inside, throbbing inside the tight sheath of the young man's passage.

The box of sounding wands was open beside where they were sitting and Hardesty was on the third, ever thicker and longer one, twirling it down into Kim's urethra channel and slow fucking the young man's penis, before he started asking questions. Kim was panting hard and making clear he was loving every minute of it.

"Tell me more about the visits by what you call the spooks and the Russians. Did they come at the same time?"

"No, always separate—and I got the impression they may not have known about each other. Oh shit, yes, that feels so . . . so . . . yesss."

"Where did Victor fit in?"

"He's Mr. T's gofer guy. Does everything for him. Brought me in from Justine's—and then, later, Leslie and Jan. Haven't seen him here since Christmas, though. He must have gone back to the Russians."

"Back to the Russians? He was with them?" It appeared that Kim didn't know yet that Victor and Leslie were dead—or at least was pretending he didn't. He wouldn't tell him unless he had to.

"Yes. He is Russian. I always thought he was with them. He was never here when the spooks visited."

"And Talmadge's wife. Were you kept entirely separate from her?"

"Talmadge's wife? You mean Maria? Oh, shit, oh shit." Hardesty had moved on to the next larger sounding rod.

"Mr. T didn't have a wife. Maria was more for when he needed to pretend he had one. A real cunt that one. They fought all the time. Had quite a row right before the last time I saw him, he said. waved a gun around at him. He said she wanted to send me and the others away. She always seemed to know what was going on here, according to what Mr. T said. I think she and Victor had something going. She's Russian too, you know . . . Oh, fuck. I think that's enough. I think I'm gonna blow . . . oh fuck, yesss! It's so thick. God, you know what you're doing with these things."

"I hear tell that you waved a gun around at him yourself the night before he died."

"So what? We fought now and again too. Victor took the gun from me. Doesn't matter much, though. Mr. T died of a heart attack, didn't he? Didn't he? Oh, fuck, I'm going to come . . . I'm going to fuckin' come."

And then he did, his cum already burbling out of his hard cock as Hardesty pulled the rod out.

Then, reaching down and releasing Kim's ankles and moving out from under the young man's bound arms behind his back, Hardesty pushed Kim belly down on the mattress on the foot of the bed, his wrists still bound behind his back and his ankles and thighs bound together, buried a fist in Kim's back to pin him to the mattress, mounted his ass, and fucked the shit out of him with a monster cock moving in a tightly constricted channel.

He left the young man spread-eagled on the bed, restraint free, of course, on his belly, purring and grinning.

* * * *

Hardesty left the townhouse and climbed into the unmarked cop car he had parked next to a hydrant, confident there would be no ticket because beat cops had lists of the license plate numbers of unmarked cop cars. Scanning the area as was his habit, he looked to see if a black Escalade was still monitoring his movements. It was. He wondered if these guys would follow him now or would stay parked. They remained parked as he pulled away from the curb. But, as he moved down the street, he whistled, seeing that a black side-door van pulled out of a parking space down the street and was following him now. A tag-team operation? How did he rate such attention, he wondered.

He needed to do some thinking. There were too many candidates floating around for having been the shooter in this case, and some of them were government and some of them were international goons. He had to go over all of it in his mind again. Instead of going directly back to the department, he drove over to the nearby Georgetown boathouse. The boathouse was closed for the winter, so he could wander around the scene of the crime and down to the water's edge by his lonesome. The university was out of session for Christmas week and there was no boating run from the boathouse in this season anyway. Talmadge had been an exception. Those managing the boathouse said that he had gone out in his kayak nearly every day of the year no matter the weather and had special privileges at the boathouse, having keys and being able to get all of his gear himself.

Talmadge was a special privileges kind of guy. So why was it, Hardesty wondered, that he had wound up dead, with a bullet in his back, in the shallows on the Virginia shore of the Potomac? Was it espionage or something domestic? The accompanying deaths of his Russian gofer and of a rent-boy had to play out logically in the scenario. Talmadge had his boating gear on when they found him. What would be the sequence of him in the act of shoving off into the water with his kayak, with his Russian gofer at his side, to take a bullet and slip under the ice and yet there to be a rent-boy in the backseat of his car, naked, and shot in the act of sex? Would Talmadge have left a dildo up the young guy's ass and a sounding rod in his penis, gotten dressed for exercise, and been ready to go into the river when Leslie was shot in the car? Would Leslie have left the dildo and sounding wand in place after Talmadge had played with him and left the car? This didn't all fit together.

When Hardesty was ready to leave, he realized that he had been wandering around the scene of the crime and thinking it through—without being any more clear about events than when he'd come here—for over an hour. He was cold as ice and he saw that the black van was still lurking about. He was not a happy camper.

When Hardesty got back to the squad room, Glen Whitehall was sitting at his desk, leaning back in his chair, with his feet on his desk, and looking all fat and happy. There wasn't much new in that, though.

"Was she as good the second time?" Hardesty asked.

"Better. She rode me," Glen responded, a Cheshire cat expression on his face. "And rode me and rode me."

Hardesty's attention went to what was laying on Whitehall's desk blotter: a pistol, with a silencer—a Ruger SR22, to be exact.

"Where's that from?" he asked, giving Whitehall a sharp look.

"Just where you suppose it's from. It's from the nightstand next to Maria Talmadge's bed."

"You know it's not legal—it won't hold up in court, if that's the murder weapon—that you took it to check it out."

"I didn't take it illegally. I found it while she was in the bathroom and when she returned, I quizzed her about it. She said she's scared—and she certainly acted like she was. And I know why too. But I read her a line. I told her it wouldn't do her any good the way it was now, that something had happened to it the last time it was fired. It needed some work on it to be able to fire again. It was a load of bull, but she swallowed it. She let me take it to fix for her and return it."

"So, why haven't you sent it for a ballistics check yet?"

"I wanted you to see it—to gloat a little bit about the sacrifice I had to make to get it."

"Fuck that. You enjoyed the hell out of screwing her."

"I enjoyed her screwing me more. Drains a man dry. But it was all for the job. I was busy pursuing why she was so scared. She's not who she was pretending to be."

"I know that. Talmadge's live-in punch, Kim—who is male, by the way, of the small, blond rent-boy type—told me she wasn't really Talmadge's wife."

"She's more than that. I had her prints run quick quick, and—"

"How'd you get that done so quick? It's only been a couple of hours."

"Thanks to you. I told Larry you needed the prints run yesterday, and after the slight embarrassment, he got them run immediately."

"Small embarrassment?"

"Her print was on an open condom packet. I had to tell Larry that it was my condom packet to bring him out of a snit in thinking it might have been yours."

"Ah," Hardesty said, and laughed.

"As I was saying, the print was run quick quick. She isn't Maria Talmadge. The name came back on a Russian who came here on a tourist visa four years ago and was never recorded leaving the country. Her name—get this—is Nadia Stanislova. Get it?"

"No, what's the kicker?"

"Stanislova. Same name as Victor's real name, taking Russian forms into account—Pieter Stanislov. Sister or wife, maybe? More controllers of Talmadge than servants, maybe? Russia or the Russian mob?"

"Shit," Hardesty said.

"Yes, shit. What have we gotten ourselves into, Hardesty?"

It wasn't something Hardesty could answer. He was still mulling it when he hit the pavement to drive out to Wesley Heights and have another go at Maria, or Nadia, or whoever she was. Thus, he wasn't sharp enough to observe until it was too late that a black van with side sliding doors pulled up beside him on the street; the door opened; two goons dressed in black jumped out and grabbed him, pulling a hood over his head and handcuffing his wrists behind his back; and pulled him back into the van, which sped on down the street, hardly having stopped at all for the grab. They slammed him to the floor and he felt the weight of four size thirteen shoes pinning down his twisted body.

* * * *

He could have been handled more delicately to be sure, but the ride was to a building, with a familiar sound in the background and not to the edge of a river, so he wasn't in the mood to complain much. He was dragged out of the van and into a building and plopped down on a folding metal chair. He didn't have any trouble discerning where he was. He knew that the sound was of a bowling alley, and that he heard the roll of the ball start in the farther distance and hit pins in the nearer distance told him that he was somewhere behind the pin-setting machines.

The hood was pulled off and he was sitting, facing a big, fat thug, with two goons, younger and in better shape, standing to either side of him and between him and the desk that the thug was sweating behind. They all looked Slavic. The Russian mafia element was revealing itself. And they were all trying to look mean but not terminally mean—terminally for him. He sensed this was more of a social call than a last-ride meeting.

"Good that you could join us, Detective Hardesty," the thug said. The goons hadn't said anything in the van—they'd put him on the floor under their legs, with someone else driving—and they didn't say anything now. "I won't keep you long. I just wanted you to know that I am sincere in what I'm going to tell you."

"OK, I'm listening," Hardesty answered. He checked out the pieces the two goons were packing. They both were lovingly caressing .357 Magnums, the revolver of choice for thugs everywhere, especially Russian ones. It wasn't the caliber Hardesty was shopping for in this case.

"You being here in my house, where I could do as I like with you means you can believe what I say."

Yeah, if you can convince yourself so, Hardesty thought, but it's not what he said. "Shoot," is what he said.

226

He only thought later that that might not have been the best choice of words.

"I'll only say it once. There are rumors that you are liking my guys for icing the old spy and the guy named Victor."

"You mean Pietr? Pietr Stanislov?"

The thug looked a little surprised. "Whatever," he said. "You need to know that this wouldn't have been in our interests. We were happy with Talmadge, and Victor was one of ours. So, we need to be looking elsewhere for who's behind those hits."

We? Hardesty wondered what that meant but didn't pursue it. He was more interested in trying something else out. "And Nadia Stanislova too? Is she one of yours? A babysitter for Talmadge?"

"I think we've discussed enough," the thug said. "And you can just sit back and watch now. This hit was in my house, and we can take care of it faster and more quietly than the D.C. cops can. So, don't get in our way."

"It's my case. I don't really want help."

"I was afraid you'd need some convincing. You live in a fancy apartment across the river, don't you?—with your son."

My son? Hardesty thought. These guys are dumber than I imagined. "It's not any of your business where I live—and who I live with."

"Your son's a hooker. Did you know that? I'm gonna have my men here take you home and give you a taste of what we can do. After that maybe you'll take us serious and stay out of our way."

Hardesty was about to say something smart back to him, but whatever he said was muffled by the hood coming back down over his head and him being hustled back out of the building and onto the floor of the van.

At his apartment door, he refused to produce a key, so Goon Number One just pulled him around in front of the peephole and Goon Number Two rang the door buzzer. And then again. After the third ring, the door opened to Toby, dressed just in a silk robe, starting to say "Forgot your key?" before, .357 Magnums waving in the air, the goons pushed Hardesty into Toby as they threw themselves into the apartment. Toby was pushed as far as the ottoman, where he landed on his back. Goon Number Two landed on top of him, between his legs, and it was immediately evident he was going to stay there for a while.

Goon Number One pulled Hardesty, his arms still tied behind his back over to where they stood by the kitchen counter. "You get to watch this a while," the goon said.

What "this" was was Goon Number Two holding the barrel of his .357 Magnum to Toby's head and unzipping himself and pulling out his own gun, which was erect, as the goons probably knew what they planned to do before they got here. It wasn't hard to gain access to Toby's ass, as he'd only been wearing a short, silk robe anyway. Toby didn't fight the goon as the man, crouching between Toby's thighs with Toby lying on his back on the ottoman, positioned himself, spiked Toby, and began to plow him. The goon got into the fuck so much—and Toby was taking it so well—that the .357 Magnum found its way to the floor beside the ottoman.

Goon Number One only forced Hardesty to watch Toby being fucked for a few minutes before he started pushing Hardesty over toward a couch. "Now you," he said. "Bend over the arm of the couch. It's gonna be me and you."

Now Hardesty did panic. He wasn't a bottom. He had fleeting thoughts of trying to get to the gun he kept on a shelf on the other side of the kitchen island, but he was being shoved in another direction from that, and there was the little problem of his wrists being tied behind his back. Goon Number One had him bent over the sofa arm and was lying on top of him and pulling his trousers and briefs off his buttocks, when the situation changed.

"OK, let's stop this party right here," a voice boomed out from across the room. Paul, naked as a jay bird had come out of the show bedroom. He was holding a revolver of his own that trumped where the goons had theirs. He approached Goon Number One and pulled him off Hardesty while rummaging around in the seat cushion where his revolver had been dropped in his excitement and quickly had possession of the one Goon Number Two dropped beside the ottoman as well.

"Now, you two stand away, over by the door."

Toby piped up, though. "Aw, Paul, I think this one is about to blow. Let him finish first."

So Goon Number One was hustled over to the door, Paul released Hardesty's wrists and gave him one of the .357 Magnums, and they all stood around humming, as Goon Number Two resumed humping Toby to an ejaculation. When he was done, Toby pushed the goon off him, surprised him with a pop in the mouth with his fist, and growled, "That's for not asking nicely."

"Just to call a truce, I'm going to let both you boys go home in one piece," Hardesty said, restoring their revolvers, without the bullets, ushering them— embarrassed—out of the door with a "You don't need to tell your boss you didn't fully accomplish your mission. But my son enjoyed Egor's attentions. Looks like he has a nice cock and a decent backswing. He fuck you well, Son?"

"Yes, he fucked me very well . . . Dad," Toby answered as the men were hustled out of the apartment and the triple locks were thrown.

Toby was giving Hardesty a funny look, but it was Paul who asked, "Son?"

"You had to be there," Hardesty answered and then laughed. "But did we interrupt something going on in the bedroom."

"We were waiting for you," said Toby.

"Not really," Paul answered. "But we're happy to cut you in. Jan's back in the bedroom too."

It was the first time Hardesty and Paul shared in doubling, doing Jan first and then Toby.

* * * *

It was still dark and had only been a couple of hours since the Russians retreated, but Hardesty had dozed off and was awakened by the buzzing of his cell phone on the night stand. The lamp on the stand was on, set on low, so it wasn't totally dark in the room. Hardesty was stretched out on his side next to Jan, who was on his back, his arms stretched over his head and his wrists tied of on the headboard. His ankles were tied together too. He was asleep and didn't waken at the sound of the cell phone. It was likely that he was exhausted. The open box containing sounding wands rested on the other side of his thighs from where Hardesty was stretched. Five of the wands were out of the box and scattered around on the bed. Hardesty had used five of them before Jan had shot his load, and Hardesty had stroked himself off in sympathy.

The bed was swaying again. Toby was lying on his back on the other side of Hardesty, his butt on the edge of the foot of the bed, and his heels rubbing on Paul's hips, as Paul crouched over him, fists buried in the sheets on either side of Toby's biceps, and was fucking Toby in long, languid, smooth strokes.

Hardesty reached up and released the restraints on Jan's wrists and continued his hand motion over to the cell phone. Putting it to his ear, he growled, "Speak."

"It's Glen. Time for another trip back to the yellow house in Georgetown. I think it's the guy you called Kim. Shot between the eyes in his bed. Pretty messy. It looks like he was tortured first."

"Shit," Hardesty whined as he started crawling over Jan's still-sleeping body.

Chapter Six: All Fall Down

"What's your guess on the caliber of the weapon?" Hardesty asked the medical examiner. They were standing in the bedroom where Hardesty had that afternoon been playing sounding games with the victim. Kim was back in his black silk lounge suit—at least the top half of him was. He was posed on the bed on his back, propped up by pillows, with a pillow under the small of his back, and his legs spread and bent. It was like he'd positioned himself to receive a lover—a male lover. His first problem was the assortment of items scattered around on the bed that had been used on him as dildos. His second problem was that there was a bullet hole in his head between his eyes.

Hardesty had castigated himself during his race across the district into Georgetown at dawn the second day after Christmas. Had he embarrassed the Russian mafia goons so badly that they'd immediately taken Kim out, out of spite, thinking the young man was the shooter in the Talmadge case? He hadn't been high on Hardesty's list of candidates for that. But if the Russians thought Toby was his son, they may have screwed up who had killed Talmadge, Victor, and Leslie, as well because of misconceptions.

"What are you looking for?" the ME asked.

"I'm thinking about whether it could have been a .38—maybe a .357 Magnum," Hardesty answered.

Glen Whitehall gave him a quizzical look. Hardesty hadn't mentioned his encounter with the Russians yet. "Or a .45. We have the possibility of a G30S involved in the case."

"A Glock G30S?" the ME said, with surprise. "Isn't that mainly a government gun?"

"Yeah," Hardesty said. "I'm afraid we haven't ruled out government involvement if this is related to the Talmadge shooting—and it's hard to think it isn't involved."

"Well, both a .38 and a .45 would be messier than this," the ME said. "My guess is a .22. I'm told that's what the slugs were that were taken out of the three bodies in the Talmadge case. So that would seem more likely if this killing is connected."

"Yeah, except we've had the suspect .22 weapon sitting on my desk in police headquarters since this afternoon," Whitehall said.

"Which leads to the question of time of death," Hardesty said. "Within the last couple of hours." He was still looking at the Russians as having done this after they let him loose earlier in the evening.

"No, no," the ME said. "This guys been dead for a good ten or twelve hours. Shot sometime yesterday afternoon."

Both his and Whitehall's cell phones sounded off. Whitehall answered his. Hardesty was a bit in shock and let his ring.

"Shit," Hardesty exclaimed. He'd been here fucking Kim's dick with a sounding wand in the afternoon. It must have happened shortly after he'd left. The black Escalade that had dogged him to Georgetown from Wesley Heights but that remained at the Georgetown townhouse when he left came to mind.

He was about to ask another question when Whitehall broke in with a "shit" of his own. "Gotta go, Hardesty. A shooting at the Wesley Heights house. A very messy one."

* * * *

233

The sun had just made an appearance and they could see that there were two areas roped off with yellow tape at the front of the Wesley Heights house as Hardesty and Whitehall drove up, not just one, and they'd already been told that Maria Talmadge (or Nadia Stanislova) had been shot inside the house, not outside. They passed the first taped off area, a black van, parked half a block down from the house. Despite the head shots, Hardesty recognized the two goons—the two Russian goons he'd danced with the previous evening. They were leaning into their respective windows in the front seat, looking all surprised and very dead. Neither would be doing any more dancing.

Crane was in the front yard of the house, along with a dozen assorted detectives and cops, standing around another dead guy who was rimmed with yellow tape. This one was dressed all in black, was spread-eagled all akimbo just at the bottom of the steps up to the front door, and had several front-loaded bullet holes in him. Hardesty didn't recognize him, but he recognized the black Escalade pulled up at an angle on the sidewalk in front of the house and looking like a ride set up for a quick getaway that didn't happen. Hardesty wondered if the body went with the Caddie.

"You slowed down passing the van down the street," Crane said to his two detectives as they walked up the incline of the lawn to him. "Recognize them."

"Yeah, I did," Hardesty said. "They are part of the Russian mafia mob in this area. Connected with Victor, who we now know was really named Pietr Stanislov. Probably also connected with Nadia Stanislova, purported wife of our mysterious CIA vic, Curtis Talmadge, who was going by the name of Maria. She inside?"

"Yes. It's less messy in there. Professional hits, I'm sure. She's in the upstairs hall. Bullet between the eyes. Still has the cell phone in her hand from the 911 call, although she'd already pushed a panic button, which is why the local cops got here so fast."

"You said 'hits'," Whitehall asked, his voice almost a whisper. He was looking a little white around the gills. He'd been humping the woman the previous afternoon.

"Yes. Collateral damage—maybe. The maid got it in the foyer—several shots. But the maid had a gun in her hand. Chances are good she was more than a maid."

"And this guy?" Hardesty asked, gesturing at the guy in black on the ground at the bottom of the entrance stairs. It wasn't lost on him that he had a Ruger SR22, with a silencer attached. in his hand. There was another pistol in a holster in his armpit too. From what Hardesty could see, it might be a Glock G30S. Another government issue piece?

"We don't know who he is, and I'm not sure we're going to know," Crane said. "We sent in prints already and all sorts of bells went off and we were blocked out of the system. I guess we both know what that might mean. Anyway, the cops arrived fast and this guy came out of the house with a gun waving, but it must have jammed or something, because the cops brought him down before he could do any more damage."

"I guess we better look inside," Hardesty said. As he and Whitehall mounted the front steps, Crane got a call on his cell phone and walked off into the yard to take it. His responses, which the detectives heard before they got in the house, were distinctively profane.

"I think I'm going to be sick," Whitehall said, as they stood over Maria's body in the upper hall. "If I hadn't taken the Ruger from her, it would at least have been a fair fight."

"We don't know that. It's just as likely that she wouldn't have used the time to call in the cops fast enough for him to be taken down. Then we'd never know. You know we're not going to get any farther with this, don't you? That we're not going to know who he is. At least we know he's dead. And it explains some things to me."

"What things?"

"The whole setup at the boathouse. We thought Maria took them out, mad at Talmadge for fucking around with young men and at Victor for letting him do it."

"We did?"

"I did. Didn't you? She's the one who had a gun to fit."

"Yeah, I guess I did."

"But what we had wrong, and we'll be able to prove that, is that it wasn't her Ruger SR22 that did them in the boathouse. The stiff out there on the lawn did that one too—with the .22 he's got in his hand. And putting a man at the scene rather than Maria makes the rest of it fall into place. The other night Jan mentioned a guy hanging around Talmadge who might be this stiff. Kim mentioned him too when I questioned him. Talmadge knew the shooter and I'll bet the meet at the boathouse wasn't just for Talmadge to go kayaking on Christmas morning. They met—Talmadge, Victor, and this other guy. Then Talmadge gave the shooter privileges with Leslie in the backseat of the Mercedes while he changed in the boathouse and got the kayak out.

"The shooter was there to do more than meet with Talmadge and play hide the sounding rod with his rent-boy, though. He was there to terminate whatever arrangement Talmadge had—probably with the Russians through Victor. The shooter popped Leslie while playing with him and then came to the river's edge and popped Talmadge and Victor. What he did in the two days after that was cleanup. Kim, the Russian goons looking out for Maria, and Maria—and the maid just because she answered the door—or maybe because she answered the door with a gun. It's what makes sense. And there isn't much doubt what agency would be included in whatever Talmadge was doing and then interested in ending it with no one left to talk about it."

236

"So, what are we going to do?" Whitehall asked.

"You're going to go into the bathroom and soak your face in cold water—you are looking green around the gills. I'll think about options for as long as they let me think about them, which shouldn't be long . . ." He brought Glen's attention to the black Escalade parking in front of the house that they could see through the fan window above the door in the foyer. ". . . and probably not much longer than it takes us to walk out of the house again."

The late arriver was the Secret Service agent Hardesty had already met at the boathouse crime scene and then again in Crane's office. He was talking with Crane, whose jaw was set. Other black vehicles were showing up and men in black were coming out of them. Crane had already pulled the policemen and detectives who had been at the scene away from the body at the bottom of the steps. The Black Escalade that had been on the lawn—the one the shooter probably came in—was already gone. Crane was holding the Ruger SR22 that had been in the shooter's hand in a plastic bag.

"I'll just say it, although I don't have to," the Secret Service agent said to Hardesty as he and Whitehall walked up to him, "that this isn't our operation in any sense of the word. We were just called in to clean it up as quietly as possible. Tell him, Captain Crane."

"Upstairs has called us off on this, Hardesty," Crane said. He didn't sound happy, but he sounded resigned. "From our perspective we will have gotten our man, though. There's that. We need to be happy with that and not make it go any further."

Hardesty was hearing him loud and clear. They had their shooter of the citizens who were important to them and he wouldn't be doing any more shooting—in fact some men in black were already rolling him into a body bag. Others were working at the Russian van. If they made waves on this, there could be more collateral damage. This was bigger than the D.C. police department.

"And the gun in the plastic bag?" he asked Crane.

"Agent Smith here wants to maintain good will. He knows we want to be satisfied beyond a shadow of doubt. We've been lent this gun to do ballistic tests to assure ourselves this was used at the boathouse. Then I have to give it back to him. It's the best he can do. It's going to have to be good enough for us, Hardesty. Right?"

"Sure, Captain," Hardesty said. He recognized that this was as good as it was going to get. He had another reason not to make waves, though, and the faster he got to that the better, so, to Crane's surprise, he just saluted to Crane and the agent and dragged Whitehall off with him to their car.

He dropped Whitehall off at the squad room to get Larry busy doing the ballistics tests on Maria's gun and then hightailed it back to his apartment.

He found the apartment empty, with a note from Toby that he was out on a job with a visiting German industrialist and would, no doubt, be bringing the guy back to the apartment later. So, business as usual there with Toby.

But it wasn't Toby he wanted. He left the apartment and went down the hall to Paul's apartment.

At his knock and after a yell who he was, Paul told him to come on in. Paul and Jan were on a sofa, both naked other than short silk robes. Jan was in Paul's lap, sideways, with his legs streaming out along the sofa and his arm around Paul's shoulder. Paul's hand was lost in the folds of Jan's robe, but from the rustling there it was evident that Jan was getting a hand job. This obviously was preliminary to something else, as Paul's plow belt was bunched on the floor in front of the sofa.

"I've got to talk to Jan about where he goes from here," Hardesty said. "I don't think he can go back to Justine's now."

"Great minds," Paul said. "Jan and I have been talking. He doesn't want to go back to Justine's and I don't want him to go back. He's agreed to live with me here. I have connections. I can keep him in clients as wealthy and as safe as Justine's done—and probably with fewer physical demands on him."

"You'd become Jan's pimp?"

"I'm retired and have time on my hands. Can you see any reason why I shouldn't?"

"Well, I understand it's against the law and there are police arresting people for it in D.C."

They both laughed.

"Then you think it's a fine idea, I take it."

"There are complications. Jan has to become someone else."

"We've already decided he has to stop being Jan. Conveniently that's not his real name anyway. He's Dean. Dean Burton. From Atlanta. No small town where everyone knows you. It's a nice name, isn't it? He has kept that documentation."

"Is that who Justine knows him to be?"

"No, Justine doesn't know who I really am," the young man who no longer was Jan piped up. "She thinks I'm someone else altogether."

"Well, I guess it can do for now, but we'll get you a whole different background and name. You'll have to lay low for a while. Someone may be looking for you who you don't want to find you. Luckily, I think it will be people who aren't supposed to track down people in the United States, so maybe it won't be easy to find you. Can you stay hidden for a while?"

"Yes, I guess I can," Dean said, sounding a bit dubious.

"I think the problem is that our little friend here is highly sexed," Paul said. "If I can't hook him up with outside clients for a while, I guess we'll have to have inside clients for him. I can do my part, but I'll need help."

"Well, if you need the help . . ." Hardesty said, with a grin.

"We were about to use the plow belt when you came in," Paul said. "Perhaps you'd like to start helping with that right now. What do you think, Dean?"

"Yes, please," Dean said, with a smile.

"But you haven't worked out a price structure for him yet, have you?" Hardesty asked Paul.

"For you, for now—and because I've been using Toby for free—mercilessly, I might add—this could be a gift. A Christmas gift."

"I've already had my Christmas gift from Jan," Hardesty said, smiling at the young man, who grinned back.

"But this isn't Jan. This is Dean now," Paul said.

"That's true. And I suppose we could say it was a New Year's gift."

"It's not New Year's yet. I'm sure Dean will be interested in your attentions at New Year's too, eh, Dean?"

"New Year's Eve and New Year's Day both," Dean answered, licking his lips in anticipation.

"That certainly makes sense to me. Anything to help, then. I have vacation time coming to me. We could start now and just work our way right through New Year's Day," Hardesty said, as he started stripping down. Mission accomplished, he reached down and picked up the plow belt. "Where? In the bedroom?"

"Why not right here?" Paul said. "I would like to watch. Compare techniques and all, you know. You first with your technique, which I understand can be quite demanding, and then perhaps you'd like to see mine, which I think is distinctive for its duration."

240

"Sure, I have all evening. Toby is going to be using the apartment."

"Have you done a double with the plow belt?" Paul asked, as he handed the young man up to Hardesty.

"No, do you know how that works?"

"But of course."

Dean moaned as Hardesty bent the young man over the leather strip on his belly, grasped the two handles, and flipped Dean over, lifting both his feet and his hands off the floor.

~

About the Author

Habu is one of the pen names of a former supersonic spy jet pilot, intelligence agent, male model, movie actor, and diplomat. A wild youth in Southeast Asia was spent enjoying whatever sexual opportunities came his way, and much of his gay male writing is about recalling incidents from those days and inventing ones he'd perhaps have liked to experience. He now leads a very quiet and ordinary happily married family life.

An American, he is a published mainstream novelist and short story writer under another name and in another dimension of his life. He has written or cowritten (with Sabb) approaching 1,000 published short stories and over 100 published erotica e-books, primarily of gay fiction but also memoir, straight fiction and ménage fiction. His hand and creative writing can be seen in stories and books by habu, sr71plt, Dirk Hessian, Shabbu, and Stephen Kessel— among unrevealed others that might surprise readers. The fictionalized GM memoir *Flying High, Diving Deep* is loosely based on his life experiences. He can be found at the adults only gay male site www.BarbarianSpy.com, which he shares with Sabb and Dirk Hessian.

Our authors always like to receive feedback, and appreciate it when readers post reviews at distributors and other sites.

BarbarianSpy

FOR LITERARY HEAT

Not all books listed below may currently be on release.
* indicates the book is available in paperback and e-book.

BOOKS BY CHRIS CROSS
Multisexual Adult Romance
Pulaski Square
Chocolate in Vanilla (MF)2
Christmas with Chris (MMF) (MM) (MF)

BOOKS BY ALEX LOCKHEED
Transgender Romance
Meeting Jenna
Transgender Other
Being Sarah

BOOKS BY DIRK HESSIAN
Xtreme Historical Erotica
Dirk's Ancient Times Collection (Print only Bundle)*
The King's Men
Shores of Tripoli*
Prophecy of Noto
Pretender's Fate

General Historical Erotic Romance
Dirk's America's Founding Collection (Print only Bundle)*
Soldier,Spy
Ridden West
Deliver a Virgin
Clouds and Rain
Confederate Gold
Puttin on the Ritz
To the Hessian Hills
Fire Down the Valley*
Constantinople*
The Beautiful Way*
Blue and Gray
Colonel's Treasure
Beginning of Time
Labyrinth

BOOKS BY HABU
Gay Erotica
Memoir Faction

Flying High, Diving Deep*
Xtreme Erotica
Fist of Gold
Liaisons
Chain Gang Banged (Short Story)
Tramp Steaming*
Escape to Girne
Silas' Choice*
Last Call
Choke Hold
Apyko: The Greek Pimp
Visits of the Schlange
Second Coming: Emile La Cour Unleashed*
Vortex: Sacrificed by Curiosity*
Dark Angel Sounding *(in e-book & included in Sounding:Ultimate Control paperback)* *
Sounding: Ultimate Control (*Print Only*)*
Sounding Five *(in e-book & included in Sounding:Ultimate Control paperback)* *
Romance
The Aviators
Poison Pen
Need to be Needed
Key Westing (short)
Finding a New Sam
Bangkok Summer Seduction
The Photograph
Inevitable Case
Turn to Love
Rain Check
Built for Pleasure (Sci Fi)
Danny's Choice*
Pull of the Groove
Sugar n Spice Christmas
Friday Nights with Lenny (Christmas Romance)
Snowy, Snowy Nights (Christmas Romance)
Tank n Bull
Sail to the Sun
War Letters
Ravens Roost
Caribbean Cruise Top to Bottom
Arena Stage
Trading Partners (Valentine's Day)
Four Coins
Lower Than the Heart (Valentine's Day)
Brambleton

Finding Amnad
Platres Conclave
Other Novels/Novellas
Also Want to Thank
Ranger Guided
Key Westing
Syrian Ram
Temptation's Clutches*
Descent into Chaos
Escape to Girne
Journey Through Abilene
Harmony and Dissonance
Stallion Station
Racing With the Devil (espionage suspense)
Prepared in Cape Verdi
Gilded Cage
House on Park*
Anything for Ambition
Dance of the Ravishers
Hard Knocks U*
My Neighbor's Spa*
Man's Man: Tales of a High Priced Gay Hooker*
Trip Money
The Indian Doctor
Sailorboy
Home to Fire Island
Murder Mysteries
Hardesty X3 (Paperback only bundle)*
Retribution (Hardesty)
Snitches (Hardesty
Gotta Keep Trying (Hardesty)
All Fools Day Foolery (Mike Kavanagh)
Inevitable Case (Mike Kavanagh)
Vanishing Laura
Death on a Ping Pong Table
Clint Folsom Mysteries Compendium Volume 1*
Death to Blonds - Stolen Judgment (Clint Folsom Mystery)*
Clint Folsom Mysteries Compendium Volume 2*
Gay Erotica Anthologies
Earth Cry*
Shunga
Habu's Christmas Balls
Eight in D*
DevilMENt
Silas' Choices*
Stallion Station (A Novella in Parts)

Eleven to the Dogs*
Fifty Seventy*
Spy Tails 001*
Spy Tails 002*
Doubled*
Doubled Again*
Tails in the Tropics*
Tails in the Med*
Tails in the West*
Rough Riders*
Grab Bag 1*
Grab Bag 2*
Grab Bag 3*
Grab Bag 4*
Grab Bag 5*
Grab Bag 6*
Grab Bag 7*
Grab Bag 8*
Grab Bag 9*
Grab Bag 10*
Grab Bag 11*
Beyond the Beaded Curtain*
The Sporting Life*
Fetish Galore!*
Literary Gay Erotica
Cairo Surrender*
The Handyman*
Homeward Bound
Journey to Mirage*
Bisexual/Menage/Multisexual Erotica
And Eat it Too
Two Men, One Woman*
Every Which Way
Summer of Denial
Death on a Ping Pong Table
Cruising Gigolo
13 Ways for Halloween
Luther*
The Indian Prince*
BOOKS BY SABB
Driver Reliever
Hiring in Hollywood
The Legend of Holleystone Grange
Surprise Encounters*
She is He
Wrong Man

Loyal to his King
Barbarian Tales - Book One - Traveler's Tales*
Barbarian Tales - Book Two - Journeys Begin*
Barbarian Tales - Book Three - The Inheritance*
Barbarian Tales - Book Four - Road to Persepolis*
BOOKS BY SHABBU
A Season in Galicia*
Blind Dates*
Velvet Interrogation
Finding Jason
Dirty Pool
Operation Black Jade
Cigars!*
Angel in the Barn
Gayly Complicated*
Despoiling David
The Tree of Idleness*
I Met a Man
Rough Road to Happiness
BOOKS BY STEPHEN KESSEL
Gay Romance
The Forever Man
Two Chances
BOOKS BY KIM BLACK
Lesbian Romance
Transfixed on Tammie (F/T lesbian)
~